Praise for Kelly Long

"*Arms of Love* is rich in the historical details of the Amish in America in the 1700s."

—*Romantic Times*, 4 stars

"There is a beautiful love story that unfolds within the pages . . . I was vested in the lives of these characters."

—Beth Wiseman, best-selling author of *The Wonder of Your Love* regarding *Arms of Love*

"[In *Sarah's Garden*] Long writes with a polished style that puts her in the same category as the top Christian authors."

—*Romantic Times*, 4 stars

"Long's easy style creates a richly detailed, charming tale. The sweetly developed romance illustrates how love can grow from friendship."

—*Romantic Times*, 4 stars, regarding *Lilly's Wedding Quilt*

"Kelly Long has hit it out of the park, *Sarah's Garden* is rich with Amish detail and an endearing romance. I highly recommend!"

—Beth Wiseman, best-selling author of *The Wonder of Your Love*

A Marriage of
the Heart

Also by Kelly Long

Arms of Love

THE PATCH OF HEAVEN SERIES
Sarah's Garden
Lilly's Wedding Quilt
Threads of Grace (Available February 2013)

NOVELLAS FOUND IN
An Amish Christmas
An Amish Love
An Amish Wedding
An Amish Kitchen

A Marriage of the Heart

Three Amish Novellas

Kelly Long

Thomas Nelson
Since 1798

NASHVILLE   DALLAS   MEXICO CITY   RIO DE JANEIRO

Published in Nashville, Tennessee, by Thomas Nelson. Thomas Nelson is a registered trademark of Thomas Nelson, Inc.

Thomas Nelson, Inc., titles may be purchased in bulk for educational, business, fund-raising, or sales promotional use. For information, please email SpecialMarkets@ThomasNelson.com.

Scripture quotations are from the King James Version of the Holy Bible.

ISBN 978-1-40168-756-4

Library of Congress Cataloging-in-Publication Data is Available

Printed in the United States of America

13 14 15 16 17 QG 6 5 4 3

Pennsylvania Dutch Glossary

ach—oh

aenti—aunt

bensel—hard to handle; a handful

Budget, The—a weekly newspaper serving Amish and Mennonite communities everywhere

bruder—brother

daed—dad

danki—thank you

Derr Herr—God

Englisch or *Englischer*—a non-Amish person

gut—good

hiya—hello

kapp—prayer covering or cap

kumme—come

milch—milk

narrisch—crazy

nee—no

Pennsylvania Deitsch—Pennsylvania German, the language most commonly used by the Amish

rumschpringe—running-around period when a teenager turns sixteen years old

sohn—son

was in der welt—what in the world

wunderbaar—wonderful

ya—yes

Contents

A Perfect Secret · 1

Christmas Cradles · 127

A Marriage of the Heart · 203

A PERFECT SECRET

For my girl, Gracie

In Hebrew, perfect means "whole or complete." It is God's desire for our lives that we become perfect or whole in Him. He is slowly revealing His perfect secret for each of our lives.

Prologue

"THAT'S IT? THAT'S MY WEDDING PROPOSAL?" NINETEEN-year-old Rose Bender stared at her best friend in the waning light of the cool summer evening.

Luke Lantz's dark blue eyes held steady as always. "*Ya*, what more do you expect?"

Rose half bounced in the buggy seat, trying not to let Luke's typical calmness rile her into a temper that would match the unruly black curls tucked beneath her *kapp*. What more did she expect? It was a fair question.

She'd known Luke for all of her young life, and he was right—a marriage was something that would please both of their families and have the strong foundation of their friendship at its base. It would also unite two lands, the rich soil that ran parallel in property. And, perhaps most importantly, it would bring a woman's touch to the motherless Lantz household. But it might have helped if Luke could have conjured up a few romantic words to add to the moment. Yet, at twenty-three, he was what he was: Placid. Faithful. Secure. And when Rose was with him, it was rather like skating on a pond that had been deep-frozen for months—no chance for a crack in the ice. Perfectly safe. Not that she should desire anything more.

"I accept," she said with determination and not a little defiance. She wanted to silence the doubts that echoed inside—that suggested she knew him too well to have a romantic marriage. And the realistic fears that she could never live up to the legacy of domesticity and kindness his mother had left behind just two short years ago. She told herself that it had to be more than enough to fulfill the expectations of Luke's father and her parents and to find a strong base in a wealth of memories—school days, sledding and ice-skating together, long walks and throwing horse chestnuts into the pond, and serious conversations about life—though not necessarily about love.

"*Gut*. I thank you, Rose. I believe, with *Derr Herr*'s blessing, that it will be a successful match."

She nodded, then slid closer to his lean form, reaching to trail her fingers in the brown hair at the nape of his neck. She felt him tense, but she ignored it.

"Luke," she whispered, "now that we're engaged, maybe we could kiss a bit more?"

His strong jaw tightened, and he turned to peck neatly at her lips, moving away before she could even close her eyes. He disentangled her hand from his hair and gave it a cool squeeze, then picked up the reins. "We'd best move on," he said. "It's getting late."

And that's that, she thought ruefully, comforting herself

with the knowledge that he would be too dutiful to maintain such distance once the marriage ceremony was over. She stifled a sigh at the unusually irreverent thought and focused on the dim road ahead.

Chapter One

∾

TWO MONTHS LATER...

THE SUNLIGHT OF EARLY AUTUMN FILTERED THROUGH the clear windowpanes and made passing shadows on the wide fir floor of the Bender farmhouse. The family was gathered for a hearty meal, and the *gut* smells of cooking mingled with robust conversation.

"I tell you that it's downright odd, that's what." Rose's father gestured with his fork to the lunch table at large. "Two of our hens—our best layers, mind you—a goat from the Lamberts', and the sheets from old Esther Mast's clothesline. All of it missing, and dozens of other things from the community over the past few months. I say there's a thief hereabouts, and that's the truth."

Rose's mother calmly passed the platter of sauerkraut and kielbasa to Rose's two older brothers to take seconds. Then she offered the fresh platter of airy biscuits to *Aenti* Tabitha, Father's sister, and nodded her head as her husband sputtered himself out.

"Maybe it's a Robin Hood type of thief," *Aenti* Tabitha ventured, her brown eyes shining. At fifty, she often seemed as young as a girl to Rose with all of her romantic ideas and flights of fancy. Yet her suggestion stilled Rose's hand for a moment over the salt-shaker. What would it be like to meet such a romantic figure of a man? Dark and mysterious in nature . . .

Abram Bender shook his head at *Aenti* Tabitha. "Tabby, you always have had a heart of gold—looking for the best in others. But Rob in the Hood, like the *Englisch* folktale? Taking from the rich to give to the poor? Who's poor in our community? Don't we all see to each other? *Nee*, this is just a thief, plain and simple. And I don't like it one bit."

"The weather'll change over the next month or so," Ben remarked over a forkful of boiled potatoes. "Any thief is likely to drop off in his ways once there's snow on the ground to track him."

"Or her," Rose said, for some reason wanting to provoke.

"What?" her father asked.

"I said *her*. Your thief could be a female, *Daed*." She didn't really think the thief was female, yet she had a strange urge to enter the suggestion into her father's mind.

Her *daed* gave a shout of laughter, then resumed eating. Ben turned to her with a smile while her other brother, James, just rolled his eyes.

"Rose, no woman in her right mind is going to go thieving about," *Daed* said. "It's a *gut* thing you're marrying Luke come December. Maybe he'll settle down some of your wild ideas."

"Perhaps." She smiled, her green eyes flashing heat for a brief second.

"Well," Ben interjected, "Rose's *narrisch* thoughts aside—there's a storm due tonight, supposed to be a doozy."

"*Ya*, I heard." Father rose from the table and hitched up his suspenders. "Come on, boys. We'd best tighten down a few things." He bent to pat *Mamm*'s shoulder. "*Danki* for lunch." Then he pinched Rose's cheek fondly. "And no more foolish thoughts from you, my miss. Remember, you're to be a married woman soon."

Rose didn't respond. She toyed with her fork instead, making a mash of the potato as an idea began to take shape in her head.

As Rose cleared the lunch table mechanically, she avoided her *aenti*'s eagle eyes. Ever since she'd been little, she'd felt as though *Aenti* Tabby could see the subdued thoughts churning inside her head, and just for a moment she wanted to debate the merits of her plan undisturbed. Still, she knew the intent look on her aunt's face and had to admit that the older woman's intuition had fended off trouble for her many a time. But today—something was different. Today Rose *wanted* trouble. She drew a sharp breath at the hazardous thought, but the idea fit with her nature of late. It seemed as though her spirit had grown more restless, less satisfied with life, ever since she'd accepted Luke's proposal. She'd tried to pray about it, stretching her feelings out before the Lord for guidance, but nothing had come to her.

Aenti Tabby caught her eye in an unguarded moment as they

washed and wiped the dishes. "I'd like to see you in my room, Rose, after we clean up a bit. If you don't mind?"

"Um . . . sure, *Aenti* Tabby, but I have to hurry. I'm going to bake some pies this afternoon."

"Bake? Pies?" Her aunt and *mamm* uttered the questions in unison, and Rose concentrated on dabbing at a nonexistent spot on a dish. The whole family knew that she was a hard worker, to be sure, but baking was not a skill that she possessed or an activity she particularly enjoyed.

"*Ya.*" She nodded vigorously, forcing a soft curl to spring loose from the back of her *kapp*. "I need to practice, you know? Luke likes a *gut* apple pie, or perhaps blueberry." She stretched to put the plate away in the cupboard. "But I'll be glad to come and talk with you before I start."

AUNT TABBY, WHO HAD NEVER MARRIED, LIVED WITH THE Benders and was a cherished part of the home and family. Rose and her brothers often sought the sanctuary of their aunt's room for advice, comfort, or a smuggled sweet long after supper. But Rose knew that she had been distinctly absent lately from any visits with her beloved *aenti* and mentally prepared to face what might be some pointed, but truth-provoking, questions about herself and Luke.

Aunt Tabby sank down onto the comfortable maple bed with its patchwork quilt and patted a space next to her. "*Kumme* and sit, Rosie."

Rose blew out a breath, then came forward to relax into the

age-old comfort of the well-turned mattress. She half smiled at her *aenti*, remembering times she'd jumped on the same bed and had once taken a header that nearly landed her in the windowsill. But that was childhood past—long past, or so it seemed to her heart.

"I'll not keep you long, Rose, but I want to ask—why did you agree to marry Luke?"

"What?"

The question was even more probing than she'd braced for, and a thousand answers swirled in her mind.

"Luke. Why did you accept his proposal?"

"Well . . . because he's . . . we're . . . we've always been best friends."

Aunt Tabby frowned. "I've never married, child, but I do wonder if that is reason enough to build a life together."

Rose said, "It's made both of the families happy."

"That's true, but what about you? Are you happy?"

There was a long, disconsolate silence that wrung Rose's heart as her aunt touched her shoulder.

"I'm supposed to be happy," Rose said, thinking hard.

"*Ya*, that's true."

"I just—I expect too much, I guess. Like wanting some kind of—I don't know."

"Like wanting someone mysterious and romantic?"

Rose gazed in surprise at her *aenti*, who laughed out loud.

"I was young once too, and I think it's perfectly normal to want more from a relationship than just friendship. But maybe— maybe there's more to Luke Lantz than meets the eye. Have you thought of that?"

Rose shrugged as her aunt cleared her throat. "Luke's father—well, we courted some. He was always shy, but then . . . well. He had it in him to do some fine kissing now and then."

Rose stared at her *aenti*'s flushed face. "You and Matthew Lantz? *Aenti* Tabby—I never knew you dated him. Why didn't you marry him?"

"It wasn't what the Lord wanted for me."

Rose marveled at the simple statement. She knew her people lived by the will of *Derr Herr*, but to give up a relationship because of faith was difficult for her to comprehend. She knew she had spiritual miles to go before she would make a decision like that.

"Haven't you ever regretted it? Not even when—well, when Laura Lantz died of the influenza? You're still young, *Aenti* Tabby. Maybe you and Mr. Lantz could—"

"*Nee*," the older woman gently contradicted. "I've never regretted it, not even when Laura died. In truth, I believe I would have regretted more if I had not obeyed what I felt was the Lord's leading. And just think—had I married Matthew, there would be no Luke for you."

Rose frowned. "*Ya*, you're right."

"So, you will try, Rosie? To see all there is of him?" Her aunt gave her a hug.

"*Ya, Aenti* Tabby—all that there is."

Chapter Two

A HAWK GAVE A KEENING CRY AS IT BEGAN ITS TWILIGHT hunt while the evening shadows stretched across the grass to wend through the windows of the Lantz woodworking shop. Luke closed the heavy ledger and glanced at his watch. Six o'clock. He was done tussling with another day's accounts for his family's furniture-making business, and his head ached from the numbers and the customers. But his father wouldn't trust an outsider with the books, and although Luke was as skilled as any of his brothers in woodworking, he was the only one "with a head for business," as his *daed* liked to say. So he sat in the stuffy office and dutifully did his job, though he would much rather let his hands run down the fine smoothness of a wood grain than the tally of a day's earnings.

He leaned back in the chair, letting himself drift for a moment until the familiar pleasure of imagining Rose came to mind. In truth, he couldn't believe she'd accepted his proposal so readily.

He wasn't always the most persuasive of persons, and Rose could be headstrong.

He didn't jump when his father clapped him on the back.

"Dreaming of your bride, *sohn?*"

Luke smiled, looking over his shoulder. "She's worth the dreaming, *Daed.*"

"To be sure. But now's the time to see what Joshua's managed for supper. *Kumme.*"

He followed his father into the old farmhouse and stifled the urge to look about for his mother as he came through the door. It was difficult for him to believe that she was gone, even after two years. She'd been what the Bible called a "gentle and quiet spirit," but she'd been a vigorous light to each of them as well. He knew that part of what he loved about Rose was her own light and sweetness, and that her spirit was a balm to his grieving soul. He knew she'd bring that comfort to the whole house once they married, and he mentally charged himself once again with making sure that she wasn't overtaxed physically or emotionally with the inherent burden of taking on a household of men.

His brother Joshua looked up rather sheepishly from the stove when *Daed* asked what was for supper. "Fried potatoes and bacon."

Luke stifled a groan. He longed for variety—vegetables, pie, anything. Even when kindly members of the community brought them hot meals, it wasn't the same as having someone cook for them with love. And there had been no one to maintain a kitchen garden since *Mamm* passed, so they were restricted to more plain fare. Still, he knew it was food in his belly, and he was grateful for it. And so he told the Lord when *Daed* bowed for silent grace.

ROSE SQUELCHED A SUDDEN CRY AS THE BLUEBERRY JUICE from the bubbling pie dripped over onto her hand. She hastily deposited the pie onto a rack and ran to soak the burn in the bowl of cool milk and vinegar she'd used in making the crusts. She glanced at the kitchen clock as she blew a loose tendril of hair away from her damp forehead and was glad to see that it was only just past seven. Her family was relaxing in the adjoining room after supper, and she'd volunteered to clean up alone so that she could finish her pies in peace. Now, if she could just keep Ben and James from wanting a taste . . .

She lifted her hand from the milk and gazed ruefully at the half-inch-long red mark on the back of her hand. But it gave her an idea. Taking a scrap of dough, she opened the woodstove and threw the pastry piece inside. Within seconds, the smell of burning piecrust filled the air. She smiled and scooped up the pies, this time carefully holding a dish towel around each pan as she bumped open the back screen door with her hip.

She ignored the groans of her brothers as the burning smell hung in the early evening air, then set the pies on the porch rail. Now, if only no animal would take a nibble before she caught her real prey . . .

"Rose!" Her *mamm*'s voice echoed, and Rose flew back inside, closing the door carefully behind her. The unpleasant smell had wafted throughout the house.

"Mercy, child! What are you doing? Where are your pies?"

Rose sighed. "Outside."

"Burned that badly?" her mother asked as she fooled with

the damper on the stove and waved a damp dish towel through the air.

Rose said a quick prayer for forgiveness as she delayed her response. She wasn't used to withholding the truth.

"Well, open the window then, so we can get some more fresh air in," *Mamm* urged.

"*Ya, Mamm*—open the window!" Ben bawled from the other room.

"And teach Rosie to bake before she kills poor Luke and the whole Lantz clan!" James's voice joined in the banter.

But Rose simply smiled as she wrestled with the heavy window; she had put her plan into action.

Chapter Three

IN THE CROWDED CONFINES OF THE WELL-CONCEALED tent, oil lamps held the encroaching night at a cheerful distance. A hodgepodge of gathered furniture, dishes, quilts, and other small items filled the contours of the vinyl walls, while a thick, hand-braided rug covered the bulk of the pine-needled floor.

"It's too much, really. You have to stop." The *Englisch* woman's tone was torn between gratitude and remorse as she balanced a blueberry pie in her outstretched hand and a fussy toddler on her lean hip.

Her benefactor shrugged as another child, slightly older, clung to his leg in a familiar game.

"Mommy! His shirt's all dirty. Wash it!"

He laughed and brushed at the blueberry juice stain on the front of his sweatshirt.

"Never mind, Ally." He glanced around the tent, then back to the woman. "There's a storm coming tonight. Supposed to be bad. I don't like the idea of leaving you here."

She smiled. "The Lord will protect us. You staked the tent so well, and I doubt anything can shake this stand of pines."

"Have you had any word—I mean—do you know when?" He stared with intent into her eyes.

"No—nothing."

He nodded. "All right. I'd better go." He set the other pie down on the washstand near the quilt-covered cot and noted that he'd need to bring more blankets soon. He disengaged the little girl from his leg, then bent to receive her sweet kiss. "Good-bye," he whispered.

She clung to his neck. "Thank you for the pies. Tell the lady thank you too."

"The lady?"

"Who made the pies."

He smiled. "Maybe I will."

ROSE WAITED UNTIL THE HOUSE HAD BEEN ASLEEP FOR more than half an hour before she crept from her room, avoiding the third step from the bottom of the back staircase and its telltale squeak. She almost giggled to herself as she maneuvered, remembering a time she'd sneaked out to see Luke when they were young. They thought they could catch the biggest bullfrog from the local pond, the one with the baritone that soothed the locals to sleep on summer nights, if they could only get there late at night. They'd ended up with no frog, muddy clothes, and stiff reprimands from frustrated mothers the next morning. It had been fun, but that was a long time ago.

Rose told herself that she wasn't a child anymore, looking for grandfather frogs on moonlit nights. No—she was a woman who wanted to hunt for something, someone—whose very nature seemed to call to her. Rob in the Hood, as some of her people called him from the old German rendition of the tale. She tiptoed across the kitchen floor and then gained the back porch. She switched on a flashlight and caught her breath, then smiled; both pies were gone without a trace. Of course, she told herself, as she stole into the wind-whipped air, a possum could have gotten them, but an animal would have left an overturned plate, a trail, a mess. A thief more likely would not . . .

She glanced without concern to the moon and dark gathering clouds overhead; the incoming storm suited her mood. She passed the kitchen garden, still sprawled with the bulging shadows of pumpkins yet to be harvested, then broke into a light run toward the forest that encircled the back of the farmhouse. She knew nearly every inch of the woods between her family's home and the Lantzes'—though she had to admit she hadn't been walking there in the months since her engagement. It seemed that courting, as well as the usual influx of work of the farm during harvest, had kept her too busy. But now she trod the pine-needled ground with secret delight. She could tell from the air that the rain would hold off for a while, and she pressed more deeply into the trees, certain that the best place for a would-be thief to hide would be the woods.

After an hour of actually navigating the rocks and root systems of the dark forest, she began to question if she truly had her wits about her. What had she expected? That the thief would just pop out and introduce himself? Suppose he really was dangerous and much more than a thief? She thought of the comfort and safety of her narrow bed and shivered, deciding she'd go hunting for the mystery man some other time. Then she stifled a scream as the beam of her light gave out, and a voice spoke to her from the dark path ahead.

"You're an Amish girl, aren't you? Why are you out in these woods so late and in this kind of weather?"

The voice was a strained whisper. Rose peered into the darkness, trying to see the speaker, when a helpful flash of lightning gave her a brief glimpse.

He was taller than she, clothed in blue jeans and a gray sweatshirt, its hood shrouding his face. Another white streak of light, and the breadth of his shoulders and a dark stain on the front of his shirt were emblazoned in her mind.

"You're the thief," she stated.

"What?"

"The thief who's been taking from hereabouts the past weeks. I put those two blueberry pies out on the back porch. I see the blueberry stain on your front."

He laughed, and she almost gasped in disbelief as the realization hit her with full force. *It was Luke!* Even as a confusion of thoughts rushed past her like the waters of a swollen creek, one instinctual idea took control of her brain—she would not let him know that she recognized him.

"Very smart," he said. "My compliments. But you'd better get home to your husband. These woods are no place for a lady."

Chapter Four

❦

"I've run about this land since I was a child," she announced, trying for normalcy in her tone. "And why do you assume I'm married?"

Was in der welt was he doing—dressed as an Englischer and stealing pies from her porch? He didn't seem to recognize her in the dark . . . but then why was he out talking about marriage with a strange girl in the woods?

"Aren't most Amish girls married young?" he asked in the same husky whisper that seemed to tickle at her shoulder bones in a way that his normal voice didn't do.

"*Ya* . . . Yes, I mean—some are. I'm just engaged." She almost clapped her hand over her mouth at the word *just*.

"Just?"

She wet her lips in the dark and tried to infuse her voice with warmth. "I'm going to marry my best friend in a few months."

"And does your . . . er . . . best friend realize how enthused you are about the whole affair?"

He does now, she thought, trying to keep a rein on her emotions. "I *am* happy," she asserted finally, then swallowed, finding herself voicing to the supposed stranger the concern that had haunted her for weeks. "It's just that—he—my betrothed—doesn't notice any-thing—not about me anyway. He's very—practical and smart."

She felt a palpable silence between them, then sensed him step toward her. She lifted her chin, wondering what he would do next.

"Smart or not, he's a fool—not to notice you," he muttered.

"How can you say that? You can't even see me properly," she said.

"You saw me, at least enough to know my—secret. And I saw you, like meeting destiny in a strike of lightning. White sparks and moonlight—they suit your beauty, Amish girl."

In the cascading roll of thunder that followed, she heard the deafening sound of her own heartbeat as his words penetrated. They were so unlike him. And proof that he did see her in the waxing light. Beguiled and bewildered, Rose held her breath, waiting.

Then he reached out one hand to stroke her cheek in a slow caress. She wanted to lean into the mysterious yet familiar hand, its strong warmth coupled with a heavy tenderness that transmit-ted to every delicate nerve ending the flush that she felt burning her skin.

"You don't even know me," she said, trying to keep her voice level. "Maybe I'm too wild, or a petty shrew, or just plain . . . bor-ing." She found herself citing all of the things she thought she might seem to him at times.

He laughed again, then backed away. "Go home," he said roughly.

She knew she should do as he said to keep up the charade, but there was a mystery here . . . a mystery man whom she had thought she knew so well. And for the first time in weeks she'd unburdened herself to someone, and it exhilarated her.

"I'll go when I'm ready."

"Suit yourself. Oh, and by the way, thank you for the pies."

She heard him step through a layer of dried leaves. "Wait!" she called.

"What?"

"I—do you—do you need some more?" She could have bitten her tongue at the desperation in the inane question, but he replied with seriousness.

"Apple. Any time."

Of course, apple . . . his favorite.

"All right. Do you . . ." She broke off when she sensed that she was alone, and only the sound of the wind through the trees touched her. She shivered in the dark before turning back toward home, wondering who in the world this man was that she was to marry.

Chapter Five

‿❧‿

THE RAIN PELTED IN EARNEST AGAINST THE BARN ROOF AS Luke stripped off the *Englisch* clothes. He stuffed them into the back of his buggy before changing in the chill air of the barn to his usual Amish wear. All the while, the beauty of Rose's pale face, the warmth of her skin, pulsed through his mind as he recalled the heart-stopping moments in the woods. He was sure that she would have recognized him, but she hadn't.

He was two steps outside when the thought stopped him. He stood stock-still, heedless of the rain soaking him. She'd gone *looking* for the thief . . . she had thought to find something out there, in the woods, with a perfect stranger, more compelling than she found in her own betrothed. The idea shook him to his core, but then he remembered why he was doing what he was and decided that *Derr Herr* might have plans beyond what he could see himself. He sloshed on through the mud and gained the back porch. He wiped his work boots against the ragged rug with the habit of his *mamm*'s long training and entered the empty kitchen.

THE STORM LEFT THE AREA, LEAVING BEHIND AN ALMOST luminous clarity to the following day. Squirrels hurried to replenish nut supplies across leaf-strewn grass as the neighborhood cows greeted their fodder with tail flicks and echoing bellows.

"What are you thinking of, Rose?" Luke asked the question in what she considered an idle fashion as they were out driving to survey the damage the storm had wrought. He navigated the buggy down one of myriad country roads, sending the horse around a fallen tree branch with a light touch of the reins.

"Same as usual." Her shrug was noncommittal, but in truth she hadn't been able to stop thinking of him all night—him and his secrets.

"Which is?" He grinned, and she frowned.

Tired and confused, she wondered if she should just admit the truth to him, but something restrained her. She'd rationalized her way through a hundred possible reasons why Luke would resort to disguising himself and thieving from his own people. But after a lot of prayer, she'd decided that she had to trust him until he trusted her enough to tell her his secret.

"Shouldn't you know what your betrothed is thinking, Luke Lantz?"

"What you're thinking? *Nee*—who can ever know what's in a woman's mind?"

Well, after last night . . . you should know, she thought in irritation. "Take me home."

"What? I just picked you up fifteen minutes ago."

"I don't care." And she didn't. She did not care one bit for Luke's sensibilities, not when she knew that he could be someone like the stranger in the woods who'd noticed her even in the dark. The Luke Lantz in the buggy today hardly seemed the same man. It wasn't just his Amish dress and calm tone; it was also his detached demeanor.

But then, to her surprise, Luke drew the buggy to a halt. She saw that they were in Glorious Grove—the childish name she'd given to the copse of maples that towered over the dirt road. She was pleased to see that nothing but a stray branch here and there seemed to have been hurt by the storm.

"What are you doing? I told you to take me home." She crossed her arms over her chest and glared at him, unused to his not doing as she asked.

He laughed low, and the sound caught in her mind. She blinked. She was definitely thinking too much about the thief . . . the thief in the night who'd stolen her dreams. Luke ran a hand down her shoulder to the bend in her elbow, and she snapped back to the moment.

"I'll take you home, Rose, but I've been thinking about what you said—about kissing more."

She opened her mouth in shock. "Now? Now you want to kiss more?"

"Maybe. What do you mean by *now*? Aren't we nearer still to our wedding day?"

She shook her head, confused, and he leaned closer. Against

her will, she was intrigued. Luke had rarely been the initiator of kisses in the past.

"Unclasp your arms," he murmured, sliding his hat off.

She lifted her nose in the air. "*Nee*—why?"

He smiled. "So you're not all tense."

"I'm not tense."

"What happened here?" He touched the pinkish burn on the back of her hand with care, and she had to look away from him.

"I made blueberry pies last night."

"Really?"

She'd never have guessed that he knew more than enough about her pie baking. And she didn't like his teasing tone, even if it was feigned. Sometimes there was no fun in having someone know you well enough to understand even your baking weaknesses.

"*Ya*, really," she snapped.

"I would have liked a taste," he whispered, and she turned to look at him in surprise. Was there some undercurrent of meaning in his words? She searched his familiar face; his blue eyes were as innocent as always. She almost sighed. She was definitely confused by the encounter in the woods.

Then he let his fingers play up along her shoulder to the nape of her neck and slid a curl free from beneath her *kapp*. He moved to press his lips against her hair and gave a soft exhalation of pleasure.

She drew a sharp breath. "Luke!"

"What?" He bent his head, her hair still in his fingers, and tilted forward so that his mouth hovered a bare inch from her own. "What, Rose?" He trailed the tendril across her lips and waited.

Her breath caught, and she felt a near dizzying sense of his closeness. She wanted him to move—to start, to finish the kiss. But he held back, as if he were searching for something in the depths of her eyes. She felt his weight rock against her for a moment, and he placed a very soft, almost brotherly kiss on her forehead, dropping the strand of hair. She blew out a breath of frustration when he picked up the reins with an enigmatic smile.

"We've made a start," he observed as he turned the horse.

Rose wasn't sure why she felt such a loss at his idea of a beginning.

Chapter Six

∽

It was a week later when Rose sank down at the Kings' kitchen table to visit with her friend Priscilla. There was a palpable excitement and energy in the air, and Rose wondered if her own home would feel this way when her wedding was only a short few weeks away.

"So, Rose—you've been *baking*?" Priscilla smiled and nodded toward the pie sitting on the table. "I thought you'd rather add up a page of sums than make a pie!"

"As a matter of fact, I would," Rose said flatly. "Just take it and enjoy. It's actually not half bad."

"Okaaay."

Rose took a sip of the tea Priscilla had offered her and tried not to dismiss the past few days from her mind. But a blur of brown sugar, cinnamon, flour, and apple peels swirled in her head until she thought she'd never want to taste another pie again as long as she lived. "How are the wedding plans coming along?" she asked, hoping to dislodge her sugary vision.

Priscilla was engaged to marry in just a few weeks, and Rose was to be one of the attendants. It was a great honor, considering that Priscilla's sister should have served in the position, but Hannah was due to deliver on the day of the ceremony.

Unlike Rose, Priscilla usually glowed with satisfaction over her impending wedding, but now she shook her head. "We've had a few—incidents, little glitches in our plans, but I'm sure everything will be perfect from here on out. I do think, though, that you and Luke have the right idea in marrying later in the season. It seems I can barely plan, with all of the weddings we have to attend on the weekends."

"I suppose you're right," Rose murmured, breaking a piece of crust from the pie before her and crumbling it between her fingers.

"Rose, what's wrong?"

Rose swallowed. Priscilla was her best friend, and keeping things from her was even more difficult than evading *Aenti* Tabby, but she just couldn't bring herself to tell her Luke's secret. More than that, she knew that her friend would never have gone looking for someone in the night, because she'd found the love of her life—it radiated in her face and convicted Rose's heart.

"Nothing's wrong."

"Rose—I've wanted to ask . . . does it—well, scare you a little to take on a household of four men? Is that what's bothering you?"

Rose sighed. *If only it were that easy . . .* It wasn't the responsibility of caring for a ready-made family she feared, but her own treacherous thoughts, and her mixed-up attraction to the man she thought she knew so well.

"Sometimes I'm afraid. But it's just work. I'll delegate. They're managing fine without me now, so one extra pair of hands has got to be a help. Luke would never just let them dump all the housework on me."

Priscilla nodded. "No, he cherishes you far too much for that."

Rose stood up abruptly. "Priscilla, I'd best be going. I just wanted—to give you the pie. Besides, I promised Luke I'd stop by the office and see him for a few minutes. I suppose I should do it."

"*Bensel* . . . you sound like you don't really want to!"

Rose summoned a smile. "That's silly—of course I do."

THE *ENGLISCH* SEEMED TO HAVE AN EVER-GROWING FASCI-nation with all things Amish, and Luke considered wryly that he'd much prefer to be wrestling with accounts than doing the other part of his job—dealing with customers.

He blinked from the throbbing in his temples and refocused on the woman across the desk from him. She was young and blond and had bright, carefully made-up blue eyes. She was also spoiled rotten by her husband, as far as he could tell. Mrs. Matthews had very distinct ideas about what she wanted for her own birthday gift, and apparently had even more particular thoughts about men in general falling under the spell of her obvious beauty. Luke had spent a mind-numbing half hour trying to verbally sidestep her, finally deciding that humoring her was the best possible recourse.

"So, let's go over this again, Mrs. Matthews." He leaned forward conspiratorially. "A carved headboard."

ROSE SIGHED AS SHE LOOPED THE REINS OF THE HORSE over the post outside the woodworking shop and glanced at the car parked there. The vehicle shone with discreet elegance in the filtered sunlight of the row of brightly colored oak trees that lined the Lantzes' lane. She hesitated, thinking maybe a wealthy client might be occupying Luke's time, but she had promised to stop.

She entered the side door, breathing in the pungent smells of many woods—butternut, sassafras, black walnut. The accompanying sounds of hammers and shavers echoed with familiar comfort as she turned to the office. The door to the small room was half closed, and she lifted her hand to knock when a burst of pleased feminine laughter made her jump.

"Oh, Mr. Lantz—tell me another, please. You've got a wonderful sense of humor."

"Call me Luke."

Call him Luke? Rose felt an unfamiliar pang in her chest as she stared at the wooden door.

"Go on in, Rosie," Joshua bellowed as he crossed behind her carrying a brace of two-by-fours. "He's been in there forever."

Forever? Rose frowned and eased the door open.

A blond-haired woman in faded blue jeans, fancy boots, and a becoming pink sweater sat on the edge of Luke's desk. Her betrothed had his hat off and leaned back in his chair. The deep smile on his face revealed a dimple in his cheek that Rose had forgotten even existed.

He turned easily in the chair while the woman looked up.

"Rose, *hiya*. I forgot you were coming. I don't know where the time's gone."

He made to rise, and Rose waved him back down with a quick swipe of her hand. Feelings of irritation and jealousy mingled in her mind like the dust motes in the shaft of sunlight from the small window.

"Um . . . I'll just see you later since you're busy."

But the other woman slid down from the desk, a pile of neatly organized receipts falling after her. "Oh, I'm so silly!"

The woman bent her slender form to pick at the papers, and somehow Luke bent forward at the same time so that they knocked heads, his black hair touching the blond strands—and causing a red haze to temporarily mar Rose's vision.

"Do you need some help?" she heard herself ask sweetly. But something in her tone must have conveyed itself to Luke, because he made haste to get up.

"Uh, Rose—don't go. Mrs. Matthews and I . . ."

"Barbara," the woman interjected with a purr. "Don't forget."

"Right. Barbara and I are finished, really. I was just tallying her bill and telling her some of the odd things people want carved in wood sometimes. Uh . . . Barbara, this is my betrothed, Rose Bender."

Rose forced herself to shake the hand the other woman extended and resisted the urge to squeeze like she was working a hard milking cow. She was amazed at her own temper. Luke had done nothing but laugh, and after all, he had to be polite to the customers. She felt herself begin to calm down and silently prayed for forgiveness for the way she was feeling.

She cast her eyes quickly over the receipt Luke held and calculated the total with an easy computation in her head. She murmured the figure to him.

"How'd you do that so fast?" Luke smiled his thanks, but Mrs. Matthews was giggling.

"Oh, a wedding. I love weddings. You've got to let me congratulate you both!" She stretched to brush the air near Rose's cheek with a kiss, then wound her slender arms up around Luke's neck.

Not as long as I have breath in my body, Rose thought as she took a step forward and gave a soft cry. She let herself fall with dead weight against the other woman, knocking her clean from Luke to land sideways on the desk, with Rose grimly atop her. Silently asking forgiveness for the second time in as many minutes, she took her time letting Luke help her up and couldn't resist a well-placed elbow in the design of the pink sweater.

"I'm so sorry," she murmured, hauling Mrs. Matthews upright. "I must have tripped. You are all right, *ya?*"

The *Englisch* woman looked faintly bewildered, as though she'd been sidelined by some strange forest creature. She grabbed up her purse and nodded to both of them.

"I'll call you when we have your order complete, Barbara," Luke said.

Rose thought she detected the slightest hint of humor in his voice—but she couldn't be sure. In truth, she was appalled at her reaction and hoped that it wouldn't cost the Lantz family a customer. But Barbara nodded vaguely and headed out the door. When she'd gone, Rose raised guilty eyes to Luke, but he just looked at her with a calm gaze.

"Got to get that board fixed," he commented.

"Board?"

"The one you tripped over. Might be bad for future customers."

Speechless, Rose could only nod in agreement.

Chapter Seven

⁓⁓

Rose hadn't seen the "thief" again since their encounter the night of the storm, but for the third night in a row she set a trap for him. She snuggled beneath the quilt she'd dragged out onto a chair on the back porch and listened to the forlorn sound of occasional raindrops hitting the tightly sealed tinfoil on two apple pies on the rail.

She was a fool to long after another meeting with Luke in disguise.

She thought back again to the image of him laughing with the woman in the office that afternoon and tried to sort out her feelings. She'd watched Luke at singings and youth outings all through the years, and never had she thought to be jealous of his interactions with other girls. Not that he wasn't attractive and well-spoken; he was simply too faithful a friend and follower to ever be doubted. But now . . . now, he was something else, something more. She was too curious by nature to resist another taste of his disguise. And she had to admit that as the thief he had stirred her senses in a new way. She sighed and wondered what kind of person she was to be attracted to the unknown in someone.

She distracted herself by thinking about the apple pies she'd made. She was becoming adept at the task and yielding a deft hand to the formation of the latticework top crusts. She'd kept her brothers from asking for their fair share by baking while they were in the fields and had apparently satisfied her *mamm*'s curiosity with her explanation that she was trying to be a better cook. She didn't like the deception, but she rationalized that her doings were certainly harmless enough. She was going to marry Luke, after all, so she might as well give him another opportunity to tell her the truth.

She was half asleep, somewhere between dreaming and wakefulness, when she heard the sound of foil rattling. She popped open her eyes and clicked on her flashlight. The pies were gone, and someone was moving across the yard.

"Hey!" she hissed, arcing the light into the yard. The beam caught against a pair of blue-jean clad legs, and she dropped the quilt and stood. "Wait!" she called. "Please."

"Put down the light and I'll wait."

She heard the hoarse yet familiar voice, and her hands grew damp with perspiration as she snapped off the light and put it where she had been sitting. She crept to the porch rail and then down into the yard.

"They're apple—the pies, I mean." She toyed with her fingers.

"They'll be appreciated."

"*Ach* . . . do you . . . take for your family? Because we have plenty to give . . . I mean . . ."

"What do you want?" His question was harsh but penetrating.

"I don't—know what you mean." Rose's heart began to pound, wondering if he'd figured out that she recognized him.

"Yes, you do. A good Amish girl chasing after an *Englisch* thief. Why? What do you want?"

The rain seemed to be melting her sensibilities, her defenses, the very excuses she'd sustained herself on the past months when she thought of a lifetime with Luke. Suddenly he'd become the center of something she desired with all her heart.

"I want you," she said baldly.

There was a long moment of silence, broken only by the falling of the rain.

"Me?" He laughed. "What do you know about me?"

"I want your way of being, your freedom. . . ." *Who you are right now . . .*

"If it's your engagement that you want out of, why not tell your—best friend?"

"I don't want out of it," she cried, amazed at his perception. But then, he'd known her forever . . .

"Tell him. Tell him you're so hungry to be free that you'd stand in the dark and the rain and long for a stranger's touch—his kiss."

She almost spun away from the deep voice, the mockery, and the powerful allure. *His kiss.*

She heard the shift of the foil, the damp footsteps, and then he swooped so close that she could feel his breath against her cheek, the press of the pie pans against her stomach. He smelled of the forest and something else that was tantalizingly familiar. But then his mouth was on hers, once, twice, two angry kisses, and then a yielding, a softening, and she was kissing him back with all of the withheld passion in her young soul. He broke away with a rasp in his breath, and Rose stood shivering, gasping for breath as the rain increased in tenor.

"Go inside," he ordered, moving away.

She couldn't obey, couldn't think, as she raised a shaking hand to her lips.

"Don't leave," she gasped.

She heard him inhale. "I must."

And then he was gone, running, the rain making an uneven and fading tattoo on the foil as she listened to some part of her dreams move far and away.

Chapter Eight

❧

LUKE STARED OUT AT THE GRAY MORNING THROUGH THE kitchen window and wondered if the sun would break through. Rose had promised to come and help with the cider making. He took a deep swallow of the bitter coffee his brother had brewed and tried to suppress his mixed feelings about kissing Rose the night before. To be sure, he could still imagine his mouth stinging with the contact, but he'd been furious too. He'd risked a second encounter with her partially because he'd wondered how far her interest extended to some strange *Englischer*. He also wanted to see her again as he had the night of the storm, so striking in her beauty and so much as one with the wild darkness. He wondered idly whether she'd understand if he tried to explain . . .

Joshua entered through the back kitchen door. "Saw Abram Bender out this morning."

Luke blinked as he sipped his coffee and turned to his *bruder*. "Mending fence?"

Joshua laughed. *"Ya."*

It was a gentle joke among the Lantz and Bender families how much time Abram spent mending fence. It was almost as if the man could sense a weakening in the stone or wire even before the cows could.

Luke moved from the sink basin to give his brother room to wash.

"Nervous about becoming a married man, Luke?" There was enough curiosity in Josh's voice for Luke to know he wasn't just joking.

"Maybe," he admitted, thinking of Rose kissing a supposed stranger.

"Wish *Mamm* could be here to see it?"

Luke tightened his grip on his cup. "Surely."

Joshua toweled his arms, whistling through his teeth for a moment. "Well, you still going to that *Englisch* homeless shelter to help out like *Mamm* did?"

"Nee . . . I haven't had the time of late."

Joshua nodded. "Just as well. You've enough of your own to care for without chasing after the *Englisch*, no matter how fitting the cause."

"Wouldn't *Mamm* say that helping another is always worth the doing?" Luke's voice was level.

Joshua clapped him on the shoulder. *"Ya,* she would. But not everybody's like she was."

"And that's the truth to be heard," Luke muttered.

"What?"

"Nothing. Nothing at all."

THE DAY WAS ONE TO STIR THE SENSES; BLUE SKIES AND cotton fluffed clouds. Geese flying in south V-patterns, and the mingled scents of nature in its hurried pursuit and preparation for sleep, all joined in a rapturous serenade.

But Rose was uneasy. For once she couldn't discern Luke's mood, and it made her nervous. Of course there was the guilty worry that, from his perspective, she'd been kissing a stranger in the rain. That had to make him angry, and she thought once more of telling him what she knew. But the moment passed and she focused on tossing the quartered apples into the Lantzes' cider press as Luke turned the crank handle.

The smell of ripe apples and the crispness of the fall day seemed to burgeon with life and abundance, and part of her wanted to dance with the red and yellow leaves that swirled in graceful arcs to land on the ground. But Luke was uncommonly silent, moving mechanically, almost as if she wasn't there.

"Are you all right?" she asked at last.

He glanced at her—calm blue eyes and a solemn expression. "*Ya*. And you?"

She frowned. She didn't want to talk about how she felt. "Fine," she mumbled.

He straightened and came toward where she sat on a low stool. His work boots brushed the rounded fall of her dress as it spread upon the ground, and she squinted up at him in the sunshine.

"*Ya*, you are fine, Rose," he said, reaching down to brush the curve of her cheek.

She sat still, mesmerized by his warm fingers and that mysterious side of him that teased at her consciousness.

He dropped his hand and cleared his throat. "I've been thinking of late . . . our engagement . . . perhaps we set the wedding too soon. Maybe you'd prefer another year in which to plan?"

"What?" she squeaked in dismay. *Is this why he's so quiet? Does he want to break our engagement?* Surprisingly, the thought made her sick at heart, even as she considered how she might feel if she thought he'd been kissing someone else in the dark.

He turned his back to her and ran a hand over the damp board of the press, shrugging his broad shoulders. "You're much younger than I, Rose."

"I've always been younger than you—it's never mattered before."

"*Nee*, but now . . . with all of the responsibilities of the house . . . perhaps you desire still a continued bit of freedom."

Her eyes widened in a rush of feverish thought. What had she said to him last night about freedom? Did he suspect that she knew?

She rose and touched his arm, and he turned to face her. "I want to marry, Luke. I do."

He nodded, but she felt him search her face, and she lifted her chin.

"All right, Rose."

She longed for him to touch her, but he was back to the apple press. The moment was gone, and the day seemed to lose some of its color as she shifted on her feet and tried to sort through her emotions.

WHEN ROSE STOOD BEHIND HIM, LUKE TRIED TO CON-
centrate on the gush of juice from the press and put aside the
thought of touching his future bride—kissing her as the "thief"
had last night. But he'd meant what he said—perhaps she needed
a bit more time. Maybe that's why she spoke of freedom in the
dark and yielded to—*nee*, returned a heated kiss with such passion. Yet he didn't want to complicate matters by bringing more
physicality into the moment . . .

He looked up in relief at the diversion when his brother Mark
emerged from the woodworking shop nearby. Mark was two years
older than Luke, still single, and was the family's tease. But today
he appeared frustrated.

Mark dropped onto the stool Rose had abandoned and sank a
dipper into the bucket of cloudy cider. He slurped loudly as Luke
ran the last of the apples through.

"What's wrong?" Luke asked.

"What's wrong with you two?"

Luke started to take the apple press apart to prepare it for drying and ignored his brother's question.

"You leaving already, Rose?" Mark prodded. "Seems like Luke
could do something to persuade you to stick around more often."

"She has her own chores to be about," Luke observed in a
warning tone.

"I'd imagine that a girl would want to spend every second
possible with her betrothed."

"*Ya.*" Luke smiled then. "You'd have to imagine it—since it
seems no one's standing in line to be your bride."

Rose giggled.

"Watch your mouth, baby *bruder*. Or I may have to watch it for you."

Luke laid the crank down with care. "All right. You are in a fine temper and in front of my future bride. Why is that?"

Mark sighed. "*Ach*, I messed up the piece of burled elm *Daed* had me redoing for that piano front. You know how rare that wood grain is."

Luke turned from the press. "How bad is it?"

Mark shrugged. "I don't know. I was off somehow in the scrolling design, and now the whole thing's lopsided. *Daed*'s gonna have a fit when he and Josh get back from their delivery."

"Let me take a look."

Mark shrugged. "Go ahead. It's on the second workbench."

Chapter Nine

ROSE FOLLOWED LUKE'S PURPOSEFUL STRIDES INTO THE shop. A generator powered several overhead bulbs and cast light onto the worktable that was laden with tools, wood curls, and a beautiful piece of wood. But the design clearly had a flaw. She watched as Luke picked up the foot-long panel and ran his large hands down the unusual sheen of the wood.

His eyes were intent as he scanned the workbench and chose a slender tool from among the gougers and scrapers. There was an air of suppressed energy in his movements, almost a sensuality in the way he turned the wood in his hands.

"Luke?"

"Hmmm?"

He was making small additions to the scrollwork, bending to cast an eye over the wood, then straightening to start again.

"Why don't you tell your *daed* the truth?"

He stilled and stared at her. "What do you mean?"

46

She gestured to the wood. "You love this; you always have. Tell your father so you can get out of that office." *And away from women like Barbara* . . .

He bent over the wood again with a shrug. "It doesn't matter."

She was silent, watching him work, liking the way the dust motes he stirred up played in the fall of light and landed in his brown hair. She'd rarely seen him so enthused, and her throat ached when she thought of the hours he gave without complaint to the work his father expected of him. Perhaps that was why he sought some sort of diversion—dressing like an *Englischer*, playing at being a thief. But still, it didn't quite make sense . . .

After a few minutes he looked up with satisfaction. "There." He blew the wood off and tilted it toward her as the sound of a wagon and horse echoed from outside. Luke put the wood down, stepped away from the workbench, and caught her hand. He pulled her toward the door as Mark entered, looking hunted.

"*Daed*'s back."

Luke gave him a swift cuff on the shoulder and looked out to see their father coming toward the door.

"*Daed.*" Luke greeted him calmly. "I was about to see Rose to her buggy, if you'll excuse us."

"*Ya*, surely. I wanted to see how Mark did on the—"

Rose watched as he broke off and drifted past them to the workbench. The older man lifted the wooden piece with near reverent hands. "*Ach*, Mark. What is this?"

Mark stepped forward as if to speak when Luke caught his arm.

"It's wondrous craftsmanship, my son. And I'll risk the vanity to tell you so. I've never seen the like of such an intricate design."

Rose watched Mark open his mouth again, and Luke turned abruptly. She felt the jolt through their entwined hands when his elbow connected with Mark's ribs, knocking the breath from him. Then Luke pulled her out the door and into the sunlight.

"WHAT IS WRONG WITH YOU?" ROSE HISSED. SHE SNATCHED her hand away from him as he moved to help her up into the wagon.

He swung up beside her. "What?"

"Why would you let your *daed* think that Mark fixed that design?"

Luke lifted the reins and tilted his hat back a bit, exposing his handsome profile. He answered slowly. "It would trouble my father—make him feel torn if he knew I could work wood like that. It's less worry for him if I do the books. And he doesn't need any worry—not since *Mamm* . . . well . . ."

"You miss her so much, don't you?"

She watched him reach to rub at his neck as if to soothe an ever-present ache. "*Ya*, of course I do."

"I never asked you before . . . did she know? I mean, how much you love the woodworking?"

"Maybe. I don't know. I planned on telling her once, and then there was the flu. It all happened so fast. And *Daed*, well . . . it nearly broke him."

Rose took a deep breath and a shot in the dark. "You're afraid. It's not your *daed*, Luke—it's you. You're afraid to be who you really are."

He turned to face her, blinking solemnly. "*Ya*. You're right, Rose. And you'd know, because your secret is that you're afraid yourself. So don't tell me about being who you really are."

"I know who I am," she cried, wanting it to be true. Wanting to banish the meetings with him as the *Englischer* in the woods from her mind. Suddenly, the planned footing of her future seemed treacherously slippery.

Chapter Ten

ROSE TOSSED BENEATH THE NINE-PATCH QUILT OF HER girlhood bed; she hadn't seen much of Luke the past week and felt distant from him. She sighed aloud and forced herself to focus on her prayers.

"*Ach*, Lord, help me. Help my relationship with Luke to be true. Search my heart, *Derr Herr*, and find those shadows, those secrets that I would hide even from myself, and bring them to light. Forgive me for spending time chasing after Luke as the man in the woods, and help him just the same. Free him from this stealing. Free me from wanting something like the wind, and not the steadiness of the moment. Thank You for Luke. Thank You, *Derr Herr*, for my life and my ability to make choices. Give me wisdom, Lord . . . please . . . give me wisdom."

Utterly drained, she pulled the covers up to her chin and dreamed fitfully. Tangled blue threads, the color of the wedding dress she was sewing on a bit each day, seemed to stretch from her mind to wrap around her arms and wrists. The thread was thin but confining, and she struggled against the bonds. Then a dark-hooded stranger stood before her and raised a pair of silver shears high. She felt her breath catch in her throat at the slash of silver against the white of her skin, but then the threads were gone and she was free. She called to him because he was running from her, and he turned. The hood fell away, and Luke stood before her. Then he caught her up in a swinging embrace and she laughed, free and clear . . .

Rose jerked awake and sat straight up in bed. Her heart was pounding and she stared out the window, glad to see the first streaks of the morning sun falling across the hardwood floor of her room. She decided that a walk in the woods before breakfast would clear her tangled thoughts, and she hurried to dress. She wanted to slip away before anyone would notice she was gone. She needed some time to herself to consider her dream.

But when she crept downstairs, it was to find everyone wide-awake and already halfway through breakfast at the kitchen table. "*Mamm*," she cried in dismay. "Why didn't you call me to help with the meal?"

Ben laughed. "We all called you, but you slept like the dead! Don't you remember that today's the first day of the fair?"

Rose bit her lip as she accepted a bowl of steaming oatmeal from her mother and sat down at the table. "I guess I forgot," she mumbled.

The first fall fair in the area was something her family always attended together, but after her poor night's sleep, the outing held little appeal. She kept seeing the moment in her dream when the stranger's hood fell backward to reveal Luke's face.

"As is right," her father remarked, scraping the last of his plate. "Probably dreaming of your wedding coming, like any girl would."

Rose concentrated on the wet lumps of her oatmeal and didn't lift her head. She had no desire to talk about dreaming—wedding or otherwise.

"Are you feeling well, Rosie?" *Aenti* Tabby asked softly.

A sudden inspiration struck Rose. "Well, actually . . . if you all wouldn't mind—I wonder if I might stay home today to do some sewing on my wedding dress. I've barely pieced the pattern yet, and I feel like time is running away from me."

She saw her mother glance down the table to her father's warm eyes.

"*Ya*, Rose." *Mamm* smiled. "Just for today. Some time alone may be *gut* for you."

Rose nodded. "*Danki.*"

James held his plate out for more sausage. "*Ya*, Rose, but just don't go entertaining any Rob in the Hood while we're gone. Luke Lantz might take offense."

She frowned as both of her brothers laughed, and told herself that she'd had enough of fairy tales for a while.

ONCE SHE'D HELPED CLEAN UP BREAKFAST, THEN WAVED the family off, she decided that a walk in the brisk sunshine would do her good before beginning hours of sewing. Of their own accord, her feet seemed to lead to the forest behind her home. She spent a peaceful half hour praying as she walked, collecting the reddest leaves, and daydreaming. On one level, she continued her prayers for Luke from the evening before, asking the Lord if Luke might one day escape the task of bookkeeping and use instead the ready skill he had with woodworking.

But then she became aware of a rhythmic pounding from somewhere in the distance. She stopped and listened. She couldn't imagine who'd be building on anything out this far. Her steps quickened as a childish memory of an old tumbledown shack on the Lantzes' property surfaced in her consciousness. She crept through the trees to the sunny clearing and stopped, pressing hard against an old oak.

Clad in blue jeans, work boots, and a loose white shirt, Luke was atop the low roof of the old shack. His back was to her, his head bent, as he concentrated on securing a new white pine board to the roof. The sun caught on the muscles of his arms as he lifted the hammer, and she made an inadvertent sound of pleasure at the sight. He half turned in her direction, then seemed to tense and put a foot back onto the gray wood. There was a brief cracking sound and a muffled cry. Rose gasped as the weathered part of the roof gave way beneath his weight and Luke disappeared in a rain of old wood and an ominous cloud of dust.

Chapter Eleven

ROSE RAN TO THE DOOR OF THE SHACK, COUGHING AS SHE breathed in the dust. She flung open the door and saw Luke lying facedown and still beneath a splintered pile of boards. She began snatching at the boards, heedless of their weight or the scratches from the wood on her arms.

"Luke! Are you all right?"

He gave a faint groan, then sneezed from the mess she was kicking up. "Rose—you know it's me?"

"*Ya*, of course . . . since that first time in the woods."

Luke sighed, a gusty exhalation, rolled over onto his back, and stared up at her through the dust and shards of wood. "I should have known," he muttered. He closed his eyes and slid one arm up and over his face, revealing an ugly gash on the underside of his wrist.

She dropped to her knees beside him and began to tear a strip from her apron and dab at the blood.

He lowered his arm slowly. "Don't. It needs to be washed first. And I think there's a splinter there."

Even his voice seemed different now—husky, inviting. And his dark blue eyes gleamed up at her with a knowing confidence. She let her eyes trail down his torn shirt to the low-slung blue jeans and shook her head, wondering if she was losing her mind. Was this really her Luke? The irony of her sense of proprietorship struck when she realized that no woman would take for granted the holding of the man before her.

"I—should have told you that I knew who you were," she said. "But I wanted you to trust me, to tell me what you were doing. You didn't." Her eyes met his, and he caught her hand, pulling her dirty fingertips to his lips.

"*Nee*," he murmured against her skin. "I was wrong."

He kissed her fingers with lingering passion, as she watched, mesmerized; then he let her go. She snatched her hand back as if she'd touched hot coals, feeling her face grow warm, whether from anger or excitement, she wasn't sure. Her thoughts felt thick, like the oatmeal she'd choked down at breakfast.

"Well, then—what? Why did you go on pretending with me that you were the thief?"

He smiled at her, a flash of white teeth and something fast and wolfish that made her catch her breath. "I am the thief."

"You—you touched me and kissed me, and I thought I was betraying Lu—you! Or that you were betraying me . . ." She broke off in confusion.

"Let your hair down, Rose, will you?" His eyes were intent, compelling, and she wondered if he'd taken a knock on the head when he'd fallen.

"Wh-what?"

"Please. I want to see you—revealed, like you're seeing me."

"Revealed?" she repeated slowly. "I don't even know who you are anymore."

"I'm the same person I've always been, Rose. Maybe you just haven't noticed."

She shook her head, inadvertently letting several strands escape the confines of her *kapp* and brush against his chest.

He smiled, a lazy, sultry smile that made her think of honey dripping from a comb, and she had to blink to keep her thoughts straight.

"We're nearly married," he observed, reaching to catch a stray curl and run it between his fingertips. The sunlight slanted down through the hole in the roof at that moment and fell across the tableau of her hair in his hand.

"Luke!" she snapped, breaking his reverie and yanking her hair from his hand. She ignored the sharp pain at her scalp. She was having difficulty breathing and thought that the dust couldn't be good for either one of them. "We need to get out of here."

"Probably," he murmured. "But I think my left ankle's sprained, so it may present a problem." His eyes drifted closed.

"Hey!"

"Don't worry; I'm here. Just get me up, if you can. We'll go to Dr. Knepp's."

"Fine. But you've got to tell me what you're doing with this shack—in the middle of nowhere." Her fingers pressed down his leg to test the extent of the sprain, and she wondered desperately how she'd ever move his weight.

He laughed, then groaned when she touched his ankle.

"That's another story. And don't forget my wallet and pants when we go."

"Is that all you're hiding?" she muttered, reaching to grasp at his shoulders.

"Maybe." He grinned lopsidedly. "But there might be a few more things I should confess to the bishop before we marry."

She stared at him in exasperation and wondered exactly what else her all-too-familiar and at the same time utterly alien betrothed would have to confess before she became his wife.

Chapter Twelve

SHE BREATHED A SIGH OF RELIEF WHEN HE TOLD HER that he'd hidden a horse and wagon in a copse of trees behind the shack. She led the horse round to the front of the dilapidated place, then half walked, half dragged Luke outside, trying to ignore the scent of sun and sweat that clung to his dusty skin.

"Your shirt's ruined," she pointed out. "And where are your suspenders?"

He grinned at her and gestured with his chin. "Over on that stump with my other stuff."

She went to gather his wallet and hat. Then she picked up his dark pants with the attached suspenders and turned to him with a frown. He was leaning against the horse for support, and for all of his seeming cheerfulness she couldn't help but see the tense lines of pain around his handsome mouth.

"Do you—do you want to put this on?" she questioned gruffly, extending the hat to him.

Luke nodded. "*Ya*, if you'll help a bit." His eyes danced as he swayed.

"Fine." She laid the items in her hands on the wagon seat, then came closer to where he stood, perching his hat on his head.

"Let's leave the hat, Rose. Just take a back road to the Knepps'. I feel like I'm going to be sick. Sorry."

Rose made a clucking sound of comfort and stood waiting, watching a pallor wash over him and a bead of sweat trail down his cheek. She pulled his hat back off, and he drew a deep breath.

"Do you want to sit down?" she asked anxiously.

"*Nee*, I'm all right now. Glad I wasn't sick in front of you."

"I saw you throw up from gorging yourself on watermelon when you were twelve, remember?"

He smiled faintly. "No secrets with a best friend."

"No secrets," she repeated soberly.

He exhaled. "Let's just go. I'll lie in the back of the wagon."

Somehow she managed to get him there; to half recline, clutching the side of the wagon. She used his dark pants to wrap about his ankle, then set about easing the wagon down back roads to get to the physician's home. And all the while her mind whirled with questions and emotions that she didn't care to examine too closely, choosing instead to focus on Luke's injuries and his need for care.

"A BAD SPRAIN CAN BE AS PROBLEMATIC AS A BREAK."

Dr. Knepp was a popular *Englisch* physician who'd long been accepted by the local Amish community. And if he thought it strange that Rose brought her betrothed in half dressed in *Englisch* clothes, he didn't remark on it. Instead, he hauled Luke onto an exam table and cut the pant leg of his jeans.

"Got to get that boot off, son," the doctor ordered.

"Right." Luke grimaced.

Dr. Knepp glanced at Rose. "I think you might go have a cup of tea with my wife, my dear. I'll wrap the ankle and get that chunk of wood out of his wrist."

She was about to protest when something stern in Luke's face made her leave the room. Probably he didn't want her to see him in pain. She wandered down the short hallway that separated the doctor's office from his home, entering the bright and cheery *Englisch* kitchen. Mrs. Knepp looked up from a pile of ironing.

"Rose. Come in and have something warm to drink. Was that Luke I saw you drive up with in the back of the wagon?" She set the iron aside.

"*Ya . . .*" She floundered for a moment, not knowing how to explain his injuries and not wanting to lie. "He . . . uh . . . we . . ."

Mrs. Knepp waved a casual hand. "Spare me the details, dear. That's all confidential doctor's information, right? Come have some hot cider and tell me how your wedding plans are coming along."

Rose sat down and accepted the delicate rose-painted china cup. She took a sip of the warm cider. Mrs. Knepp joined her, stirring her own cup with a stick of cinnamon.

"I hear you're to be bridesmaid . . . er . . . attendant for Priscilla King's upcoming wedding. A pity her sister's due that day, but a nice honor for you, hmm?"

"*Ach, ya.* I've known Priscilla nearly as long as I've known

Luke." Rose stared into her cider, wondering exactly how long she had known Luke—at least, the Luke who touched her hair and enticed her with his eyes.

A muffled groan from the doctor's wing made Rose stand up. Mrs. Knepp waved her back down. "He'll be fine, Rose. Just relax."

Rose sank back into her chair and toyed with the cup handle.

"Luke will do his own fair share of waiting over the coming years, I'll bet."

Rose looked at her hostess in confusion. "What do you mean?"

"Babies." Mrs. Knepp smiled. "He'll be waiting for you then, though if he's half the man he seems, he'll be right beside you, helping you along."

Rose flushed. The thought of having Luke's children sent her heart racing. Yet, up until a few days ago, she thought she'd known everything there was to him, and not much of that had caused her heart to thrill. But here she was, anxious for his pain, worried about his stealing, and in love with a part of him that she didn't even know. She took a strong swallow of cider, scalding the tip of her tongue and hastily depositing the cup back on the table.

Mrs. Knepp smiled once more. "Engagements are always hard."

Rose had to agree. "What's an *Englisch* engagement like?"

Mrs. Knepp laughed. "Oh, not so much ceremony as your own people's, I suppose, but there's still the fun . . . and the uncertainty."

"Uncertainty?"

The older woman gave her a sympathetic look. "Has no one told you, dear, that uncertainty is part of an engagement?"

Rose shook her head.

"Well, it is. How exactly are two young people supposed to look down a road where they can't see so far as the nearest prayer in the church?"

"I don't know. I guess I've struggled some with it myself."

"So you're normal. But I saw your face just now when you thought Luke was in pain . . . that's love, Rose—the worrying, the hoping."

"And . . . the future?"

"Belongs to God." Mrs. Knepp smiled and patted her hand. "And with that, we all must be content."

Chapter Thirteen

"I TAKE IT YOU'LL NOT BE EXPLAINING HOW THIS ALL came to be?" the doctor asked, a faint, telling glimmer in his eyes as he wrapped the swollen ankle with gentle hands.

"*Nee*, if you don't mind."

"Not a bit. Just a quick tetanus jab and we should be through here. Keep that ankle elevated a few hours a day, and make sure the bandages on the wrist stay clean and dry. Do you want some help changing your clothes back? I think your jeans are shot."

"*Danki*, Doc. What do I owe you?"

Dr. Knepp chuckled. "The truth—when you care to tell it. Only because I'm curious."

Luke offered his hand and had it shaken with goodwill. "Consider it a future payment then. I've got to get past *Daed* first."

"And your future bride?"

"Don't remind me." Luke sighed as he eased off the examining table.

HALF AN HOUR LATER LUKE'S HEAD WAS THROBBING nearly as much as his ankle with Rose's ceaseless round of questions as she drove him home. And the rattling of the wooden crutches in the back of the wagon didn't help matters. Sitting on the bench seat beside her, his leg extended, Luke had the sudden and pressing desire to simply kiss her quiet, but decided it probably wouldn't be quite as fair as an explanation. Still . . . he glanced at her berry red lips as she framed her next query.

He moved quickly, dipping his head and slanting his chin so that he met her mouth half open. He kissed her hard, then pulled back a fraction to smile with satisfaction at the surprised *O* her pretty mouth had formed.

She stared at him suspiciously. "Did Dr. Knepp give you something weird for pain?"

"*Nee,*" he whispered. "Am I being . . . weird?"

"Maybe. For the Luke I thought I knew . . . yes. For the other . . ." She slapped the reins across the horse's rump and tilted her head aside. "I don't know if I can say."

He laughed and withdrew. "Oh, I think you can say, Rose."

She flushed visibly at his intimate tone, and he tore his gaze away to glance at the passing landscape.

"What will you tell your family about how you got hurt?" she asked. "I certainly don't know what to say."

He tilted his hat forward and leaned back, closing his eyes. "Don't worry so much. I'll take care of everything."

WHEN SHE BROUGHT THE WAGON TO A STANDSTILL AT the Lantz home, Rose found that Luke's idea of taking care of things had little to do with explanation and more to do with exhausted dozing. And she couldn't very well give him the elbow jab he so deserved when she was confronted by Mr. Lantz's look of consternation.

"*Ach*, Rose. What is this?" Mr. Lantz whispered anxiously, peering up into the wagon seat where Luke drowsed.

"Uh, Luke and I . . ." Her voice rose several octaves. "We were, um . . ." She broke off abruptly when Luke half turned to nuzzle against her shoulder.

"Luke!" She rapped his name out frantically, and he woke with a start, blinking his blue eyes warmly at her. "Luke. Your *daed*—we're home." She pleaded with him with her eyes while he got track of his bearings.

"*Ach, Daed.*"

"Is it broken?" Mr. Lantz asked anxiously, reaching up to touch his son's leg above the bandage.

"Just a bad sprain," Luke assured him.

"You are both all right then? Rose?"

Rose could only nod, having no desire to lie to her future father-in-law. Not that she could tell him the truth anyway. She didn't know it.

"I'm sorry," she said, apropos of nothing, and was surprised to feel her lip tremble.

Mr. Lantz misinterpreted her look. "*Ach*, Rosie . . . never mind. He'll be right as rain for the wedding. I'm sure of it."

The wedding! Rose felt her heart skip a beat as she saw Luke shoot her a warm sidelong glance. Somehow she was supposed to marry a man who had become more than she could ever desire. It was enough to both exhilarate and make her feel like throwing up at the same time.

"*Danki*," she whispered.

Mr. Lantz came round the wagon and reached up to pat her hands on the reins. "Mark, Joshua!" The old man's voice carried into the workshop, and Luke's brothers appeared in the doorway. "Come—your brother's sprained his ankle. Let's move him inside the house, and then one of you can see Rose home."

"Uh, I'll walk," Rose interjected, slipping down from the wagon seat. "Really. Please—just take care of Luke." She was two steps away from the wagon when Luke's voice stopped her.

"Rose? Come and visit later?" His tone was pleading.

His *daed* nodded his approval, and she could hardly decline. But first she needed some time alone to think through this strange turn of events.

Chapter Fourteen

"Daed—I'm fine. Really."

Luke noticed that his father's work-worn hands shook a bit as they smoothed the mounded quilt under the injured ankle, and his heart squeezed in his chest. He'd never given much thought to the fact that his father was getting older. Somehow he'd believed that *Daed* would always be healthy and strong.

"*Ya*, surely you are," his father murmured, straightening.

Luke swallowed. "*Daed* . . . I know none of us has been sick or hurt since *Mamm*, but this is nothing to worry over."

"*Ya*, so they said about your mother." The older man dropped into a nearby rocker and covered his face with his hand for a moment. "Perhaps I grow old in my concern."

Remorse swelled in Luke's throat when he thought of how his selfish behavior could bring more pain to his father. It had never been his desire to assume the role he had—that of a common thief—and what's more, he knew that he'd enjoyed it. But no weight of purpose could outbalance what he'd done. He sighed softly and flexed his wrist in its white bandages.

"*Daed*, we're all a bunch of fool men in this house, who've done little to really talk about *Mamm* not being here. Rose—well, she likes to talk. I've come to learn through her that talking helps things. It's when we don't say—what we should, maybe—that things are worse."

He waited, and after a moment his father drew a hoarse breath.

"Well, I miss your *mamm*, to be sure. I thought that if I— spoke too much of it, that it would hurt you boys . . . add to your grieving. I guess I've kept the secret of my hurt inside for too long, and you're right—it's not *gut*." He took out a white hankie and blew his nose prodigiously. "*Ya*, especially with a new bride coming to bring life to these walls again. Your Rosie's got your *mamm*'s spirit, her gentleness and love of life. You're a lucky man, *sohn*—she's perfect for you."

Luke licked at a tear that slipped past his mouth and nodded. "*Ya, Daed*. Perfect."

THE MORE SHE WALKED, THE MORE CONFUSED ROSE GOT. Luke had her coming and going, and she had him in nearly the same position—except for the fact that he seemed so . . . steamy in his behavior, despite his injuries. Yet she still could explain little to nothing about why he'd done what he had the last months. And he'd kept on as though nothing had happened—except for the day he'd suggested she'd like more freedom . . .

She stopped so abruptly on the dirt road that she nearly stumbled. He'd offered her freedom, and had she taken it, he'd been willing to let her go, without any guilt or condemnation. Remorse flooded her consciousness, and she felt tears sting the backs of her eyes. What she'd taken for granted—his love—was real. It was giving and patient and all of those other things she knew from church but couldn't recall from her flustered mind.

Aenti Tabby's words teased at her consciousness with sudden importance. *What if there were more to Luke? More. More. More.*

She sighed and resumed walking, swiping at her eyes with the backs of her hands. Luke still had a lot of explaining to do . . . but then, maybe she did too.

She arrived home slightly breathless with emotion to find that the family had returned from the fair. *Aenti* Tabby was in the backyard making unrefined sugar from the bumper crop of sugar beets they'd had that year.

"*Ach*, some stronger hands than mine for the press," the older woman said with a welcoming smile.

Rose ducked her head so that her aunt wouldn't see the emotion in her face and plunged her hands into a nearby bucket of soapy water. She dried her hands on a clean towel and then took over at the apple press, which currently ran with the bright red and purple of sugar beets. Later the juice would be boiled until nearly all the liquid had evaporated, leaving rough granules of sugar for cooking. The hard part was pressing the liquid from the beets.

Aenti Tabby moved to continue cutting off the rough green tops. "So, have you seen your friend Priscilla lately? I've heard the Kings are having quite a time getting ready for her wedding."

Rose realized she had been too involved in her own issues to be of much comfort to her friend. She'd have to pay her another visit soon. To think that Priscilla and Chester's wedding was only three weeks away. The thought made her heart speed up at the seamless passage of time, and thoughts of her own December wedding to Luke flooded her mind again.

"How is your dress coming?"

"*Gut.* I've got it pieced, and I sew on it a bit whenever I can."

Rose was waiting for it—more pressing questions about Luke from her *aenti*—and decided to forestall the process by talking a blue streak. But as she opened her mouth to speak, her *aenti* gave a shocked cry.

"What?" Rose asked in alarm.

"Your hands, child! You didn't put on gloves."

Rose stared down at her hands and wrists, now stained as purple as the beet juice that gushed through the press.

"*Ach!* I wasn't thinking . . ."

"Or perhaps you were thinking too much," Aenti Tabby suggested.

Rose laughed aloud ruefully. "I suppose I can try kerosene to get it off."

"Or maybe your Luke would prefer a purple hand to hold until he's feeling better."

Rose opened her mouth in shock. "What?" How did her *aenti* know about Luke's injuries?

Aenti Tabby laughed at her expression. "Dr. Knepp stopped by before you got here to make sure that you were feeling well. Will you tell me what happened?"

Rose stared down at her purple fingers, perplexed, and thought hard about strangling Luke as she struggled for an answer.

Chapter Fifteen

"GO ON UP, ROSE." MR. LANTZ SMILED WITH WHAT SEEMED
like extra exuberance. "He's just resting that ankle a bit."

Rose returned the smile to her kindly future father-in-law and
decided Luke must have handled things all right. She crossed the
beautifully pegged oak floors of the Lantz farmhouse with a familiar appreciation. Luke had suggested that they might move into
the small house adjacent to the farm soon after they married, but
Rose wouldn't think of it. She'd loved the woman who would have
been her mother-in-law, and part of her longed to bring back the
feminine touches that were missing from the home—the watering
can of red geraniums on the kitchen windowsill; the sheen and
patina of the beautifully carved furniture, which in recent months
seemed always to need a dusting; and just the general feel of a
woman about the place to cook and clean, heal and listen. She was
no fool though, and knew that unless she drew upon *Derr Herr*'s
spirit, drinking from the Living Water to nourish herself first, she
would have nothing to bring to her new family.

This thought filled her mind as she moved to the bottom of the staircase and glanced upward. Over the years Rose had climbed the staircase to Luke's room more times than she could count, having always been treated like a daughter by the Lantzes. But today something was different as she gripped the smoothness of the simple balustrade with one hand and swiped at a stray piece of lint on her dress with the other. Today she was nervous, uncertain, and she hesitated at the closed wooden door at the top left of the steps. It wasn't just her friend who lay within, but her betrothed—and the thief of her heart.

She knocked softly, half hoping he slept, but his voice rang true through the wood.

"*Kumme* in."

She took a deep breath, plastered a pleasant expression on her face, and opened the door. Luke gazed at her with that same rich smile he seemed to have grown out of nowhere, and she felt herself flushing for no reason.

"Rose, *kumme*. Close the door and sit down." He patted the edge of the bed near his hip, and she swallowed.

"*Ya*, but maybe I should leave the door open—your *daed* . . ."

"My *daed* knows you've been up here a hundred times with that door shut, but suit yourself." He stretched his long arms behind his head so that his suspenders strained across his white shirt, and shifted so that his ankle was better positioned on the heap of pillows. "Will you sit down then?" he asked.

Rose forced herself away from the idea of the chair near the window and went to perch on his bedside, trying to keep away from the length of his black-clad leg.

"How's the ankle?"

"Not too bad as long as I stay off it a bit here and there."

Rose nodded and cast about for something else to say.

"So, it's my fault, I'm guessing," he observed.

"What's your fault?"

"You meeting strangers in the woods." He smiled up at her, but his eyes were searching, compelling.

She hadn't been sure how to bring up the subject of his disguise and her enticement with him, but since he'd provided an opening . . .

"*Ya*, it is your fault. Both for being the stranger and for being—well, a stranger to me—your supposedly best friend." Her voice wavered a bit. "But I could have told you I recognized you."

"You told that stranger you wanted freedom," he said seriously. "Why did you agree to marry me, Rose?"

She caught her breath. She couldn't tell him the things she'd told *Aenti* Tabby when she'd asked the same question, so she sat silent and miserable, staring at the quilt top.

He reached to toy with her fingers and took a deep breath. "It's not too late for anything, Rose. Engagements can be broken. Friendships can remain."

Her gaze flew to his handsome face, and her heart hammered in her chest. "Is that what you want?"

He gave her a rueful smile. "No fair, Rose. Tell me what you want."

You, her mind screamed with sudden certainty, but she wet her lips cautiously. He'd betrayed her trust, and she did want things from him—the truth, for a start. Yet she hadn't been truthful either. She decided on plowing ahead in the discussion and getting to her own accounting later.

"You have no idea how it's been for me," she declared. "I've known you forever but haven't really known you at all—at least, that's how it seems."

"So you feel like I've taken advantage of you in a way?" he asked quietly.

She blew out a frustrated breath. "No . . . *ya* . . . I don't know. And you've never seemed to well—desire me—when you were—are—really you—"

"Why are your fingers purple?" he interrupted.

"Beet juice sugaring."

"*Ach*," he sighed, squeezing her fingertips. "Well, I have taken advantage of you, I guess. I didn't mean to. And as far as desiring you, Rose—do you have any idea what it's been like holding back for all these months—these years even?"

"Then why did you?"

"Because I felt like the same kid who chased bullfrogs with you and brought home stray dogs. I felt like you'd grown into something beautiful while I was still this awkward person. And then . . . when *Mamm* died, I guess I just sort of distanced myself, unintentionally, but the feelings were there, Rose."

"Well, I thought you couldn't stand the thought of touching me, and I wanted—well . . ." She thrilled at the thought that he'd fought back his feelings for her.

His hand drifted to stroke her arm. "What did you want?"

She shook her head stubbornly in reply, and he shifted his weight fully onto his back. "Rose, listen . . . I'm sorry. I'll prove it to you. Come here." His eyes burned like dark blue flame as he reached out for her.

Rose leaned forward and reached one purple fingertip to trace the contour of his mouth. She brushed her lips against his, following the trail of her finger. His arms drew her closer and he deepened the kiss, and she felt his chest rise and fall in uneven rhythm.

Rose pulled away. There *was* more she wanted from him . . . answers, for a start.

"Luke, tell me about the thefts," she whispered. "And the *Englisch* ways of dress and doings. You were baptized last year."

"I know."

"And?" She trailed her lips to the line of his throat, finding a spot behind his ear and tasting the salty sweetness of his skin.

"And I can't go hobbling out there in the dark anymore . . . at least, not until this ankle heals up."

She broke away from him at his words, forcing herself to focus on the matter at hand.

"What were you doing in the first place? Why would you steal from your own people when they'd gladly give you anything you asked for?"

He opened his eyes with visible reluctance. "Would they?"

"*Ya*, you know that."

He shook his dark head slowly. "They'd give for me, but maybe not for someone else."

"Someone else?" Her heart began to pound in dismay. "Who else?"

"I can't say, Rose. I'm sorry."

"You can't say?"

"*Nee*, but I do need your help."

Rose was rapidly losing patience. "You need my help—but you can't say why? Are you wanting me to pick up where you left off—rebuilding tumbledown shacks, thieving from the neighbors, and pretending I'm *Englisch*?"

"Actually, something like that."

Rose bounced upward so fast that the bedsprings twanged.

Luke grimaced with pain as the pillows under his foot shifted. "Just sit down and listen."

"*Nee*. Not until you start telling me your secrets."

"It's not my secret to tell," he said finally.

She bristled at his words. "Then whose secret is it?"

"Another woman's." He looked grim. "An *Englisch* woman."

LUKE'S CALLS TO ROSE WENT UNHEEDED, AND EVENTUALLY he sank back against his pillow and covered his face with his bandaged hand. He looked up in surprise when the door creaked back open.

"What's all the fuss?" Mark asked, almost apologetically. "I was next door fixing that windowsill for *Daed*."

Luke lowered his hand, feeling like his mouth still burned from Rose's attention, and glanced at his *bruder*. "What?" he asked finally.

"She sure gets riled," Mark offered.

Luke smiled. "I like that."

"It's no wonder—you like thunderstorms too."

"Did you hear much?" Luke's brow furrowed.

Mark shook his head sheepishly. "Told you I was fixing that sill. I wasn't trying to listen."

"All right. And?"

"Josh and I have been talking. We know you don't like being cooped up in that office all day. And—well—now that you're about to marry, you might find the place even more confining. Women can be a passel of trouble sometimes . . ."

"And you know this how?"

"Shut up. I'm trying to help you. Josh and I want you to tell *Daed* how you really feel."

"How I really feel?"

"*Ya*, you know, about fooling with the books and the customers. Tell him you want to do woodworking—even if it's just part of the time. It'll be *gut* for you."

Luke smiled, but rolled his eyes. It felt good to be cared for and thought of with such kindness, even though his brothers could drive him *narrisch*. But he didn't want to listen to another lecture on doing what was true to himself. He had enough trouble just being true, or so it seemed.

"I'm fine, Mark. Really. Somebody's got to do it, but *danki* for caring."

His brother snorted. "You're not going to brush me off that easily. After I got over *Daed*'s praise—which rightly belonged to you—I found something of yours in the workshop."

Luke shrugged. "What?"

"This." Mark pulled a folded piece of paper from his pants pocket and strode across the room to hand it to Luke.

Luke opened the drawing, already guessing what it was. "I wondered where this got to. I must have left it one night." He stared down at the intricate design for a mantel shelf that he had hoped to carve for Rose as a wedding gift.

Mark cleared his throat. "That's a fine vision of work, Luke.

Better than anything me or Josh could design. You owe it to your-self to work a talent like that. Maybe you owe it to *Derr Herr* too."

Luke exhaled slowly at his brother's unusually serious tone and leveled his own voice in response. "I said I'm fine as I am. That's all."

Mark gave a wry shake of his head. "All right. I tried. Suit yourself." He cuffed Luke lightly on the shoulder as he turned from the bed.

Luke smiled at the veiled affection. Then he carefully folded the drawing and slid it into his pants pocket.

"Hey." Mark paused. "Do you want me to drive you over there tomorrow to talk to her? It's no fair runnin' away on a one-legged man."

"Would you?"

"*Ya*, but maybe she needs a while to cool down."

Luke smiled. "Told you. I like it when she's riled. Keeps me on my toes."

Chapter Sixteen

ROSE KNEW HE COULDN'T CHASE AFTER HER WHEN SHE slammed the door on his pleas. She jogged down the steps, feeling a bit guilty, and slowed briefly to say good-bye to Mr. Lantz.

"Is everything all right, Rose? I heard the door . . ." He made a helpless gesture with his hands. "I know the engagement time can be stressful."

Rose gave him a wan smile. "It's nothing. Luke is just tired, and I should leave. Please forgive me for hurrying so."

"All right, child. But if there's anything you'd like to talk about—I'm always here."

Rose nodded her thanks and slipped outdoors. She knew exactly where she was going . . .

CARRYING A FLASHLIGHT, ROSE RETRACED HER WAY through the woods. The light faded fast in the fall evenings, and the dense trees made it appear even darker. She huddled more deeply in the folds of her cloak as she approached the tumble-down shack. She felt nervous for some reason—not afraid of the twilight or the crack and rustle of small creatures among the forest branches, but rather of what she might find at the shack. It was pure instinct that drove her, searching for something, anything—a clue to the *Englisch* woman Luke spoke of and her place in his life.

Rose shone the flashlight over the open threshold of the door and shuddered a bit when she saw the pile of rubble from the caved-in roof. Luke could have been hurt a lot worse. The small circle of light played against the walls with their peeling dry wood and then back to the floor again. She almost turned away, feeling foolish, when a piece of paper poking out from under a board caught her attention. She tiptoed across the creaking floor and scooped the paper up, then rushed back outside. She had no desire for another board to come tumbling down while she was out alone.

A safe distance from the shack, she balanced her light in one hand and unfolded the lightweight paper with care. It was the page of a coloring book. Amish parents would sometimes allow coloring books and wax colors to occupy very young children during the long Sunday church service, but the pictures were of simple objects like a wagon or an apple. This was an outline of a beautiful rainbow and clouds, obviously colored with diligence and signed by its artist in uneven block letters—To Daddy Luv Ally.

Rose bit her lip to stem the sudden welling up of tears that threatened to pour from her eyes.

Chapter Seventeen

LUKE KNEW HE WAS DREAMING, BUT HE WAS TOO CAUGHT, too enmeshed in the images playing inside his mind to force himself to wake. He was losing Rose in a thousand different ways; fast-forwarded images—Rose in a boat on storm-tossed waves drifting away from him, the eerie lights of a carnival's Ferris wheel and Rose spinning high to the top in a swinging singsong motion, Rose standing on the edge of a cavernous drop while he tried desperately to reach her. Everything that was human in him recognized the fear, the distance, and he knew he had to tell her the whole truth. It was the only way he was going to be able to stay close to her, but when he opened his mouth to speak, he awoke shivering and knew that dawn couldn't come fast enough.

"SURE YOU'RE NOT GETTING SICK, ROSIE?" HER FATHER asked with genuine concern when she appeared wan and sleepy at the breakfast table.

"Nee, Daed." Though she wondered if she actually was sick, as awful as she felt inside. She had spent the night clutching the child's drawing, examining it by the light of a kerosene lamp from every angle, and was no nearer the truth than she had been standing outside the shack the night before.

She tried to think logically. Ally was not a traditional Amish name, yet she had no doubt the drawing had been a gift of some kind to Luke. It must have slipped from his jeans pocket when he fell. She noticed that the child had drawn faces on the clouds, so that their raindrops looked like tears. What would clouds weep for? And for so young a life's imagination?

And then that single word: *Daddy.* The letters had rung through Rose's mind with all the cadence of a loud and clanging bell, merciless in intensity and reverberating possibility. Luke was twenty-three . . . The child had to be at least four or five, judging from her letter formation . . . That would make Luke eighteen if he were . . . She couldn't finish the thought, not once the whole night through nor now as she tried to concentrate on her scrambled eggs.

But like a bad canker sore that attracts the tongue, her mind kept running over the possibilities with drawing pain. She and Luke had both had a *rumschpringe*, but it had been nothing like some she knew. At least for her it hadn't been . . . She'd ridden in a car once, gone to two *Englisch* baseball games, and stayed out all night singing round a campfire with some of her Amish friends. She racked her brain for what Luke had been doing and realized she couldn't fill in all the blanks of time. He'd been to her then what he always was . . . devoted. But friendship or not, she didn't see him all the time. Could he have met an *Englisch* girl? Could he have had a relationship that she didn't know about?

She poked at her eggs and wished now that she would have stayed and listened to his odd request for help instead of running away like a child. She began to pray for guidance as she determinedly ate her food under the watchful eyes of her father and thought that life could be as difficult as navigating in the dark sometimes. Then she recalled the Bible verse that said "all the dark was as light" to the Lord; it gave her something to cling to as she ate her eggs.

LUKE KNEW THAT HE WAS PROBABLY CATCHING ROSE'S family right at breakfast, but he hadn't been able to go back to sleep. Consequently, he'd poked Mark out of bed with one of his crutches just after dawn, and they now rode through the chill morning air in the buggy.

"I don't mind takin' you." Mark's teeth chattered as he spoke. "But isn't this kind of early for working out your differences?"

Luke waved a vague hand at his brother. "Never too early to make things right."

"Well, I hope breakfast is still on the table. I'd love to have a stack of pancakes made by a woman's hand."

Mark soon had his wish. Mrs. Bender hustled them in out of the cold, and Mr. Bender filled their coffee cups before they could get their coats off. Luke glanced at Rose and found, to his dismay, that she looked worn and weary. He had to get her alone to talk, but the Bender men appeared to love company at any hour.

And in truth, though he was worried for Rose, there was something infinitely soothing about the stack of pancakes that was placed before him, steaming with goodness and light as air. He toyed with his fork, wondering whether to take a bite or just ask to see Rose alone for a moment first.

"Eat up, *sohn*," his future father-in-law urged him. "And tell us how you're feeling with that wrist and ankle. Rosie wasn't quite straight on how it all happened."

Luke caught the daggered look Rose threw him across the table and decided she was still mad enough. He also had no clear idea how to answer her father. He took a careful bite of pancakes and smiled at Mrs. Bender. "Wonderful."

"*Ach, ya,*" Mark agreed with him.

Mrs. Bender gave a quick nod at their appreciation. "*Danki.* Eat hearty—there's plenty more," she said, moving back to the stove.

Luke cleared his throat and looked back to Mr. Bender as Rose arched a delicate dark brow in expectation of his response. He knew that look; it was a blatant challenge. He'd seen it enough when she'd dared him to climb higher in the old oak or to ford a rushing stream. He gave her an enigmatic smile.

"I'm feeling much better today, sir. And, of course, it really wasn't Rose's fault." He took a sip of his coffee as he let his words sink in and watched Rose turn to him across the table with a surprised glare.

Ben looked up from his cup. "Not Rosie's fault, you say? What exactly did happen?"

Luke shook his head. "*Ach*, I'm not one for telling tales on my future bride."

James laughed. "*Ya*, but she's still our sister and *narrisch* in her ways. Go ahead and tell."

"*Ya*, Luke," Rose murmured through tight lips. "Do tell, but don't leave out the bit about your behavior. I mean, just because we're to be married doesn't mean that we should . . . well . . ." She broke off helplessly, and Luke almost choked on a laugh as the attention of the whole table now turned with quiet interest in his direction. His Rose could give as *gut* as she got.

Mr. Bender fixed him with a wary eye. "Perhaps we should have the whole story then."

"*Ach*, by all means," Luke returned easily. "But I'll let Rose begin."

The attention of the table swung back like a pendulum to Rose as she gave Luke a saccharine-sweet smile. "Certainly, *Daed*. We were in the woods together, Luke and I, near the old shack. You remember that tumbledown place about a half mile back on the Lantz property? Well, the sun was shining and the day was young, and Luke thought that the place might actually be a nice place to . . ." She paused. "Won't you go on, Luke?"

"*Ya*, go on," Mr. Bender suggested, tapping his empty *kaffee* cup against the wood of the table.

Luke shrugged and took another bite of his pancakes. "I thought it might be a fair spot to build a house for Rose and me— you know, far enough away from everyone for a newly married couple, kind of a pretty spot. I suppose it was foolishness, but I wanted to surprise her with it."

"But I thought you were going to live with—" Mark broke off quickly when Luke gave him a quelling glare.

Then he smiled at the table at large. "You'll no doubt think it was too forward of me to want to lead Rose into the place, to imagine the fire in the old fireplace, the placing of furniture, and where best to carve her windows for light."

Mr. Bender cleared his throat and gave a gusty laugh. "I think that's just fine, *sohn*. Just fine."

Aenti Tabby smiled, her eyes misting, and Rose's brothers were momentarily silent. Then James harrumphed in disappointment at the tale. "Well, what wasn't Rose's fault then?"

Luke shook his head with regret. "*Ach*, she wanted me to test the roof."

The men groaned as one and turned to stare at Rose with accusation. "The roof, Rosie?" her father asked in disbelief. "How could you do that to a man?"

Luke watched Rose open and close her mouth like a beautiful, gasping fish; then she flung her napkin down on the table and ran from the room and out the back kitchen door.

"She left her cloak," Luke observed, rising to wrangle with his crutches. "I'll take it to her."

He swung himself from the room, listening to the murmured comments behind praising his romanticism and foresight, and grimaced. He had the distinct feeling that he'd won the battle but was about to lose the proverbial war.

Chapter Eighteen

ROSE TOLD HERSELF THAT IT WAS FOOLISHNESS TO CRY so, simply because Luke had bested her in an argument. Then she admitted to herself that she was really crying over the drawing in her pocket and the terrible lie he'd told when he'd really been fixing that cabin for another woman.

She nestled more deeply between the hay bales of the barn, her sobs dissolving into hiccups, as she tried to warm herself.

"This might help." Luke's voice echoed from above her, and her cloak fell about her shoulders.

She scrambled into the garment and rose, not wanting to feel trapped by the hay and Luke's presence. "Go away. You've had your bit of fun."

He sighed. "Rose. I'm sorry."

"*Ach*, yes you are, Luke Lantz—as sorry a man as I've ever seen." She pushed past him, almost knocking him off balance as she angrily swung a milk bucket down from a hook on the wall.

The barn cats begin to entwine about her as she plunked down on a milking stool near Bubbles, the *milch* cow.

"Look, I should have been more honest with you yesterday, and I shouldn't have let you take the worst of that in there. Please forgive me, and listen." His voice was the husky, cajoling voice of the stranger, and she shook her head furiously as she concentrated on the rhythm of milking, trying to ease away her hurt.

"Rose, come on, please." He bent near her.

She took deep breaths as she filled the cats' pans, then turned to look up at him from the stool. "Fine. Say whatever you like, but I already know the truth. Or . . . at least one person of it."

He straightened. "What do you mean?"

"Who's Ally?" she asked, staring him straight in the eye.

She watched him blink in surprise. "How do you—"

"Just answer me, Luke. Who is she?"

"A little girl."

"Is she—yours?"

He shook his head in obvious disbelief. "You'd think that?"

Rose lifted her chin stubbornly. "I went back to the shack last night. I found this." She reached into the pocket of her apron and withdrew the coloring sheet. She handed it up to him without a word.

She watched him balance on his crutches to open the page; then he lifted his head to stare at her, anguish and anger lighting his blue eyes.

"I was wrong," he said slowly. "I thought I was the one wearing the mask, but it's you. You, who would marry me, think that I'd leave a child unclaimed, hidden, who was my own? How little you must truly believe in me."

"Well, what am I supposed to believe, Luke?" she cried. "How does all of this look? You just told me yesterday that you couldn't tell the secret, that it belonged to another woman—an *Englisch* woman! Do you know how much that hurt?" Rose could feel the blood pounding in her ears and knew that she was raising her voice.

He drew a deep breath. "All right. You're right. I can see how this must look to you."

She rose and came to stand in front of him, her eyes brimming with unshed tears, her words softer now. "Can you, Luke? Can you understand? I don't think badly of you. I just wanted to know for sure. I—I didn't know if I could accept it, if you'd hidden her from me all this time."

"I didn't hide her from you," he whispered low. "Not intentionally."

Rose reached out to touch the coloring page. "Why is she so sad . . . this Ally? Her clouds are crying."

He stared down at the paper. "That's the part that's not mine, Rose. It's not mine to tell, but I need you to trust me. To help me, even. To help Ally and her family."

"Her family? They're *Englisch*?"

Luke nodded and met her eyes. *"Ya."*

"And they're important to you?" Rose reached her purple fingertips to stroke his hand where it held the paper.

"They were . . . important to my *mamm*."

"Your *mamm*?"

He nodded, his mouth set in a grim line.

She could have pressed him further, fought him for answers, but thoughts of what the Lord expected as far as honor and fairness in an individual swirled through her mind. She understood valor, as part of her people, to be that part of self that yields instead of fights.

Rose swallowed. "Then they'll become important to me too. I'll help you." She stretched on tiptoe and sealed her words with a kiss.

Chapter Nineteen

THE WEATHER CONTINUED TO TRACK IN WITH THE MER-
curial moods of Pennsylvania autumn. Cold to frost one day,
blazing sun the next. The trees were beginning to lose their foli-
age now, and the leaves underfoot were a sure sign that Rose had
let too many days slip past before visiting Priscilla. She knew it
for sure as she looked across the table into her friend's drawn face.

"Has it been that bad?" Rose asked, wishing she'd visited
sooner.

Priscilla nodded. "I just don't understand what all of this
means. I've tried to reason it out, and it almost seems like—well,
like maybe all of these things going wrong are a sign that I'm not
on the right path."

Rose caught her friend's hand in her own. "Priscilla, you
know you love Chester."

But Priscilla was staring down in horror. "Your hand is
purple."

"I know. Beet juice. Just think, though, if it doesn't wear off soon, it'll look really nice with the blue dress for your wedding."

"That's not funny."

"Sorry." Rose swallowed her smile.

"Well, tell me about you and Luke. How are your plans?"

Rose stifled a sigh. She'd promised to carry out hers and Luke's "plans" later on that evening, but they weren't exactly wedding related. Or maybe that wasn't completely true, she considered. She certainly was being a helpmate to Luke even if no blessing of the bishop had yet been said between them. But even so, she couldn't reveal any of this to Priscilla, who was looking at her expectantly.

"Fine," Rose murmured at last. "Plans are coming along just fine."

In truth, she knew that her *mamm* and *aenti* were the ones who were beginning to prepare for her December wedding, while she seemed to be off in a world of her own with Luke. She really needed to work on her dress . . .

"Well, your attendant's dress is nearly finished," Priscilla said with relief in her voice. "If you could come over before the wedding to try it on, that would be *gut*."

"I'll be here," Rose promised. She got up from the Kings' kitchen table, then bent to hug her friend. "Don't worry so much. Everything will work out perfectly. You'll see."

Priscilla nodded. "*Danki*, Rose."

Rose left the Kings' house feeling glad to escape the tension that radiated from her friend. She hoped her own wedding wouldn't be as complicated . . . then laughed aloud at the irony of her thought.

"I STILL FEEL NERVOUS LETTING YOU GO ALONE," LUKE commented, frowning as he watched Rose put things into her basket in the Lantzes' barn.

"It'll be light for another two hours," she pointed out as she looked toward the horizon.

Luke rubbed his chin. "Maybe I should tell Mark . . . let him go with you."

"Mark?" Rose looked up with a smile. "Mark can't be still with a joke in church, let alone keep a secret. Not that I know all of the truth myself, really . . ."

Luke ignored her comment. He'd said all he could say. Now he tried to test his weight on his ankle and was forced to catch hold of a support beam to stop from falling. She calmly handed him his dropped crutch.

"Luke, I can be up to that stand of pine trees and back before anyone will ever know I'm gone. Besides——" She grinned at him, her eyes sparkling. "I like being the Rob in the Hood."

"That may be true enough, I've no doubt . . . but you're not 'in the hood.' Won't you reconsider dressing in *Englisch* clothes, or at least like a boy?"

"*Nee,* " she answered, and he sighed in defeat.

They'd gone over this a dozen times. She wouldn't pretend to be something she wasn't when she went to see the *Englisch* woman and her children. And what could he say? He hadn't told her any more than simply that—an *Englisch* woman and her children. But she was willing to help blindly, without knowing, just trusting him. He couldn't ask for anything more.

"Well"—he balanced to reach one hand and place a thumb against her fair cheek—"no one would take you for a boy, no matter your disguise."

"Really?" She blinked coy lashes up at him, and he had to smile.

"Really."

"And why is that?" She leaned against his chest lightly and looped her basket over her arm so that she could encircle his neck with gentle arms.

He couldn't help the catch in his breath at her touch and bent his mouth close to hers. "*Ach*, perhaps it could be the tip of your nose, or the shell of your ears . . . or the taste of your lips." He kissed her lingeringly until she pulled away.

"*Ach*, but I've learned my lesson, Luke Lantz. No more kissing strangers in the woods."

"*Nee.*" He swallowed, trying to regulate his breathing. "None of that."

"All right. Then I'll be going." She patted him jauntily on the arm.

He turned to watch her go. "Don't forget," he called, unable to still a last bit of anxiety. "I'll be waiting out back of your house, and if you're not there in two hours I'll . . ."

She cracked open the barn door and gave him a sidelong glance. "You'll what?"

"Just be there."

He watched her smile and slip out into the light while he stood fretting in the dimness of the barn.

Chapter Twenty

ROSE CLIMBED THROUGH THE WOODS, EXCITED AT THE prospect of an adventure, even one as simple as bringing some food and supplies to a woman in need. Of course, she wondered why the *Englisch* woman had not gone to her own people or family, but Rose hadn't been able to press any more information out of Luke and had decided that it didn't matter. It was part of *Derr Herr*'s will that she help those who were less fortunate and in want. And surely a woman living in a tent in the middle of the forest with children was in want.

Time slipped by quickly till she came to the stand of pines. The tent was cleverly disguised from view by branches and bracken, and she might have overlooked it had she not been told it was there. She approached the blue liner of the shelter cautiously, calling out to make her presence known.

"Hello! Heelloo! I'm a friend of Luke's!" she called out, stepping closer. She noticed a goat tethered nearby and a pen of chickens.

Then she heard rustling and the high-pitched squeal of a child, and a beautiful dark-haired woman came out of the tent. She balanced a red-faced toddler on her hip and stared at Rose with worry in her dark eyes.

Rose smiled. "Please . . . it's all right. Luke sent me."

"Is something wrong with him?" The woman's tone was anxious.

Rose had to bite down on a sudden flare of jealousy; it was more than a fair question when he'd been such a help to the family. "He had a small accident. Just a sprained ankle. But he can't make it up here on crutches, so he asked me to come instead. May I come in?"

"Yes . . . please. I—I'm Sylvia. This is Bobby, my boy. My little girl, Ally, is taking a nap. There's not a whole lot for her to do when her brother's fussy." The woman held open the tent flap.

Rose entered to find a veritable storehouse of items that had gone missing from the community over the past few months. She had to marvel at the larger items, wondering how Luke had hefted them through the woods alone. Then her gaze fell on the little girl curled up beneath a nine-patch quilt. Her long, black curls cascaded over the fabric squares, and Rose felt a tightness in her chest at the kinship of the skin and hair coloring she shared with the child.

"I suppose Luke's told you everything about us . . . I mean, for one of your people to come up here." Sylvia tried to put Bobby down, but he began to sniffle, and she scooped him back up with a sigh.

"One of my people?" Rose asked. "You mean Amish."

"Yes, sorry. Does Luke have good friendships with the Amish?"

Rose placed her basket on a small chest of drawers. "Luke *is* Amish," she said.

The woman laughed low, revealing a devastating smile. "Luke? Amish? Are you sure we know the same person?"

Rose began to unpack her basket, not knowing what to say. Part of her wanted to retort and part of her wanted more of the truth. To this woman and her children, Luke had been *Englisch*. He'd explained to her that the disguise made it easier to move about without attracting curiosity, both in town and in the woods, but she still couldn't help wondering if that was the full reason.

"Hey, I'm sorry if I said something wrong. Maybe Luke just seems different to us." Sylvia's tone was genuine, but her words pricked at Rose's heart.

"It's no matter. Look, I'll probably come again soon. Is there anything else you need?" *And can you tell me why you're here . . . in the middle of nowhere, with my betrothed as your provider?*

"The Lord has blessed us already with Luke's providing, and now yours. We're grateful for whatever you bring. Hopefully, it won't be much longer until Jim . . . well, you know."

Rose wanted to say that she had no idea what *until* meant or who Jim was, but she was glad that the woman's tone had lingered longingly over the man's name. She also felt chagrined that the woman mentioned the Lord with such genuineness while she was hardly having Christian feelings herself. Still, Luke could have told her more, since Sylvia didn't seem to have a problem with her knowing.

She'd just placed the final jar of preserves on a stand when a small, cherubic voice spoke up from the little bed.

"Mommy . . . who's that?" The little girl scooted up to grab at her mother's jeans.

"A friend of Luke's," Sylvia responded, stroking her daughter's hair.

"I'm Rose."

The child's eyes grew wide with interest. "Your hair's like mine. Does Luke think it's pretty too? Why are you dressed up all funny? Did you see my pet goat? Is it Halloween yet? Mommy, when can I have a costume?"

"Shhh," Sylvia admonished.

"It's all right." Rose smiled. "But I need to be going before it gets dark."

"Wait!" Ally cried. "I always make a picture for Luke to take when he visits my daddy. Shall I give it to you?"

"Certainly," Rose said. She accepted the coloring sheet the child tore painstakingly from the book and made a mental note to bring more toys and things to occupy the little girl the next time she came. *"Danki,"* she said. "That means thank you." She chuckled as Ally tried to get her tongue around the strange syllables.

"Thank you again," Sylvia said as she lifted the tent flap. "And be careful."

"I will. Don't worry." Rose waved good-bye and set out down through the maze of trees, so deep in thought that she didn't notice when she took a wrong turn.

Chapter Twenty-One

LUKE HAD DRIVEN THE BUGGY ROUND THE BACK WAY OF the Benders' property at the expense of his ankle and now swung along between his crutches, anxious and in pain. It was already over two hours since Rose had left. *I never should have let her go,* he berated himself.

He kept searching the distant tree line when a voice behind him nearly made him jump out of his skin.

"Is that you, Luke?" *Aenti* Tabby asked with curiosity.

"*Ya,* ma'am . . . I was just, uh, waiting for Rose."

"Behind the barn? And with your ankle? Wouldn't you be more comfortable inside?"

The older woman walked up to him with a smile, but her eyes were keen. Luke sighed inwardly. It was next to impossible to keep a secret from *Aenti* Tabby.

"Rose went up to the woods to gather . . . um . . . late berries or something, and I said I'd wait here until she—"

Tabby crossed her arms over her ample bosom and har-rumphed loudly. "Luke Lantz! Has Rose run off because you two were arguing? Is she out alone this time of the evening?"

"Uh . . . that sounds reasonable, doesn't it?"

"I'll get the boys to go and find her then," Tabby said.

"That would be *wunderbaar*," Luke agreed, relieved that someone could search for her.

"Who needs finding, *Aenti* Tabby?" Rose asked breezily as she came soft-footed from the dark field.

Luke blew out a sigh of relief, but he wanted to holler at her too, for looking so casual and pretty when he'd been worried sick.

"There you are, child!" *Aenti* Tabby exclaimed. "And a *gut* thing too. It's never wise to run off when you're having a bit of a spat. It's better to stay and work things out."

Luke threw Rose a pleading glance as she slowed her steps and brought her swinging basket to an abrupt halt.

"Uh, *Aenti* Tabby, it was my fault, in truth," Luke supplied.

"As usual," Rose murmured, and he had to suppress a smile.

"Well, it's too cold out here. Come inside and warm up, the both of you." *Aenti* Tabby turned to go.

"We'll be along shortly," Rose called.

Luke watched her approach warily, wondering how the time at the tent had gone. Then he caught the heat in her green eyes and thought they wouldn't be going into the house anytime soon.

ROSE WATCHED HIM STANDING IN THE TWILIGHT AND thought how handsome he was, then frowned at the thought.

Why her mind would drift to how he looked when she had a thousand questions to ask was beyond her understanding.

"How were they?" he asked.

"Beautiful," she said shortly, speaking the first word that came to mind.

He smiled. "Ally's like you, I think."

She shrugged, flicking her flashlight on and off for a moment. "Sylvia didn't know you were Amish . . . You are Amish, right?"

He laughed. "*Ya*, Rose."

"It's not funny. Besides the excuse of moving about, why else did you pretend to be something else . . . *Englisch*?"

He sobered suddenly. "You seemed to like it well enough at times."

She didn't appreciate the reminder and bit back an angry retort, remembering what the Bible said about a soft answer turning away wrath. "That is true. But I hope that it was the real you, no matter your dress, who touched and kissed me those times."

"It was. I'm sorry."

"So, will you finally tell me about Sylvia?"

He sighed. "Her husband's name is Jim—she probably mentioned that."

Rose nodded.

"Well, Jim knew me as *Englisch*, or at least I thought he did . . ."

He stopped, and Rose sighed and slapped her hands against her sides. "Luke, I know you say this isn't your secret to tell, but I'm involved now. I've seen that woman and her children. They shouldn't be living alone—it's dangerous."

"Do you think I don't know that? Don't think about it a hundred times a day?"

"Then tell me why they are there." She waited.

"All right. All right." He took a deep breath and turned away from her to face the dark fields. "Before I joined the church, and after *Mamm* died, I sort of lost things in my head. One part of me did all the right things—saw you, went to church, worked; but one part of me was wild with pain and anger. But I had to keep that part of myself secret. I couldn't hurt *Daed* . . . or you."

"Maybe I would have understood," she said softly.

"No, not when I didn't understand myself. So I just kept up two parts of me, two lives . . . I started going into town and running around with this gang of *Englischers*. They had no idea I was Amish, but this wasn't like *rumschpringe*. They were a dangerous lot . . . drugs, drinking, crime. When I began to see how they really lived, I backed away. Most of them were homeless, so when I would head back to my warm bed at the house, they were sleeping under bridges, trying to avoid the shelters because they thought they didn't need the help." He pivoted on his crutches to face her. "My *mamm* volunteered at one of the homeless shelters in town. Did you know that?"

"*Nee* . . . an *Englisch* shelter?"

He gave a bitter laugh. "*Ya*. How many homeless Amish do you know?" He exhaled. "I'm sorry, Rose. I didn't mean to snap."

"And I didn't mean to question . . . I just . . . your *mamm* was so busy about her own house."

"She was, but she found time to give to others too . . . even if it was unusual to find an Amish woman volunteering alone at a place like that."

"Did your *daed* know?"

"We all did . . . we kind of teased her about it too—'going looking for trouble,' I said once." He looked grim. "When she got sick, she had me take some jellies and things down there. At first I didn't want to go. I thought it was a dirty place, foul smelling . . . full of *Englischers* who supposedly wouldn't work. But later I discovered the truth . . . the secret that nobody *chooses* to be homeless, at least not at first. *Ach*, there were the boys I ran with, to be sure, but there were families too . . . children."

"Ally?" Rose asked softly, trying to piece the story together.

"*Ya* . . . the shelter is okay, but it's no place for kids, and every family only has so much time that they can stay. When Sylvia's time ran out, I just thought . . . I don't know what I thought—that I could honor my mother by helping Sylvia have some type of home . . . Jim got into trouble with the law a couple months back. He's in the local jail waiting for trial—I go see him when I can. Take him Ally's pictures."

Rose frowned. "But surely there are other *Englisch* means of help—housing, medical insurance . . ."

"Jim was afraid they'd lose the kids—if the police knew Sylvia was in the area and could question her, he was afraid they might charge her too."

"Charge her with what?"

"Robbery. A series of home robberies. He said he was innocent, and I believe him."

"But then you robbed from your own people to help them. Why didn't you just go to the bishop and tell the truth?" Rose asked.

"The bishop . . . who'd want no part of *Englisch* law. Who'd not hide a woman and children—"

"You don't know that," Rose cried. "You've not only taken on the role of thief but also judge—of your own people, your own community. You've tried to do this all alone, and it's not going to work anymore, Luke. Cold weather's going to set in, and then what?"

"I don't know," he said. "But I ask you to keep the secret, Rose. Just a little longer. The trial's bound to be soon."

"And if Jim is found guilty? What will you do then?" she asked, closing her eyes against the thought.

"Please, Rose. Just keep the secret. Let me worry about the rest."

"I don't know what to do," she said miserably.

He moved closer to her, and she could feel the heat from his body through his heavy black coat. "I shouldn't have involved you, but this will work out. I promise."

She looked him in the eyes and said the only thing she could think of. "I'll pray."

Chapter Twenty-Two

~~~~

LUKE CONCENTRATED ON A PARTICULARLY COMPLICATED gouge in the wood he was working for Rose's mantelpiece wedding gift. It didn't help that he had to do it by candlelight and so late at night, but he couldn't risk starting the generator up and waking his father.

He hadn't seen Rose for a few days . . . not since the conversation behind the barn. And he wasn't sure what she might be feeling about him at this point. She'd raised a lot of issues that made him think, but the thing that struck home the most was her idea that he was judging his own people.

He wasn't sure when or how it had happened, but some way or another he'd come to a place in his head where he believed that the community would fail him. He sighed as he moved the lantern closer and bent over the wood.

"It was you, my *sohn*," said a voice behind him.

Luke turned to blink at his father. "*Daed?* Why are you up?"

"I might ask you the same thing. But I can see by that workmanship that it was you and not Mark who did that burled elm piano front. It's the truth, *nee?*"

Luke laid the tools carefully on the workbench and braced his hands on his crutches, shifting his weight from where he'd been leaning against the table. "It's just a hobby, *Daed.*"

His father stepped closer and lifted the lantern high over the table with a work-worn hand. "A hobby? Such gifts from *Derr Herr* should never be wasted on a hobby. Wasn't it you who told me something about speaking the truth and releasing pain? I'm afraid you've hidden much pain from me, Luke. And I've been too blind and selfish to notice."

Luke met his father's eyes in the light of the lamp. "I never wanted you to know, *Daed.* I am content to do the books. I know it's a help to you."

"Content? Perhaps, but not joyful, my *sohn.* Not working with joy and purpose as the Lord would desire."

Luke hung his head. "*Nee,* sir."

He heard his father put the lamp back on the table, then looked up as he was caught in the older man's loving embrace. "Forgive me," his father whispered.

"There's nothing to forgive. Please don't worry, *Daed.* We can go on as before."

His father stepped away and clapped him on the shoulders. "Not one minute longer. We'll find someone else to do the books. And you will take your place as a carpenter . . . as The Carpenter would have you do."

Luke's eyes welled with tears. He felt undone inside, like

his secrets were slowly being revealed by *Derr Herr*'s hand, one by one.

"*Danki, Daed. Danki.*"

AFTER EVERYONE HAD GONE TO BED, ROSE BEGAN TO work on her wedding dress in earnest. She'd been to see Sylvia and the children only once since she and Luke had last talked. And she wasn't sure how he was feeling, since she'd had no word from him. She sighed as she fingered the cloth of her wedding dress, wondering what the future held for them. Shadowy images of dark-haired children danced through her mind. Then she looked up from the kitchen table in surprise as Luke maneuvered himself inside the kitchen door with his crutches. She blinked, feeling her heart begin to pound, and wondered if she simply imagined his presence.

"*Hiya!*" He smiled brightly.

She glanced with dismay from her wedding dress pieces back to his handsome face and blurted out the first thing that came to mind. "Nobody's up. And I'm working on my wedding dress."

"Well, that's nice, isn't it?" He slipped his hat off.

"*Ya* . . . I mean, no . . . I can't ask you in. I told you—I'm working on my wedding dress. I thought it would be a surprise."

He glanced at the fabric and pattern pieces spread about the table and turned his head a bit. "Suppose I don't look? It's blue, right?"

"You know every wedding dress is blue."

He balanced on his crutches and swung his injured ankle

absently. "True. But there're all kinds of blue—the sky on a summer's afternoon, the smoky blue of a kitten's fur, the creek when the light dances off it until it stings your eyes with its beauty . . ." His voice dropped an octave. "Your eyes, when they're a sleepy blue-green after you've been kissed."

Rose's mouth went dry as she tried to shake off the spell of his words. Since when did he know how to speak so . . . like he was touching her, though he stood across the room? She cleared her throat and clutched the pair of shears in her hand closer to her chest.

He smiled. "Nervous, Rose?"

"*Nee* . . . I just . . . need to get this work done," she whispered.

"Speaking of work—I took your advice and told my father the truth. I've got a new job."

"What?"

"He's going to hire someone else to do figures for him. I want to work the wood. My hands ache for it."

She couldn't help glancing down at his strong hands as he spoke and thought about the moment in the old shack when he'd wound her hair about his hand. "I'm so proud of you," she said and meant it.

"Are you? That's *gut*." He swung himself around to her side of the table and placed a finger against her lips when she tried to protest. "Shhh. I'm not looking."

She fell silent under his touch and barely noticed when he reached with unerring fingers to lift a spool of blue thread from the table. He balanced on his crutches and started to unravel the thread.

"Luke . . . what are you doing?"

She watched him trail the end of the thread across her bare wrist, which was still the lightest purple from her sugar beets encounter. Then he feathered the blue line up across her arm and shoulder and used it to tickle the tip of her nose. She felt curious, like she was watching herself outside of her own body and could only follow in sensory delight wherever he led the thread. When he traced her lips, she closed her eyes, and soon his mouth followed where the blue had been. She lost herself in the deep silence of the kiss.

When he broke away, his breathing was ragged. "Guess I'm helping you thread your wedding dress."

She bit her lip as an impulse shook her and she picked up the piece of thread where it trailed against her shoulder. "Are you? Then maybe you should do a little more work."

She twirled the thread between her thumb and forefinger, then let it drift up across the high bones of his cheeks. She smiled up at his surprised grin and ran the thread behind his ear. Stretching on tiptoe, she let her lips follow the blue tendril down his neck, and he made a rough sound in his throat.

"Any work you like," he whispered.

But the moment was broken by a frantic knocking on the back kitchen door.

Rose dropped the shears and brushed past him, pulling off the thread. Who could it be at this time of night?

She opened the door to reveal a bedraggled and panicked Sylvia. The woman held Ally in her arms and Bobby was asleep in a backpack on her back. "Please," she gasped. "I just took a chance that this might be Luke's house. Please do something. Ally's having a bad asthma attack. She can't breathe!"

Chapter Twenty-Three

ROSE TOOK THE LITTLE GIRL INTO HER ARMS, ALARMED AT the bluish tinge and the rasping intake of the tiny lips.

"Dr. Knepp's," Luke ordered. "I've got the buggy outside."

"*Nee*, it's too far." Something compelled Rose's heart. "We'll go to Bishop Ebersol's. His wife is an excellent healer."

"All right," Luke agreed reluctantly.

"Please, hurry," Sylvia urged.

Luke made short work of the drive despite his ankle, and Rose flew from the buggy with Ally in her arms. She climbed the familiar steps of the Ebersol farmhouse and kicked at the solid front door.

A lamp soon cast eerie shadows on the porch and the shimmering fall of the child's hair as Mrs. Ebersol stared out at them.

"Please," Rose gasped. "She can't breathe."

Mrs. Ebersol was nothing if not practical; she urged them all inside at once. "Is it asthma like our John? Or the bronchitis?"

"Asthma," Sylvia half sobbed.

Luke had taken Bobby from her back and stood with his weight on his ankle holding the sleeping child.

"The child needs steam to breathe in and some menthol. Our John used to have bad attacks. Bring her in here to the kitchen . . . I'll wake the bishop when we're through, though he's probably already up."

"Right here." Bishop Ebersol moved quickly, bringing more lamps.

Mrs. Ebersol flew about the kitchen bringing various salves and herbs to where Rose sat holding the child at the table.

"Teakettle's always on the boil when you're a bishop's wife. Now let's make a little tent with this cloth and get her face as near to the steam and herbs as possible. The menthol and peppermint oil act like bronchodilators. Fancy word for opening the airways. That's it. Breathe it in, little one."

The kitchen was quiet as the child's breathing slowly eased. Within minutes, Ally opened eyes and then coughed heartily, trying to pull back from the steam.

"No," Rose crooned, gently holding back the small hands. "Just be still, Ally. It will help you breathe."

In another ten minutes the asthma attack was under control. Everyone sat drained and silent for a moment when Mrs. Ebersol eased the teakettle away.

"What you folks need is some hot chocolate," the bishop's wife announced, tightening the belt of her voluminous housecoat. She rose from Ally's side and laid a reassuring hand on Sylvia's shoulder. "It's all right now."

She and the bishop moved about the kitchen with the accord

of those long married, and soon steaming mugs of cocoa were placed on the table. Rose gave Ally back to Sylvia to hold when the child fussed for a drink.

"Let her have a sip," Mrs. Ebersol suggested. "Is your car somewhere about? You're welcome to stay here for the night. Perhaps Luke and the bishop might bring in your things."

Sylvia raised a worried gaze to Luke and Rose. "I—I don't have a car."

Luke rose to his feet. "Bishop Ebersol," he said clearly. "Might we talk for a few minutes in private?"

"*Ya*, certainly. Come this way."

The bishop lifted a lamp, and Rose met Luke's shuttered gaze as she began to pray for him and the words he might feel convicted to say.

Chapter Twenty-Four

THE NEXT DAY WAS CHURCH SERVICE, AND BEYOND DRIV-
ing her home and telling her that he would speak at the end of the
service, Luke didn't go into what he and the bishop had discussed.
Rose felt it within her spirit that it was not a time to question, so
she went quietly to bed.

"What was all the ruckus last night?" her *mamm* asked when
Rose entered the kitchen the next morning. "I thought you and
Luke might have been having an argument."

Rose sighed. She'd decided last night that the next time she
was asked a direct question about what had been going on lately
that she would give a direct answer. She found herself telling her
mamm, and the rest of the family as they entered for breakfast,
about Sylvia and the children.

Her father pointed with his forked bacon. "You mean to say
that Luke has been the Rob in the . . . the thief hereabouts?"

Rose shrugged. "For a cause."

Her *daed* considered. "Well, Bishop Ebersol's a wise man;

he'll handle it all right. But you, young lady, had no business out in those woods alone."

Rose was struck by a sudden inspiration. "I did say that your thief might be female, *Daed*. Perhaps I just had to prove my point."

Her *daed* stared at her, then laughed aloud as she'd hoped he would. Her brothers joined in reluctantly. Even her *mamm* and *Aenti* Tabby smiled.

So they went in good spirits to the buggies and on to church, which was being held at the Lamberts' that morning. Joseph Lambert greeted them with a warm smile at the door.

Rose hoped that her marriage might go as well as that of Joseph and Abby. Abby Lambert certainly looked happy as she sat in the married women's section, her stomach rounded with obvious pregnancy. Rose pushed aside the thought of carrying Luke's child and made her way to sit down next to Priscilla. Rose squeezed her friend's hand and decided that Priscilla was looking better, though still too pale, as the wedding loomed.

Then the service began, and Rose was lost in the ancient soothing rhythm of the hymns and the message of Scripture. Then, at last, when she thought Luke must have been mistaken about speaking, the bishop rose to address the community.

"Before we would dismiss, there's a matter of confession that's come to my attention. Young Luke Lantz would ask your patience while he speaks." The bishop sat down, and the crowd rustled with curiosity as Luke made his way forward to the head of the benches.

Rose's heart ached at his pallor, but she knew his eyes were steady and clear. Priscilla now clasped her hand, and Rose was grateful for the support.

Luke began to speak in a strong voice, and the general

rustlings of the crowd ceased as his words burned into Rose's heart.

"I have betrayed you all," he began. "All of you, but especially those I love. It's easier to tell what you may think is the heavier offense—that I've been the one who stole from you these past months."

Rose couldn't ignore the faint gasps of surprise, and swallowed hard.

"Why I took from you doesn't matter. I did it. It was wrong. I confess this wrong and beg your forgiveness. But . . . there's more . . ."

Rose felt his gaze rivet to hers across the space of crowded benches.

"I've betrayed you by expecting little from you as a community, as a people. The truth is . . . the truth is that I've been angry at *Derr Herr* since my mother died. And I've been angry at all of you. I started to believe that if you didn't have the power to save my mother, then you had no power together at all. And that is so wrong. Someone very wise told me that I had judged you, and it's true. I might have asked for your help for a woman and family in need, but I didn't. I believed I could do it alone . . ."

His voice broke a bit, and silent tears slipped down Rose's cheeks. Priscilla squeezed her hand harder.

"Alone is not what our people are about. Our strength lies in our community. I have wronged the community. I confess this before you all and ask for your forgiveness." He dropped to his knees and bent his dark head.

The bishop rose and placed a hand on Luke's shoulder. "Is it the will of the community, then, to grant Luke Lantz the forgiveness he begs for?"

There was a general assent of *ya*'s, and Rose breathed a sigh of relief.

"Then," the bishop continued, "please come forward following our dismissal to greet Luke Lantz with renewed goodwill and acceptance."

Rose received Priscilla's hug, then wended her way forward to stand next to Luke. He caught her hand in a fierce grasp, which she returned as people began to come forward.

"Stole my best linens, young man?" Esther Mast inquired with a glint in her faded blue eyes.

"Yes. I'm very sorry," Luke said steadily.

The old woman sniffed. "Well, keep 'em. Probably for a *gut* cause. Would have given 'em to you had you asked."

"I know that now."

"Hmmm," Mrs. Mast mused, ignoring the press of the crowd around her with the distinct dignity of the aged. "Seems like I've got some more linens in a trunk upstairs. They'll make a fine wedding gift to go with what you already got." She gave Rose's hand a squeeze with her bony fingers.

"*Danki,*" Rose whispered.

Joseph Lambert was next. "Hey, anytime you want to talk, friend, I'm here. *Ach*, and keep that old goat of ours too. Kicked me once too often." He shook Luke's hand and winked at Rose.

They came, one after the other, to forgive and to give, telling Luke to keep all that he had taken and offering more should he need it.

Rose thrilled in heart and praised the Lord when Luke turned to her and whispered, "You were right, Rose."

Chapter Twenty-Five

❧

WORD OF THE DETAILS OF SYLVIA AND THE CHILDREN spread about the community, and Luke was inundated with offers of places to stay, clothes for the children, and a hundred other small kindnesses that made abundance seem too small a word.

In all of the details, he barely had time to talk to Rose and sheepishly asked Joshua one morning if he'd do a favor for him.

"Flowers?" Joshua snorted. "Weeds, you mean? There's nothing much growing now . . . Why not ride into town and get her something?"

"Just get a bouquet of something pretty. She likes the outdoors, and I want to get over there this evening and see her alone."

"Suit yourself. I'll have it ready."

That evening Joshua thrust a thick bouquet into the darkness of the buggy.

"*Danki.*" Luke sneezed, wondering exactly what his brother

had picked. He drove the short distance to the Benders', glad to be rid of his crutches, and went to knock softly on the back door.

Rose opened it with a shy smile, and he produced the bouquet, watching her face light up as she stepped back into the light of several lamps. Then he noticed what she held and dashed the flowers from her arms to the floor.

"Luke? What—are you—"

"*Ach*, that *bruder* of mine! It's poison ivy, Rose."

She gasped and ran to the sink. They both knew that she was badly allergic to the stuff, and somehow Joshua had grabbed a strand as background to the Queen Anne's lace and ragweed. She scrubbed frantically at her wrists and hands.

"I think I got it all. I barely held it."

Luke scraped the would-be bouquet from the floor; he was not allergic to the annoying weed. Then he bundled the stuff together and stalked toward the door. "So much for romance," he muttered.

"It's the thought that counts," Rose called with a smile.

He laughed as he went outside with the offending gift, then returned to wash his hands at the sink. She caught his arm and pulled him to a set of rockers in the living room.

"Everyone's gone to bed, but I wanted to show you the coloring pages Ally's been sending over from the Ebersols' house." She opened several wildly colored scenes, and he nodded.

"Nice."

"You're not getting it." She poked his ribs. "Her clouds aren't crying anymore."

"Oh, I didn't notice—but wait. I thought the clouds were crying for her daddy?"

Rose shrugged. "Maybe. Or maybe just for a sense of home or"—she blinked her green cat's eyes at him—"or community."

He reached over, and with one hand pulled her easily onto his lap. He nuzzled her throat cheerfully until she laughed and tried to push him away.

"Luke!"

He was concentrating on her hair, taking deep breaths of its heady scent. "Hmmm?"

She sighed and relaxed back against him. "Nothing."

THE NEXT DAY WAS FRIDAY, AND ROSE WOKE WITH HER mind set to keep her promise to Priscilla and go and pick up her dress for the wedding. But when she sat up in bed, it was to look with horror at her wrists and inner arms.

"*Ach, no,*" she whispered aloud.

She dressed hurriedly, biting her lip in an effort to make no move to scratch, but the long wool sleeves of her dress were torture against the rash. She made her way to Priscilla's in near tears from the sensation and knocked hurriedly at the back door, shifting her weight from one foot to the other.

"Rose? What's wrong?" Priscilla looked like she was prepared for anything from an ostrich to an airplane landing, and Rose plastered a smile on her face.

"Nothing," she managed. Then she could stand it no longer and burst into a spat of intense itching that made her jump and then wriggle with short-lived satisfaction.

But Priscilla's mother must have recognized the outlandish

movements, because she soon rooted in her herbal closet and sent Rose off with her attendant's dress and some salve that she guaranteed would help the affliction.

Rose danced out onto the back porch, then gave in to another fit of intense itching, all the while praying silently that the salve would do something miraculous.

Chapter Twenty-Six

THE WEATHER HAD TAKEN ON A DISTINCT CHILL, THE spiny spindles of tree limbs forming bare arms raised in supplication to the still bright sky.

That afternoon Rose opened the door to Luke, but knew that she probably looked distracted.

"Rose? Are you all right?" Luke took his hat off and stepped aside to reveal a thin *Englisch* man. "Rose, this is Jim. He was released yesterday and made his way out here. He was found not guilty."

Rose snapped herself back from her meditations on not scratching. "*Ach*, that's wonderful. Please come in."

She held the door wider, but Luke shook his head. "We can't. He's got a car and is going to pick up Sylvia and the kids. They're going to Colorado for a new start where his parents live."

Rose bit her lip as the desire to scratch radiated along her arms, but she didn't want Luke to know and feel bad. "That's great," she burst out, reaching to shake Jim's hand.

And then she could stand it no longer and nearly doubled over with her efforts to get at her arms to her satisfaction. Luke groaned.

"What's wrong?" Jim asked.

"Poison ivy," she heard Luke mutter. "Rose, don't scratch."

"Don't scratch!" She rounded on him, then smiled again at Jim, lowering her voice. "Don't scratch? I'll scratch you, Luke Lantz, if you don't . . ."

Apparently, her betrothed knew when to beat a hasty retreat. She waved good-bye to a bemused Jim.

"Is MRS. KING'S SALVE NOT WORKING?" AENTI TABBY ASKED from where she sat reading her Bible near her bed.

"I want to believe it's helping." Rose sighed as she maneuvered onto her aunt's bed, rubbing her woolen clad arms against the quilt.

"Well, let's talk about something to distract you then . . . Tell me if things are better now that you know a little more about Luke."

Rose flopped on her belly and regarded her *aenti*'s merry face. "I have the feeling that there's a lifetime of things for me to learn about Luke."

"That's as it should be—like the Bible says, 'new treasures out of old.'"

Rose gave in to one delightful scratch. "Then I'll pray that we have a lifetime of treasures together, *Aenti* Tabby."

The older woman smiled. "You will, Rose. You will."

ON MONDAY MORNING, LUKE'S FATHER TOLD HIM TO step into the office. "Just go along and have a hello with our new bookkeeper."

A new bookkeeper? What was his *daed* talking about? Luke shrugged and knocked on the office door with good grace, then, when no one answered, opened it slowly.

The back of a dark head and *kapp* greeted him.

"Rose?" he asked in disbelief.

She spun in a new swivel chair and smiled up at him, pencil in hand. "*Hiya!* You've always known I have a head for figures."

He smiled slowly. "So you do, but what about . . . ?"

"The house?" she queried. "I can do both, Luke Lantz. Women are great at multitasking."

He had to laugh, then bent close to her. "Is that your secret, Rose? Being able to do two things at once?"

"Maybe. What did you have in mind?" She blinked bright eyes at him, and he lowered his mouth to hers.

"*Ach*, I don't know," he whispered, pressing his lips to hers. "Maybe this . . . and this . . ."

"And this," she added, drawing him close again until he had to sigh aloud.

Reading Group Guide

GUIDE CONTAINS SPOILERS, SO DON'T READ BEFORE COMPLETING THE NOVELLAS.

1. Why do we often pretend to be someone different, in some aspect, even with those we love?
2. How does Luke's mother's death undergird his decisions in life?
3. Why does Rose enjoy being the "Rob in the Hood" for a change? What does this say about her personality?
4. What is it about your life that God is perfecting at this time?
5. What is potentially dangerous about secrets in a relationship?
6. How does Rose's relationship with her aunt Tabby bring balance to her life? Who helps you in this way?
7. Why do weddings create such stress and expectation in life?

Acknowledgments

I'd like to acknowledge Beth Wiseman and Kathy Fuller, who were a treat to work with on this novella. These ladies are smart and supportive, as always! Thank you to Natalie Hanemann for her keen insight and to L.B. Norton for her deft editing. A big thanks to my critique partner, Brenda Lott, for her scene insight and to my mother-in-law, Donna Long, for her marketing support. As always, thank you to my Amish readers and especially to my family. I love you, Scott.

CHRISTMAS
CRADLES

For Anna and Sam Locksley

Chapter One

The fading light played with the reflection of the kerosene lamp against the window of the old Amish farmhouse and illuminated the stray snowflakes just beginning to fall. Inside the warm and simple room, Asa Mast bent his broad back over his father's bed and lifted the older man into a more comfortable position against the pillows.

"*Danki*, Asa." Samuel coughed, giving his son a bleary-eyed look. "The flu is bad this year and it moves fast, or else I'm growing old."

Asa sat on the edge of the bed and poured a fresh glass of water from the pitcher his sister-in-law had just brought.

"You seem as young to me, *Daed*, as the day you took me out behind the barn and tanned my hide for driving the colt through *Mamm*'s kitchen garden."

Samuel smiled as Asa knew he would, his fever-bright eyes, so dark and so like his son's, growing warmer for a moment. "*Jah*, to think that you were ever that young . . ."

They sat in silence for a moment, remembering. Then Asa lifted the cloth napkin from the tray on the bedside table and saw untouched thin slices of ham, mashed potatoes, pickled beets, and a wedge of apple pie.

"Can't you bring yourself to eat anything, *Daed*? Would you like something lighter, maybe broth?"

"I'm not an invalid; I asked for all of that. I guess my eyes were just bigger than my stomach."

Asa recovered the plate. "I hate to leave you alone tonight, *Daed*."

Samuel waved the words away. "Your *bruder* and sister-in-law are here; they will care well for me."

"I know, but I guess I'd feel more comfortable if you'd let me take you to the hospital to get checked out. I don't like the sound of your cough."

"Ha! Going to the hospital for the flu, and on First Christmas too. I don't think so. And I made a promise to *Frau* Ruth; you must keep it for me."

Asa sighed. "I know, but . . ."

Samuel tapped his son's large hand. "You're making excuses. Perhaps you don't want to go because it's a woman you'll be helping. Hmm?"

Asa's dark eyelashes drifted downward.

"So that's the truth of it?" Samuel smiled as he settled back once more against the pillows.

"*Nee* . . . it doesn't matter."

Samuel snorted. "Women always matter."

"I'm going to point that out to *Grossmuder* the next time she visits."

"Bah, and I'll point out to her that you've yet to get over something that happened more than a decade ago."

"I didn't think you'd kept track."

"Your *mamm* did," Samuel rasped. "She worried for you. Now that she's gone, it's my job."

"I'm over it, *Daed*. There's nothing for you to worry about." Asa touched his father's arm.

His father sighed. "We celebrate Christmas, my son. A sea-

130

son of expectancy, of hope. But you, I don't think that you expect anything wonderful to happen to you in your life. You don't look at your days, or your nights, with the hope of *Derr Herr.*"

"I know *Derr Herr* has a plan for my life."

"Then look for it. Watch for it, like a candle in the snow. This is what your *mamm* would want for you. It's what I want for you."

"*Daed.*" Asa smiled. "I'll think about it. And I know you miss *Mamm*—I do too."

"Now you're changing the subject . . ."

Asa got to his feet and adjusted the quilts, tucking them around his father's shoulders but leaving room for his long, gray beard to stick out. "*Nee*, now I'm going to keep your favor—woman or not. Happy Christmas, *Daed.*"

The old man sighed. "Happy Christmas, *sohn.*"

Anna Stolis breathed a prayer of gratitude when the large white van took the last corner around Lincoln Street and came to a ragged halt in front of Dienner's Country Restaurant. She'd endured the *Englisch* teenager's reckless driving for two and half hours. At the last minute her transportation from Pine Creek had canceled, but she had needed to get to her *Aenti* Ruth, who was due to leave town for a brief but much needed vacation.

The *Englisch* boy grinned at her. "You're a pretty good sport. A couple of those turns were icy coming down the mountain."

"Thanks." She adjusted her *kapp* and reached into the side pocket of her large midwifery bag and paid him the agreed-upon amount plus a tip. "Drive back safely."

"No worries. Merry Christmas. Hey, and I'll pick you up the same time tomorrow evening." He grinned, cranking up the radio, and she could only nod to him through the deafening sound. The van sped away, and she stepped back in relief.

She entered Dienner's Country Restaurant, glad that it was open for a few hours on Christmas Day to cater to those who had to work or just wanted time out. She took a deep breath of the fragrant air, happy for the opportunity to warm up. She caught sight of her *aenti*, Ruth Stolis, seated at a table near the window, and she hurried to shake out her cape as she crossed the room to greet her.

Ruth Stolis was a comfortably round, keen-eyed, middle-aged widow. And at twenty-six, it seemed as though Anna might follow in her *aenti*'s footsteps, as she already had an intelligent mind, generous curves, and lack of suitors on the horizon. Still, she possessed the proper training to practice midwifery in the state of Pennsylvania, and she told herself with stout reassurance that was worth ten men. Though the wishful thought did pass through her mind that if the good Lord saw fit to send her a husband, she'd be more than grateful.

Ruth rose to enfold her in a warm hug. "I was getting worried, Anna, but I should have known better."

"Midwives always deliver." Anna grinned and they shared a smile of camaraderie as they sat down.

"How was your First Christmas? And my favorite *bruder*?"

"*Daed* and *Mamm* are doing well, but I had a delivery call just after I'd helped *Mamm* serve the noon meal. And it was twins, no less. I didn't see that coming, as I'd only had two prenatal visits with the mother. I'm still not comfortable delivering twins outside the hospital, but our women would much rather stay at home. What about you?"

"Only one delivery. My quietest Christmas ever. I relaxed by the fire, then stopped in to visit with my friend Rachel Fisher for a few minutes. You remember I wrote you a few years back to pray for her *sohn*, Seth, who was in that accident? Anyway, she would have liked me to stay longer, but I wanted to get home and curl up with Bottle."

Anna grinned at the image of her *aenti*'s cat. "You're lulling me to sleep right here."

"Well, it'll be the first Second Christmas I've spent with my daughter since she married. I'm excited, but I wouldn't be able to do it without you. Even with the other midwives in the area and the local hospital, it's hard to get away, even for a day."

"My pleasure, and I know what you mean. Although, there is a new *Englisch* physician in the area who is a great help; he's an older man and he's got an intern with him for a time. They're covering for me tonight and tomorrow."

Anna ordered a roast beef sandwich from the *Englisch* waitress, then took a sip from the thick mug of coffee. "*Ach*, I almost forgot . . . I brought a gift for my favorite *aenti* . . ." Anna reached into her oversized midwifery bag, which looked more like a folded piece of flowered carpet with wooden handles. She withdrew a small package with festive wrapping and a flattened bow.

"*Danki*, Anna . . . you didn't have to. Just coming is enough." But *Aenti* Ruth's fingers moved with happiness as she opened the gift. She laughed aloud when she saw what it was.

"A retractable tape measure—in pink and blue. Do you know how many tape measures I go through?"

"Me too." Anna smiled.

Ruth reached across the table to squeeze Anna's hand. "*Danki*, Anna. This is one I will not lose." She bundled her gift back up, then folded her hands, obviously preparing for a more serious discussion. "Now, I'll be back by seven o'clock tomorrow evening, providing everything goes well. And I want you to know that anytime you want to have a partner or just get away, I'd love to share my practice with you here in Paradise."

Anna's gray eyes shone with gratitude. "*Danki, Aenti* Ruth. *Derr Herr* has blessed me with your love and your friendship."

"All right." Ruth patted Anna's hand. "Here's my list of potential deliveries. Three possibilities. Two are further than remote."

Anna rolled her eyes at the suggestion that any possibility was remote in the realm of pregnancy and delivery. Her *aenti* laughed.

"Sarah Raber, age thirty-two, fifth child. No previous problems. Probably could deliver without you if she had to.

"Mary Stolis, some vague cousin I bet, age thirty, three children. She had a miscarriage late term last time, but she would not allow an autopsy, naturally. She's healthy as a horse, as she likes to say, on this go-around. I don't foresee any difficulties, but if she does put in a call, you'll want to keep a sharp eye."

Anna nodded.

"And Deborah Loftus. Twenty-three. First baby. Still two weeks out. Just in case."

"Just in case, hmm? Isn't it always the 'just in case' ones that deliver early?"

"Yep." Ruth's eyes twinkled. "And Samuel Mast will spend the night in the barn and drive you out if any calls come through. His kids are all grown and pretty much gone from home, and his wife passed last year. It'll make him feel good to have something to do at the holidays besides visiting. Here's the key, and the supply room is well stocked. Just make yourself at home after dinner. Folks are saying it'll snow, but Samuel knows every inch of this area. Hopefully there'll be no calls."

They both had a hearty laugh at the idea, then Anna bid her *aenti* good-bye, promising to pray she would have a safe trip. Anna sat down and finished her sandwich, savored a last cup of coffee, and made her way to the yellow house and small attached barn that her aunt rented on one of the back streets of the town. The weather looked grim, but lights burned with good cheer in storefronts and upstairs apartments.

She removed her glove to fit the key into the icy lock and entered to Bottle's purr and caress. She bent to stroke the animal and glanced with pleasure at the banked fire burning in the grate. She laid her bag on a chair and had just stretched her hands out to the warmth when a heavy banging on the front door interrupted her.

"Well, that was all of two free minutes," she muttered, going to open the door.

A tall Amish man stood in the shadows of the street lamp, and she searched his handsome face to assess the possible status of any pregnant wife. She saw nothing but calm, deep brown eyes, which made her think of dipped chocolate, and a thick fringe of lashes like icing on the cake, so to speak. She blinked. He looked rock steady, so his wife was probably just experiencing Braxton-Hicks or practice labor. Anna assumed a professional manner.

"Please, come in, Mr. . . . ah?"

"Mast. I'm Asa Mast, Samuel's son. *Daed*'s down with the flu. He sent me out to drive you tonight if need be." His voice was husky, inviting, making her think of the steady creak of well-worn rockers moving in unison. Anna decided the ride in the cold van had done more than rattle her nerves. She had never reacted like this to a man's voice; the truth was she usually saw men as vague nuisances, always underfoot when she had work to do.

"I'm, uh . . . Anna, Anna Stolis. You must know my Aunt Ruth well. Please come in out of the cold." She held the door open wider, but his tall form didn't budge.

"*Daed* said I was to sleep in the barn."

"*Ach*, right—I forgot. I mean, of course. If you'll wait, I'll get some blankets—"

He held up a large gloved hand. "No need. I'm warm."

His words caused her to inadvertently trail her gaze down his high, ruddy cheekbones to his sculpted chin and on to his broad, bundled chest. He did radiate a certain warmth; she fancied she could feel it from where she stood. And he smelled as clean as Christmas, like pine and snow.

Anna decided she was truly addled.

"Well, all right then, Mr. Mast—"

"Just Asa. Mr. Mast's my father." He gave her a warm smile.

"Right. Asa . . . I . . . call me Anna. I'll, um . . . I'll wake you if the need arises."

"Afraid I'll have to wake you most likely, ma'am—Anna. The phone's in the barn. Your *aenti* has a keen ear . . . or a sixth sense, they say." He smiled, a flash of white teeth, and a stray dimple appeared in his chiseled jaw. "She left my *daed* an extra key. I'll just holler up the steps, if that's okay?"

"Fine . . . fine." She watched him tip his black hat, then step off the porch; he was probably married, she thought, and the idea depressed her. Still, she decided she'd sleep in her clothes. She told herself that she had no desire to have Asa Mast "hollering" to her while she was in her nightgown.

A candle in the snow . . . Asa shook his head as his *daed*'s words echoed in his mind. He tried to relax against a pile of hay in the small barn, but the image of the nicely curved midwife danced before him like shadows thrown from a lantern. He couldn't remember being so struck by a woman, not for years, not for a decade. It made him feel like a teenager again, and that, in itself, was something to pray about.

Anna was dreaming. It was summer, incredibly hot, and she was debating the merits of removing her shoes and socks to dip her toes in Pine Creek. It would only make her want to swim, she decided, something that adult women were forbidden to do in her particular community, and yet she felt herself searching the bushes with a furtive glance. She was far enough away from any of the farms for anyone to see her, and her dark skirt was dreadfully warm. She fumbled with the waist, frustrated by the weight of something more than the skirt, when she heard her name being called in a low tone. She jumped, snapping her eyes open. She realized that she'd been in a deep sleep, buried under clothes, quilts, and her aunt's cat, and that Asa Mast stood near the bed, holding up a kerosene lamp.

"What's the matter? Is it a case?" She flung back the covers and the cat and made to rise.

"You sleep in your clothes?"

"All midwives do," she quipped fuzzily.

"I never knew."

"Trade secret."

"Interesting."

Anna sank back down on the bed, trying to get her bearings.

"Here . . . I brought you some hot chocolate." He offered the mug and she took it with grateful hands. She loved chocolate.

"*Danki.*"

"You sleep like the dead. I tried hollering, but it didn't work. I'm sorry to have startled you."

"No problem."

He smiled down at her. "Were you dreaming?"

She burnt her tongue on the chocolate. "Hmm? What?"

"You seemed all ruffled, like . . . I don't know."

Ruffled? She put a hand to the mousy brown hair escaping her *kapp* and looked down at his mammoth boots. Honestly, the man would be hard to dress in proper clothes at his size. She found a knot in the back of her hair and pulled.

"Here, don't do that." He put the lamp on the bureau and moved so fast she didn't realize what he was doing. He pulled her hands down and quickly worked the knot loose with his long fingers, then stepped away. He cleared his throat, and Anna thought he seemed as surprised as she was by his actions.

"Your hair's as fine as corn silk," he said, seeming to try to explain his impulsive movement. "Pulling on it won't do any good."

She was mesmerized. *Corn silk*. No one had ever said anything as direct and complimentary about her before. And the way he touched her—as if she were a porcelain doll, not the hearty and capable woman she knew herself to be. There had to be a sin involved in this thinking, she considered, her thoughts muddled.

"*Danki* . . . for helping me . . . my hair . . ."

He nodded as a brief look of sadness crossed his face, but then he changed the subject. "The call's out at the Loftuses'."

She wracked her brain. Deborah. Two weeks out from delivery. First baby. Probably lots of time, but you never could tell. She pulled on her cape and her bonnet and picked up her bag, which she'd prudently filled with supplies before she lay down. Asa went ahead of her down the narrow staircase, holding the light high. She glanced out a window, and in the faint moonlight she saw that the snow had picked up.

"What time is it?" she asked, peering at her brooch-pin clock.

"Nearly ten."

She nodded and yawned, then glanced around, trying to think if she'd forgotten anything. "We'd better go then."

"I've got the buggy pulled up. My horse, Dandy, doesn't fuss much, no matter the weather."

A gust of wind nearly snapped the door out of his hand, and Anna had to catch her breath at the biting cold. She recognized more ice than snow in the air.

"He must be a *gut* friend then," she shouted. He nodded and flashed her a fast grin, and then the giant of a man swept her up and into the warm buggy.

"How far to the Loftuses'?" she asked, attempting to break the intimate quiet of the buggy as they started off. She felt as though she and he were the only two alive in the world at that moment, insulated by the press of the weather.

"Five miles, give or take."

She nodded, understanding "give or take" to mean anything from nearly another whole mile to less than a quarter of a mile farther. She watched him handle the reins with ease.

"You cold, Doc?"

She turned, surprised, when he addressed her so. No one back home could get past her being Anna Stolis, the eldest of three sisters, even though she had her training and had delivered babies as regular as rain for the past two years.

"I'm not a doctor," she said, feeling obliged to make this known.

"Close enough for Miss Ruth to leave—that's saying something. What's your husband think about you being gone?"

She started at his question. "I'm not married."

He grinned. "Me neither."

She gave a tentative smile back and then looked out the small side window. It occurred to her that she'd never once thought of herself as a pretty woman. Passable, yes, but too curvy in the bosom and hips to be of interest when other women were as slender as reeds. But here she was, sitting in a snowstorm with an unmarried man and a dependable horse, thinking for the first time in the twenty-six years of her life that she actually might be pretty.

"Are you cold?" he asked again.

"I'm okay."

He pulled a neatly folded Jacob's Ladder patterned quilt from beneath the seat and began to spread it across her lap with one hand.

"*Ach*, it's beautiful." She loved quilts as much as she loved hot chocolate, and she ran her gloved hands over the fine workmanship, apparent even in the half-light. The color-play of the triangles somehow made Anna feel comforted, soothed.

"My *grossmuder*'s. She gave it to me last year before she died."

"Really?" Anna asked, knowing that quilts were usually left to female relatives.

"Yep. Said I should carry it with me to—" He broke off, almost in confusion.

"To what?" Anna couldn't contain her curiosity.

"Well, she said I should carry it with me in my buggy to warm the girls up. She was afraid I'd never . . . marry." He stumbled over the last word.

"*Ach*."

"I'm sorry—I've never told anyone that. I didn't mean to be forward."

Anna's heart warmed to him even as she blushed. "Please

don't mind. People tell me lots of things in my role as a mid-wife . . ."

In actuality, her mind was alternating between the images of girls snuggling with Asa beneath the quilt and her curiosity as to why he hadn't married yet. He was probably her age at least . . .

"Twenty-eight." He smiled.

"Girls under the quilt?"

He laughed, a sound that managed to tickle her spine.

"*Nee*, I'm twenty-eight, and you're the first girl to have ever used the quilt."

"I'm twenty-six," she confessed.

He nodded.

She stared at his perfect profile, the dark edges of his hair standing out only a bit lighter than his hat. He'd called her a girl . . . *a girl* . . . who was long past marrying. She'd even taken to sitting with the married women during church meetings, and nobody seemed surprised. Girls got married at twenty or twenty-one, or sometimes twenty-two—but not twenty-six. And, if he was telling the truth, that she was the first female under this warming quilt . . . her mind spun with stars and dreams and things long forgotten.

"Why haven't you married?" she asked, deciding she had nothing to lose by being so bold. She'd be going home tomorrow and would never see him again.

At first she thought she'd offended him because he didn't answer right away. But then he smiled and gave her a warm look and a sidelong glance that made her clutch her hands beneath his grandmother's quilt.

"I'm just picky, I guess."

She shook her head, feeling sleepy and spellbound. Surely he couldn't be implying that he was being preferential in showing attention toward her.

"Is that your only reason?" she asked, refusing to allow herself to give in to the pull of his words.

A tightness seemed to come over his strong features, but then she decided she'd just imagined it when he gave an amiable shrug.

"That and the fact that I'm not very good at being anything but myself. You don't get to practice charm when you're just a farmer and the hind ends of horses are all you see for half the year."

"What?"

"Guess that didn't come out right." He chuckled, and she shifted on the seat, clapping a hand over her mouth to suppress a giggle. A giggle . . . she, Anna Stolis, Anna the serious, the studious, the stern even, was giggling.

"I'm sorry, I'm not laughing at you." She took a breath. "I— I've just never met anyone like you."

He swallowed, his throat working. "Well, like I said— you're the first one under that quilt."

She savored her surprise at his response, not even caring when the snow picked up. A dim light shining in the distance alerted them to the turn, and he swung the horse with ease. He drove down the short lane, stopped the buggy, then jumped out to come around and help her. He lifted her down as though she were weightless, then grabbed her arm and her bag, steering her to the porch in the thickening snowfall.

"Step!" he hollered when they'd reached the porch, and she did.

They piled in through the front door as an anxious Amish man opened it, his light hair and fine blond beard betraying his youth and concern.

"Miss Stolis? Your aunt told us before that it might be you. I'm John." His voice quivered a bit.

He shook her hand, then Asa's. "Asa? Your father is ill, I heard today?"

"*Jah*, making tough weather of it, but he'll pull through. *Danki*. How is Deborah?"

Anna glimpsed the anxiety in John's face as he took her wet cape and hung it on a hook behind the door. "I'm not sure . . . We hosted the family here, but then everyone left early because of the storm. Deborah seemed fine, but then she started feeling sick and her contractions started."

"It will be all right, John. You'll see. I'll just go and put the horse up." Asa excused himself and went back out into the swirl of snow.

"First pregnancies are always difficult to gauge. Has she been having regular contractions?" Anna slipped off her boots and gathered up her bag.

"*Jah* . . . they were six minutes apart . . . but . . . that's not all. She's in here." He led the way to the master bedroom as Anna registered his vague comment. Concerns were already swirling through her mind when she heard the cough followed by a faint groan from the woman in the bed.

"Hi Deborah, I'm Anna, Ruth Stolis's niece. I've delivered a lot of babies, so you're in good hands." She entered the bedroom with deliberate cheerfulness, talking as she walked, and glanced around at the variety of inhalers and prescription wrappers on the carved wooden bureau. "Do you have asthma?"

Deborah was pale and obviously between hard contractions. "*Jah*." She coughed.

Anna got out her stethoscope and approached the comfortably piled bed, a fixed expression of encouragement on her lips.

Chapter Two

Asa led his horse into the Loftuses' warm barn and turned up another kerosene lamp. He stared at the small, glowing flame for a moment and thought about Anna Stolis's generous red lips and the flash of her smile. She'd appeared from behind Ruth Stolis's door like some sparkling thing, the catch of sunlight on a white splash of creek water, or the freshly washed windows of home in the springtime. But in the few minutes of knowing her, she'd also managed to bring back all of the hurt and pain he thought he was good at hiding—even what he thought he was over. But it was there, raw and open and aching until he had to bend his head against the warmth of Dandy's side to regain control. And even then the memory of his intoxicating *rumschringe*—deceptive in power and poignancy, like dandelion wine on a hot day—forced images of Jennifer back into his head and heart.

Jennifer and her incomparable beauty, her way of smiling and making others serve her, her whispered words and his desperate desire to do anything she wanted, no matter the cost. His horse shifted and he lifted his head, wiping the damp sleeve of his coat across his face as he realized he'd wasted precious moments when the midwife might need help inside.

He made his way back out into the storm and considered what everyone else had told him over the last few years—that he was going to end up an old bachelor. He'd come to rather believe it, he supposed, and viewed the girls at meetings or hymn sings with a detached interest. Truth was, he'd rather go fishing than spend time with any of the ladies of his community, but maybe that was because *Derr Herr* had never allowed anyone like Anna Stolis to cause him to think beyond his own hidden self.

He stomped his snowy feet on the porch and opened the door. It was quiet inside the house except for the sound of the wood burner popping. He slipped off his boots and placed them on the mat by the door, then hung up his heavy coat and took off his hat. He felt like he was intruding somehow and wasn't quite sure what to do with himself. He padded over to a rocking chair near the stove and eased his large frame into the carved wooden seat. He jumped up a moment later though, when a door opened and Anna walked briskly from a room off the kitchen.

"What's wrong?" he asked in a low voice, searching the tense lines of her face.

She walked toward him, and he was surprised that he had to resist the urge to look at the sweetly curving swells and sway of her body. He concentrated instead on her expression. She reached his side, and he had to bend from his much greater height to hear her whisper. Her breath smelled like summer, and her gray eyes, with their tangle of lashes, held his steadily.

"She has asthma, but I think it's gotten worse because she's caught the flu too. Her regular medication isn't getting her breath where it needs to be. I have a small portable tank of oxygen in my bag; I think that should help. Once the baby comes, I'll give Deborah a steroid shot, which should also help, but I don't want to worry John about it now. I told him to sit with her. The baby should come anytime. John suggested a few poultices might work to clear her chest, so I wondered if you'd help him brew up some things. They can't hurt and might help; that way I can focus on Deborah and the baby."

Asa nodded, then caught her arm gently when she turned away. "You're a good doc."

She flushed. *"Danki."*

He watched the fabric of her skirt swish against the end table as she walked back to the bedroom, then pulled himself up to start on his task. John emerged a few moments later from the bedroom, his blond hair rather on end and his eyes dazed.

Asa approached him the way he would a riled-up horse and laid a hand on the younger man's shoulder.

"Doc says we should make up those poultices for Deborah's breathing. I know a few remedies from taking care of *Daed* in the past. Can you show me where things are?"

"Jah." John nodded. "I'll be glad of something to do. We've got a cabinet of herbal medicines stocked, but maybe we should have gone to the hospital . . . I should have suggested that."

"Should haves are worthless in life, I've always believed," Asa said. "You just keep moving forward into what the Lord gives you." The words convicted him even as he spoke, as he realized he had spent years doing the exact opposite.

"You are right, Asa. *Danki."*

The two men soon had multiple kettles on the boil full of wild cherry bark, honey, and melted horehound candy. Ground mustard, cinnamon, cloves, ginger, allspice, and lard were also brewing, and John was beginning to look more relaxed. Asa glanced now and then at the closed door of the master bedroom and prayed that all was going well for the Doc and her patients.

～

Anna ignored the abrupt sound of a branch scratching the window and concentrated on the pale face of the woman in the bed. Deborah's reddish brown curls had all but escaped her *kapp*, and her traditional long-sleeved white nightdress was damp with perspiration. Anna slid a long plastic drape beneath her and arranged it to fall over the bottom edge of the bed. Then she opened packages of large, flat, absorbent pads and arranged these as well. As she expected, Deborah's water broke after the next few contractions.

The young woman instinctively gasped at the rush of fluid.

"It's all right, Deborah. Your water's broken, and I have a feeling that things are going to move fast now. You're doing great! Do you want me to get John?"

Deborah shook her head as she inhaled from the oxygen cannulas. "*Nee*, not yet—he gets sick to his stomach, even at calvings." Her faint smile melted into a grimace as she arched against another pain.

Anna strained with her. "Hold my hands. Let me carry the pain with you, just like *Derr Herr* does, *jah*?"

Deborah gasped. "*Jah*, you are right." She regained some composure after a moment. "Do you have children of your own?"

Anna shook her head. "*Nee*, so I don't know quite how you feel, but I can imagine."

It was a question that she was asked often. Each time she

answered, she had to remind herself that the Lord had blessed her with the chance to serve others and to see new life come into his world. But there was one part of her that longed for a husband and children of her own. Sometimes the most elated moments in her practice were also the loneliest, when the new baby came and she watched the mother take it to her breast. It was like there were two Annas—the professional and the woman . . . or the girl, as Asa Mast had called her.

Deborah's sharp cry brought her back to the moment. Realizing that the contractions were becoming more intense, she glanced around the cozy bedroom, with its simple, carved cradle, seeking a distraction for Deborah's mind, when she noticed the Turkey Tracks patterned quilt hanging on a display frame near the bureau. The wide, feathered patterns in each square did indeed resemble turkey tracks, but Anna knew another story about the quilt.

"You have a beautiful Turkey Tracks quilt, Deborah."

The woman glanced in the direction of the bright red pattern and nodded, the tension in her brow easing a bit.

"*Jah*, John's mother gave it to us . . . a wedding gift. I forget now what she said about it . . ."

Anna breathed with her through another contraction and then began to speak. "Actually, one of the first names of that pattern wasn't Turkey Tracks—it was Wandering Foot. The story goes that any boy who slept beneath the quilt was destined to lead a life of endless wandering, never having a home or family. So mothers renamed the pattern."

Deborah smiled. "That's right . . . and my John would never wander. *Danki* for reminding me." She grimaced again, and Anna adjusted the pile of quilts that covered her patient's chest. She bundled up the plastic sheet and put it in a trash bag she pulled from her midwifery case. Then she put down sterile towels and pulled on a pair of sterile gloves. She began laying out supplies from her bag, including the antibacterial wash.

"Deborah, I'm just going to check you again because I think you're very close, okay?"

"*Jah*, I think—I have to push."

"Okay, just hold on." Anna was quick. "You're right—it's time to push. Do you want John?"

Deborah nodded with visible concentration.

Anna opened the door and peered out into the kitchen where Asa and John were talking to each other by the stove.

"John, it's time now."

Anna took in the blanched face of the father-to-be and ushered him to the door. Then she saw Asa's encouraging smile, as if he held her responsible for the whole moment to come. She quickly checked her vanity and reminded herself she'd be returning the next day to Pine Creek. The thought sobered her as she eased the door closed on the man she'd just met but who had made a surprising impact on her. She refocused and followed John to the bed.

She turned up the oxygen to three liters and concentrated on encouraging Deborah. Anna always made it a habit to allow the couple to feel comfortable and in control of the moment while she was there to provide reassurance and spiritual, mental, and physical support. When John looked rather lost as to what to say as his wife squeezed his hand, Anna suggested that he climb behind Deborah in the bed and be a support for her to lean against. John latched onto this idea, and soon both husband and wife were working together as Deborah delivered a healthy first-born son to the Loftus house. Anna laid the baby on Deborah's belly and then clamped the umbilical cord and worked on her own chores with the afterbirth as the new parents murmured thanks to *Derr Herr* over their child in soft Pennsylvania Dutch.

"Would you like to cut the cord, John?" she asked after a few minutes and was surprised when he nodded and snipped the area between the two clamps with calm precision. Anna smiled as she made a brief examination of the child. She lifted the baby onto the portable sling scale. "Seven pounds, five ounces," she announced as she laid the baby on the end of the bed to clean and dress him in the traditional tiny undergarments, gown, and head covering that had lain waiting in the cradle. Then she swaddled him in a yellow patchwork baby quilt and handed him to John, who'd moved to stand by the bed, while she finished her cleaning and eased Deborah into a fresh nightdress. John laid the infant in his wife's arms, and Anna smiled in satisfaction.

"You both did great! Now I'm going to check Deborah's lungs and give her a little shot to help her breathing and we'll see if we can't get the oxygen turned down. But"—she eyed John—"I want them both to be seen tomorrow at the hospital in Paradise, just to make extra sure that everything's all right."

John gave a solemn nod, seeming to have grown older in just a few minutes. "We'll be there, Doc."

"Great. Now what are you going to name this handsome little man? I've got to fill out the paperwork."

They spoke in unison, "John Matthew."

"After his father," Deborah murmured.

Anna nodded. It was common to have three or four people with the same name in an Amish community, and it made it all the more confusing when a midwife got a nervous phone call and someone forgot to leave an address. "All right, I'll give you three some alone time." She walked toward the door, then turned back around with a smile. "By the way, I have to make it a habit to check my watch at each delivery. Your son was born on Second Christmas, 12:05 a.m." She closed the door on the happy family and walked out to the kitchen table, which was laden with covered trays of Christmas cookies that Deborah must have prepared before her labor began. She saw Asa folding white tea towels and dipping them with tongs into the steaming kettles, which filled the room with rich, spicy scents. He must have taken her instructions about herbal remedies to heart. He turned and laid the tongs aside when she sat down.

"How did it go, Doc?"

She smiled up at him. "A healthy baby boy. John Matthew Loftus."

Asa leaned back against a counter and half-closed his eyes in consideration. "The babe will be the sixth John Matthew Loftus to bless the community."

Anna laughed. "I wondered how many there might be." She drew the necessary paperwork and forms from her bag and began to write in her copperplate handwriting.

Asa came forward and put a cup of coffee in front of her. "Here. Now, tell me—how are you?"

She paused in her writing as his question penetrated. She couldn't recall a time that anyone had ever asked her that after a delivery . . . not even her mother when she returned home.

The simple question brought a rush of emotion and longing with it, sharp and piercing in its intensity. How was she? She bit her lip as the birth certificate blurred before her eyes.

He sat down at the table next to her. "Did I say something wrong?"

She shook her head, then realized he was waiting for a response.

"It's just that . . . you'll think it's silly, but it's just that no one's ever asked me that before and I've never realized how lonely a job it can be . . . I mean, people say thank you and are so grateful, but right after a birth no one's ever asked me how I was. Thank you." She looked away, hoping he wouldn't notice the tears that she barely held in check.

He repeated his question in a soft whisper. "So, how are you?"

She laughed, feeling jubilant in her spirit with a realization from the Lord that tomorrow didn't matter, nor the rest of the night; this moment was enough. She met his gaze, drowning in the dark depths of his eyes. "I'm—fine, tired but so happy that everything went well."

"*Gut*," he murmured. "That's good. I'm glad." She caught her breath as he leaned closer to her, and for a wild moment she thought he might actually kiss her, but then the bedroom door opened and John emerged.

"They're both asleep. Thank you again, Doc. Deborah wanted me to offer you some cookies, or would you like a sandwich?"

Anna penned out the remainder of the paperwork with haste. "Cookies would be good . . . to go." She glanced at Asa.

"Actually, I'd like to check on another patient my aunt told me about, depending on where she lives. I just feel a responsibility to *Aenti* Ruth to make sure all of her possible deliveries are okay."

John shook his head at the darkened window where the snow beat without mercy. "It might be better for you to stay until morning, Doc. The storm's bad." He looked at Asa over the top of her head, and Anna turned to Asa.

"*Nee*, if the Doc says we go, we go. I trust her instincts. Who is it?"

Anna thought. "Sarah Raber."

John looked relieved. "*Ach*, that's only a mile away then."

"*Gut*." Asa rose. "I'll bring the horse and buggy out of the barn while you get ready."

"And I'll have one last look at Deborah and the baby." Anna bustled into the bedroom, much more pleased with Deborah's eased respirations. She reminded John about the hospital, then stuffed the side pockets of her bag with the cookies he pressed on her. He opened the door and held a lantern high as she stepped out onto the porch, rocked by the combination of wind and snow. Asa moved like a huge shadow in the blur of white, coming to the steps and leading her into the buggy while his horse stood still. She waved toward the light of John's lantern, then refocused on the bleak road before them, but Asa was energetic and cheerful.

"That was great," he announced as he tucked the Jacob's Ladder quilt across her lap once more. She tried to focus on his words instead of his gloved hand and nodded in agreement.

"It's always something wonderful when it's a first baby, but each one is special."

He was navigating the buggy through the blowing snow with apparent calm.

"I think it's a *gut* plan to stop by the Rabers' tonight. The weather's not going to give any. I can't believe there are so many women due to labor tonight."

She decided not to tell him about the third possibility at that moment. "Babies don't wait on the weather or holidays," she pointed out instead.

He grinned at her and once more she had to resist the myriad of sensations that danced across her usual reason. Her gaze dropped to his mouth, and she imagined what it might be like to steal a kiss from him. She'd only been kissed by two boys during her young adulthood, and both were memorable for their sloppy lack of prowess. One had been from a boy who'd called her stuck up and who'd kissed her out of taunting more than desire, and the other had been from a youth one year her senior who'd been on his *rumschpringe* and smelled of sweat and alcohol. After that, Anna had focused all of her mental energies on her studies once she'd gained her parents' approval to proceed. She'd had no time for men, but now she discovered that she had a great potential for fantasizing. She could imagine Asa sleeping somewhere, maybe in a grassy field, and her leaning over his firm mouth to . . .

"*Ach*! We can get through!"

She jumped in her seat and he regarded her with a quizzical smile.

"Dreaming again, Doc?"

She blushed and was grateful for the dim interior of the buggy.

"No . . . I, ah . . . was thinking about . . . ah, what we might find at the Rabers'." Her voice ended on a squeak and she swallowed hard.

He eased on the reins and pushed his hat back a bit, exposing more of his dark mane of hair and strong brow. "Hmm . . . well, *Derr Herr* has his plans for what we'll meet at the Rabers', but I know that I do a fair bit of daydreaming myself, especially when I'm plowing."

"What do you daydream about?" she ventured with a guilty conscience, considering the train of her own thoughts.

His laugh was husky, causing a knot of feeling to tighten in her stomach. "Weird things, I guess, like picturing the sky a different color, or the way dew bounces on a spider web, or just remembering climbing trees when I was a kid . . ."

She was silent, drinking in the unconscious poetry of his words.

"Think I'm *narrisch*?"

She shook her head. "I think you're—real." *Real as honey on hot bread*, her mind whispered.

"Thanks." He smiled. "If I ever told any of my brothers what I just told you, they'd take me down to the creek and give me a good dunking to fix my addled brain."

"How many brothers?"

"Four. I'm the second oldest. What about you?"

"Two younger sisters . . . both married." She felt she should add their marital status for some reason.

"Does that make them more 'real' than you somehow— that they're married?"

She looked at him in surprise, amazed at his intuitiveness. "*Jah*, but why would you ask me that? How could you know?"

"My own brothers are married and neither they nor their wives ever stop pointing out to me that I'm missing out on real life because I'm not married."

She laughed aloud. "And are you?"

He looked at her and again she thought she saw a shadow pass over his face, but he just shook his head. "Maybe I've never considered it fully until now."

She found that she couldn't proceed with her line of questions without blushing and felt relieved when he turned the buggy into a drift-deepened lane. Anna marveled at how well the horse responded to the control of its master as it navigated through the snow. "You're a *gut* driver."

"Thanks, but a buggy's the best way to travel in snow this deep. After that, you need something from the *Englisch*." She felt him study her profile and tried to sit up a little straighter.

"Is this your first winter delivering babies?"

"*Ach*, no . . . my second, but I didn't expect Paradise to be having a storm like we do up in the mountains at Pine Creek."

"It's a doozy, all right. You drive yourself at night?" he asked.

"*Jah*, it's safe."

He grunted but didn't respond.

"*Ach*, that must be the house, and from the looks of things, we might be just in time," Anna said as she peered through the haze of snow at the farmhouse and saw that all the downstairs windows blazed with kerosene lamps. Even the barn door, farther on, revealed a thin line of welcoming light.

"I'll get you in there first and then wipe down Dandy." Asa leaped out of the buggy as she folded the quilt back. She waited only seconds before she felt him grasp her around the waist. Somehow, even through the bulk of her clothes, she could feel the warm press of his hands and the length of his leg as he hugged her to his side and swept her onto the porch.

She glanced over her shoulder to watch him stride against the wind and back to the buggy before she knocked at the front door. She decided that no one could hear her over the subdued din of the storm, so she pulled off a glove with her teeth and tried the knob. It gave with no problem and opened to a typical Amish kitchen: neat, well ordered, warm with light, but silent. She tiptoed inside, recalling her aunt's primer that Sarah Raber already had four children, and hoped she wouldn't wake anyone. Considering the hour, perhaps everyone was asleep and they'd just left lights burning because of the storm.

She was debating whether to knock on the master bedroom door or head back out to the barn when the door burst open behind her with a gust of swirling air.

"Anna," Asa gasped, his cheeks flushed, light snow dusting his face. "Sarah and Ezekiel are in the barn. They were trying to make it to the hospital or her *mamm*'s, but she's in their buggy . . . I think the baby's coming now!"

Anna pulled the edges of her cloak together. "Let's go."

The wind was piercing in its intensity. Even a few moments of respite from the cold hadn't prepared Anna for heading back outside. She caught her breath when Asa lifted her with ease off her feet, bag and all. "I'll carry you; you'll stay drier," he yelled.

Anna forgot about the cold and wished the few feet of being held against his chest could go on forever. His damp wool coat rubbed against her tender cheek like a hushed secret.

And his purposeful steps made her wonder what it would be like to have someone to help carry her through life's burdens, or at least through clover fields in high summer. She smiled and knew she'd remember this Second Christmas for as long as she lived.

He bumped open the barn door with his hip, then slid her to the ground, twisting to shut out as much cold as possible. She was surprised at the overall warmth of the barn, its walls insulated by the hay, the feed bags, and the animals' bodies themselves. She noticed Asa had withdrawn his quilt from beneath his coat and laid it on a clean hay bale. Lamps burned, highlighting the hay and the shadowy movements of the animals' bodies, as cows chewed from their mangers and horses shifted with gentleness. Asa had stabled his horse in a stall to her right and must have left the buggy outside, though she'd been in no frame of mind to notice it.

But now, Anna couldn't help but compare the comforting warmth of the scene to the one so long ago, on that first Christmas. Only the starkness of a woman's cry brought her back to reality and reminded her that her Lord and Savior had few of the comforts that lay before her. The Rabers' buggy was hitched and ready to go with one door still wide open. Mr. Raber, a middle-aged Amish man with a blue shirt and black suspenders, was running his hands through his hair and speaking in earnest, soft Pennsylvania Dutch to the occupant of the buggy while Asa stood tense with his back turned.

Mr. Raber caught sight of Anna and hurried over, his hand extended. "You are Anna, *Frau* Ruth's niece, *jah*? Thank *Derr Herr* you've come. How did you ever know?"

He wrung Anna's hand with goodwill, and she caught a firmer grip on the handle of her bag. She smiled with reassurance. "The Lord is in control. So this is your fifth child, Mr. Raber? May I examine your wife? I take it that things have moved rather fast?"

He led her to the buggy. "*Jah*, so we thought, but something is wrong now." He kept his voice low, then stepped away to unhitch the horse, who was beginning to dance restlessly.

Anna peered inside at the laboring woman. She met the anguished green eyes of Sarah Raber and recognized worry mixed with pain in equal amounts. Her first job was to calm her drained patient.

"I'm Anna Stolis, Sarah. Have you had problems or delays with your other deliveries?"

"*Nee.*" The woman shook her head and put a hand up to push her *kapp* back on her head. "And we thought this one . . . would be as easy, but . . . we got into the buggy and I felt like pushing, but nothing's happened. I'm afraid it's been too long . . ." Tears dripped from her eyes as she clutched the sides of the buggy seat with white-tipped fingers.

"*Aenti* Ruth said that you could probably deliver without me," Anna told her with a heartfelt smile. "Now, let's just see what's going on, shall we?"

Anna disinfected and pulled on her gloves, praying as she went through her comforting preparation rituals. She had a sick feeling of what might actually be wrong.

Lifting her head a few moments later, Anna kept a reassuring smile plastered on her face. The baby was Frank breech, and Sarah was right: time was growing short. She thought for a moment, knowing there was no way to get the mother and baby to the hospital in time.

Just then the barn door slid open, letting in a blast of snow. A wide-eyed girl of about ten stood in her nightgown, over-sized boots, and a shawl.

"*Was en der welt*, Esther?" Mr. Raber exclaimed. "You will freeze, child!"

"I had a nightmare, *Daed*. I called for you and *Mamm* . . . what's wrong?"

Sarah spoke to her husband in quick Pennsylvania Dutch from inside the buggy, and Mr. Raber went to gather up his daughter. "I will take her back and tuck her in."

Anna spoke in soothing tones to the laboring woman when he'd gone. "Sarah, your baby is breech. Do you understand what that means?"

Sarah choked on a sob. "*Jah*, we will lose the child. My best friend's baby was breech—she couldn't make it to the hospital in time."

"Well, as the Lord wills, you are not going to lose this child." Anna spoke with confidence. She rummaged in her bag and opened a sterilized kit containing a gown, mask, pads, and another pair of gloves. "I've delivered three breech babies in the last two years. It will be okay—you just listen and do what I tell you to, all right?"

"All right," Sarah gasped.

Anna smiled, then called for Asa to come nearer the buggy.

He came reluctantly, clearly feeling it was not his place.

"Sarah, Asa Mast is here," Anna said from behind her

mask. "He drove me tonight. I may need his help if Mr. Raber doesn't come back right away. We have to move fast."

"It's—okay—just please help my baby."

"Asa," Anna said in a low tone. "Sarah's baby is breech. Put on a pair of gloves from my bag and find something warm . . . your coat . . . and get ready to take the baby when I hand it to you."

"Breech . . ." he said, meeting her eyes, and she couldn't look long at the fear she saw there.

"*Derr Herr* will not abandon us. Hurry."

"*Jah*," he murmured, turning to do as she asked.

Anna prayed as she began the delicate delivery, closing her eyes and visualizing the anatomy of mother and baby.

"Everything's fine, Sarah. Don't push, not yet. Just breathe." *Please, Lord, help this baby's head to not be too large. Please let it pass easily . . . help me, Lord, please . . .*

Sarah drew deep, wrenching breaths as Anna manipulated the small bottom and limbs, wishing she could give Sarah something for the pain. But she'd probably refuse it, and there was no time.

Then everything began to move at once, and Anna took a deep breath when she felt the size of the baby's head. "Okay, Sarah, just a little push . . ."

Sarah pushed and Anna strained to put subtle pressure on the head. Within seconds, the squalls of a newborn baby girl echoed in the vastness of the barn, mixing with her mother's sobs. Anna cut the cord, suctioned the breathing passages, wrapped the baby in sterilized pads, then turned to transfer the bloody, squalling scrap of humanity into Asa's outstretched hands, which were covered by his *grossmuder*'s quilt.

Anna met his brown eyes, finding them welled with tears. "To keep the girl warm," he murmured, wrapping and cradling the baby in his strong arms.

Anna swallowed hard and turned back to Sarah. "It's a girl, Sarah. She looks great; I'll check her over. Let me just see to you for a moment."

Sarah rested her head back against the buggy door, breathing soft prayers of thanksgiving as the barn door opened and Mr. Raber hurried to the buggy. Anna watched Asa hold out the bundle in his arms from the corner of her eye.

"A girl," Asa told him. "Congratulations, *Daed*."

"And Sarah?" Mr. Raber moved to look inside the buggy.

"She did a wonderful job," Anna said.

"*Gut*," Mr. Raber choked. "That's good."

"She was breech, Ezekiel." Sarah sniffed. "We could have lost her . . . but *Derr Herr* . . . he was with us."

"He is always with us, Sarah," Ezekiel Raber whispered as he stared down at his new daughter. "He gives and takes away, but praise him for giving this night."

Sarah nodded, then stretched to pat Anna's hand. "And you, and Asa Mast—we could not have done this without you both."

Anna smiled and finished with the usual post-delivery chores, pleased that Sarah did not bleed too much with the delivery of the placenta. She covered the new mother with her cloak, which had dried somewhat, then cleaned everything in sight. She turned to see Mr. Raber's eyes filled with tears as he rocked from side to side with his new daughter.

"*Danki*, Anna, and Asa too."

"What will you name her?" Anna asked after examining the baby again. She had drawn the birth certificate forms from her bag and watched from where she leaned against the top of a bale of hay.

Mr. Raber rested against the buggy and stared with love at his wife. "What will it be?"

Sarah Raber spoke. "That quilt she's wrapped in—where did it come from?"

Asa had turned his back to the buggy once more but came forward to answer. "It was my *grossmuder*'s. Please, I want you to keep it—for her hope chest maybe." He nodded at the cherubic face, half revealed. Anna smiled.

"What was your *grossmuder*'s name, Asa—I can't seem to think straight." Sarah laughed.

"Rachel."

Sarah and her husband smiled, and Anna began to letter the birth certificate even before they spoke.

"Then Rachel it shall be," Sarah announced. "Rachel Anna Raber."

Anna looked up in surprise and felt a thrill of delight. She'd never had a namesake, and now she felt the page in front of her blur with the onset of tears and weariness, which she swiped away before they could smear the ink. "Time of birth . . . 2:20 a.m., Second Christmas. Congratulations."

"Thank you." Asa humbly bent his head at the couple and Anna nodded. "*Jah*, thank you so much."

Chapter Three

Asa helped Ezekiel Raber harness the horse to the buggy again as Anna made Sarah and the baby as warm and shielded as possible inside. The trip from the barn to the house was only twenty-five feet or so, but Anna wanted there to be no opportunity for either patient to take a chill. She also made Sarah lie on a makeshift stretcher, created from a wide, thin roll of plastic window insulation that Ezekiel had found and made more secure with two blankets he'd tramped back to the house to get. Ezekiel got up on the buggy seat to drive as Asa went to open the barn doors.

Asa paused a moment, wanting there to be no mistakes now that everything had gone so well. "I'll hold the horse's head, Ezekiel, if you like. Just in case he balks."

"*Gut* idea. The storm is more than anything I've seen in years."

Asa caught the bridle with a soothing sound, glanced back for Anna's nod to proceed, and opened the barn door. The wind whipped inside with wild abandon and the horse attempted to rear. Asa held firm, though he felt like his arms were going to be wrenched out of their sockets, and the horse seemed to relax when it realized that neither man panicked. Asa pushed through the thick, wet snow as tiny pieces of ice, like shards of glass, drove against his face and down the neck of his coat. He felt as if he were wading through freezing maple syrup when they finally got to the steps, and that was the easy part. They still had to get mother and daughter safely and pain-lessly inside.

~

It hadn't been easy, Asa reflected as he walked to the whistling kettle at the stove. He decided he never wanted to be responsible for transporting a new mother again, unless, his mind drifted with sleepy lassitude, it happened to be Anna. The thought jerked him wide-awake, and he moved the kettle with more force than he'd intended, sloshing the boiling water over the side of the cup. He put the back of his hand to his mouth and gave it an instinctive suck.

"Here . . . don't do that." Anna sounded worried, and he felt himself flush as though she could read his thoughts. She rose to go to the Rabers' icebox and brought him a clean towel with ice.

"Let me see your hand."

"It's fine."

"Now, please." She smiled sweetly but wearily at him.

He sighed and extended his burned hand. She wrapped it in the ice-cold towel, and he watched her delicate fingers press here and there against his work-roughened hand as she secured the fabric. It made him feel hot behind his collar, and he could only nod when she told him to be still while she hurried to get antibiotic ointment from her bag. It was a blessing that Ezekiel, Sarah, and the baby were in the master bedroom, resting after the precarious trip out of the buggy and up the steps. The wind had almost tipped the stretcher, and Asa's heart had ached at the involuntary moan of pain Sarah had emitted against the wind. They'd finally gotten her inside and into bed, and Anna continued to check between mother and daughter. Ezekiel had hastily shown Anna and Asa where to find the coffee and cookies and then had gone to be with his wife.

Asa held the wet towel in place until Anna crossed back to him with her bag.

"Seems like you must have everything but a church meeting going on in there," he joked, trying to regain his equilibrium of thought.

She nodded with an absent *mmm-hmm*. She was clearly in Doc mode. But he didn't feel dismissed when she gently peeled back the towel and began to massage the clear ointment over his hand. In truth, more than the sudden sparks of sensation her touch sent down his spine, an expanding, ridiculous urge to cry rose up in his chest.

He bent his head and wet his lips as a wash of images invaded his mind. He remembered how he'd wrenched his hand fixing the axle of the car he'd bought and hidden from his family when he was seventeen. It had been one of the first times he'd gone driving with Jennifer. He'd asked her for help as the blood had rushed from the deep laceration, but she'd glanced away, looking disgusted. So he'd wrapped his own hand, using his teeth and a rag, and had decided that such common things were beneath anyone so wonderful as Jennifer. He grimaced now at the irony of it all and forced himself back to the moment as he realized Anna had just spoken.

"Uh, I'm sorry—what?"

She'd turned his hand over, exposing his palm and the long, jagged scar. "I asked how you got this. It looks like you never got proper first aid."

He pulled away a bit and fisted his hand from her gaze. "I was young. It was something stupid."

"Well." She gathered up her supplies. "The burn should heal well."

It will. Because of you.

～

Ezekiel Raber had just carried the polished cradle into the master bedroom, then returned a few minutes later to refill their mugs. A sudden grinding sound and a flash of lights passed by the dark kitchen windows, illuminating the still-falling snow.

"That'll be Joe Grossinger, a *gut Englisch* friend of mine. He runs a plow for extra money during the winters and always does our drive for free. He'll only accept a cup of coffee to warm him up," Ezekiel explained.

Anna rose to her feet in obvious excitement. "Is that a dump truck he's driving?"

Ezekiel nodded. "*Jah*, with a plow on front, and he drops cinders or gravel from the back. Why?"

"*Jah*, why?" Asa asked Anna, who swallowed under his alert gaze.

In hindsight, perhaps she should have told him straight off about the three possible labors, but she hadn't thought the storm would be so bad. And in her experience men could usually only handle one labor a night, though Asa had already proved her wrong.

When she didn't respond, Ezekiel lit another lantern and went to the front door. She clasped her hands in front of her and looked at Asa.

"Well, it's just that . . . *Aenti* Ruth told me that there could be one more delivery tonight, and I thought . . ."

He raised his dark brows and half groaned. "Another delivery? Is all of Paradise due to deliver tonight? And when exactly do you sleep, Anna?"

"I . . . don't . . . at least, not a lot. Look, you don't have to go with me. I can ask Mr. Grossinger if he will take me and then I'll . . ."

He straightened up in his chair. "Do you think I'm letting you go off with some stranger—an *Englischer*—in the middle of the night?"

"Well, you were a stranger too . . ." She trailed off, thinking she felt as if she'd known him so much longer than just a few hours.

He must have caught the look in her eye because he leaned forward and searched her face. "And am I still a stranger, Anna?"

She caught her breath at his words, amazed that they shared the same thought. She shook her head as she returned his gaze. "*Nee*, you are no stranger."

She might have gone on if Ezekiel hadn't led a tall, lanky *Englisch* man into the room.

"Joe, this is Anna and Asa . . . they helped Sarah give birth a couple of hours ago. A little girl this time!" Ezekiel beamed.

"Well, shoot!" Joe exclaimed, whipping off his ball cap to reveal an unruly crop of dark curls. "That makes five, don't it, Zeke? I've got to say that I envy you and the missus." He gave Ezekiel a back-slapping hug that was returned enthusiastically, then he stretched big, dirt-stained hands to shake with Anna and Asa. Anna found herself enjoying the open personality of the *Englischer*, who had just plopped himself down at the kitchen table and accepted his mug of coffee as if he'd been there many times.

"How's the storm looking?" Ezekiel asked. "Anna wants me to take both Sarah and the baby into town tomorrow for a checkup at the hospital."

Joe laughed. "I'm about as lonesome out there as Santy Claus, and him a day late. It's bad. But I'll be glad to come back out and get you folks tomorrow morning when it slows down a bit."

Ezekiel smiled. "I think it'll be all right."

Asa cleared his throat. "Well, actually, Ezekiel, Joe . . . uh . . . Anna's got to check on one more woman who could deliver this morning. We were thinking of asking maybe to keep the buggy here and to see if Joe might drive us to—" He glanced at Anna, who had a slight smile on her face.

"The Stolises'," she supplied. "Mary Stolis."

Asa and Ezekiel groaned aloud in perfect unison.

"What?" Anna and Joe asked at the same time.

Asa sighed. "Mary and Luke Stolis are a nice couple. Everyone in the community mourned when she lost the last baby. The Stolises run a big woodworking shop out of their house and outbuildings. A lot of brothers, sisters—"

"So?" Anna queried.

"It's Luke's mother, *Grossmuder* Stolis, who runs the house and kind of makes things difficult for people. She's . . . older, lost her husband, and she's kind of stern."

"Mean," Ezekiel clarified.

"Got a few relatives like that myself," Joe commented with a chuckle.

"Well, I've dealt with plenty of strong-willed older folks up at Pine Creek," Anna said, shrugging her shoulders. "She can't be that bad."

Again, Asa and Ezekiel looked rather like they'd both eaten a bad pickle.

"Well, I'd sure enough be glad to get you there," Joe offered. "I know where that big woodworking outfit is, though I can't promise the lane might not be drifted over."

"Oh, we'd be so grateful." Anna clapped her hands.

Joe drained his cup. "All righty then. Let's get to it. Zeke, tell Sarah congratulations and I'll swing by again to check on you all when it lightens up."

Anna went to examine Sarah and the baby once more, then pulled on her boots and cape and grabbed her bag. She felt a renewed energy, though she could tell that Asa was dragging a bit as he adjusted his hat and gloves.

"Be careful. And *danki* again." Ezekiel shook Asa's and Joe's hands and patted Anna's shoulder, then opened the door to the frigid air once more.

Chapter Four

Anna had never ridden in a dump truck or any kind of truck for that matter, and she was delighted by the new experience. Joe had left the engine running, and he climbed into the driver's seat while Asa led Anna to the passenger door and then boosted her up to the high seat inside.

She breathed in the heavy scent of the heat that blew from the truck's vents, feeling drowsiness seep into her with the warmth. Then she'd had to crawl over empty plastic water bottles, potato chip wrappers, and an assortment of tools to get to the middle of the seat.

Joe stuffed as many of the oddities as he could behind the seat as Anna got situated. Asa climbed in beside her, and she found herself squashed between the two men with her bag situated on her lap. Joe turned a knob and the blaring sound of Christmas music faded.

"Sorry for the mess."

"No problem." Asa laughed. "You should see the back of my buggy sometimes."

Anna watched as Joe backed the truck down the lane, a loud beeping sound accompanying the movement. She had to press against the seat as he swung the huge steering wheel, his bony elbows protruding here and there. Then he backed onto the lane and began a slow pace across the treacherous piles of icy snow.

"Did you have a good Christmas, Joe?" Anna asked.

"As good as can be. I went to church—I know you folks are big on that. Then I had dinner at my momma's and watched some TV."

How lonely, Anna thought as she considered all of the family she had.

"Oh," she murmured.

Joe sighed. "I used to have a wife but she run off. Took the kids with her. It's not been the same since."

"I'm so sorry," Anna said.

"Ah, it's not so bad. I do have a girlfriend now, but I'm kind of takin' it slow like. I don't want to make another mistake like before. You know what I mean?"

Asa cleared his throat. "*Jah*, you are a wise man to be cautious—and a good man, to help Ezekiel and us too."

Anna considered Asa's use of the word *cautious*, but Joe had resumed talking.

"I like your kind, the Amish. You seem—real to me. That matters."

"Thank you," Asa replied with quiet sincerity.

Joe adjusted the plow, then whistled for a few seconds. "So, you folks got kids of your own?"

Anna spluttered at Joe's assumption that they were married.

"Uh . . . no . . . we—"

Joe grinned. "Well, they'll come along, right as rain. Happens that way, you know." He resumed whistling, and Anna couldn't find the voice to correct him. She noticed Asa's silence as well and tried to ignore the warm press of his body against her side.

"Okay," Joe announced after a few long minutes, slowing the vehicle. "I think this is it." He began to turn cautiously into the lane but soon shook his head in frustration.

"Their lane's a lot narrower than Zeke's and the drifts are huge. I wish I could get you a bit closer." Joe tugged on his ball cap and stared out at the blinding white illuminated by the headlights of the vehicle. "I can't take a risk going off the lane; I'd never get her out. I don't know if you should try and walk it."

"We'll get through," Asa said. "Thank you very much."

"I'll keep the lights on high 'til I see that you're near the house, but you'd better move fast. Those drifts look chest deep in some places."

"Thank you." Anna smiled, laying her hand on Joe's arm as Asa lifted the large latch on the door and swung it open, letting in a blast of cold air and a heavy fall of snow onto the vinyl seat. Anna tried to brush it away.

"Aw, leave it," Joe said. "Go on now. I'll keep watch."

Asa swung her down into the snow, and she was amazed that it reached as high as her waist. The cold engulfed her as Asa closed the door and then took her bag and her arm.

"I'd carry you," he called over the wind, "but I don't want to take the chance of dropping you in a drift. Can you make it?"

"*Jah!*" she yelled back as they waded out into the twin beams of the truck's headlights, which reflected a good distance ahead.

Anna gave vague consideration to how quickly she ceased to feel her feet and then noticed that her heartbeat, after a few slogging steps, began to shift from hard pumping to a slow lassitude. She tried to concentrate and took deep breaths of the biting snow, then started reciting anatomy facts as the first insidious thoughts of sleep whispered at the back of her consciousness. She shook herself and almost went down in a drift but felt strong hands hauling her back to her feet.

Asa shook her. "Come on," he called. "We can do this."

She nodded, but it must not have satisfied him because he shook her again, and this time she felt her teeth rattle.

"Anna Stolis!" he yelled. "I am not going in this house, where that wiry old woman lives, to deliver a baby alone! I don't know how—so stay awake!"

"All right," she snapped, and he dragged her on.

Soon they were out of the reach of the truck's lights. Anna felt a moment of fear as the snow swirled with blinding force around them, but she found herself remembering that all was light to *Derr Herr*. He knew the way they were going, and he'd apparently revealed it to Asa as she felt herself yanked along. Soaked to her neck, she staggered, then came to an abrupt halt when she ran into Asa's broad back.

"Are we lost?" she yelled.

"No—clothesline." He reached above his head, and she had to laugh at the thought of Asa getting clotheslined by a diligent housewife in the middle of a blizzard. A few steps more, and Anna saw the reassuring bulk of the house. From a distance, they heard Joe honk his horn as he pulled away, and Asa pounded on the door where only a dim light shone from the inside. Again, Anna hoped she'd not brought them on some fool's errand in the small hours of the night, but the door opened with abruptness.

They staggered into a large, dim living room and Anna tried to steady her breathing. She wiped the wet snow from her face, and it became apparent that, although few lights burned, the room held three women who stared at Anna and Asa as though they were apparitions.

Asa spoke first. "It's Asa Mast and *Frau* Ruth's niece, Anna Stolis. We thought we'd come check on Mary . . ." He trailed off when no one responded. Only Anna's deep intakes of breath could be heard.

Then the oldest woman gave a crack of harsh laughter. "The clock says close to four a.m., and there's a blizzard. Are you drunk or just fools?"

Anna felt Asa stiffen beside her but decided it was a fair, albeit rude, question.

"Neither, ma'am," she said politely, coughing a bit and trying to reach the snow that trailed down her neck with a discreet hand. "I felt a responsibility to *Aenti* Ruth to check on all of her possible deliveries tonight, especially because of the storm, to make sure all was going well."

"Well, all is not well, missy. Luke Stolis is in bed with the flu, as are his brothers, two of the children, and my two sisters. The rest of us, myself and my two daughters, are just sitting here waiting to get it."

"*Grossmuder* Stolis," Asa said with resignation. "I'm sorry you're going through this; my *daed* is down with it too."

"*Humph*—time was nothing could get Samuel Mast down. He's getting old."

Anna heard the small rumble that escaped Asa's lips and ignored the steady drip from her freezing nose.

"Please excuse me, Mrs. Stolis, but you didn't mention your daughter-in-law, Mary. Is she feeling well?"

"Who are you?" The old woman leaned forward with an ominous creak from her rocker.

"Anna Stolis, from Pine Creek. As Asa said, I'm Ruth Stolis's niece and have taken over her midwifery duties for this night."

"Pine Creek, hmm? No relation that I can think of just now."

Anna sneezed, and Asa made an impatient gesture with his arm. "We are soaked and freezing. How is Mary?"

Anna felt his frustration but clung to her diplomacy, not wanting to alienate one of *Aenti* Ruth's patients' family members. But she needed to know how the pregnant woman felt so they could march with good conscience back out into the freezing cold.

"Mrs. Stolis, I've been practicing midwifery successfully for the past two years in Pine Creek, and *Aenti* Ruth briefed me on Mary's last pregnancy. I'm sorry that she lost the child."

"There is nothing to be sorry for in the will of *Derr Herr*."

Anna did a mental count to ten and tried to wriggle her toes. She knew she had to get past the older woman, but her patience was running out.

"Of course the Lord's will is best, but we've come far tonight. Could you just tell me that Mary is doing well?"

A woman sniffed from the shadows. "As well as can be expected for a body nine months pregnant and in labor."

Dead silence reigned in the room for all of three seconds, and then Anna's patience exploded.

"That's it!" Her voice bounced off the walls, and the two quiet sisters jumped in their chairs. She felt Asa start beside her as well, but she didn't care. She pulled off her icy gloves with her teeth, letting them fall with wet plops onto the hardwood floor. Her cape, scarf, bonnet, and boots followed in quick succession, building an inelegant, dripping pile. She hopped gracelessly from one foot to the other as she peeled off her soaking knee socks, flinging them backward to splat low against the wall. Then she grabbed her snow-covered bag from Asa's hands.

Anna stepped forward into the gloomy room and caught up a lantern from a side table, turning it to its highest flame, then setting it back down with a thump. Her gaze swept the room until it came to rest on the older, black-eyed woman sitting in full Amish church-meeting dress, who was regarding them without emotion. Anna swept toward her, ignoring the two other women, and moved to drop her bag on the floor in front of the matriarch.

Anna caught the arms of the rocking chair and knelt to give an even glare into the dark eyes. "Now let me make myself clear, Mrs. Stolis. I don't care who you are or who you think you are in this family, but—as *Derr Herr* wills—this baby will not die under my watch. So unbend your stiff neck for two minutes and take me to Mary, or I'll search every room myself."

There was an infinitesimal pause.

"You're not married, are you?" Mrs. Stolis asked.

Anna would have given the chair, possibly even the grandmother herself, a good shake had she not heard Asa's sudden choked laughter.

She whirled to shoot him an accusing glance, but he held up a placating hand.

"What," Anna snapped, "is so amusing?"

Asa shook his head. "Ask *Grossmuder* Stolis."

"*Jah*," the older woman said with what could only be described as suppressed mirth. "No one's spoken to me like that in a good long time. Not since Henry died. I—I've missed it, truth be told. He kept me in line, and I've become a shrunken apple without him." She gave a wry glance at her frozen daughters. "There's not much fruit on the trees around here. But you, Anna Stolis from Pine Creek, you just gave me the nicest Christmas gift I've had in nearly fifteen years."

Anna sank to her heels with a shiver and pulled her bag back on her lap. "So, where's Mary?"

"I haven't abandoned her, if that's what you're worried about. I want to keep the flu away from her—her husband has it. So she's comfortable in a bedroom on the third floor. One of us goes up to check on her every few minutes."

Anna was already on her feet. "I'll just have a look."

"You're going to freeze to death, Anna," Asa pointed out. "Your clothes are soaked."

Anna glanced down at her blouse and skirt, which clung stubbornly to every curve she had, and sighed. First, she'd lost her temper in front of the only man who'd ever given her a second glance, and now her generous shape was portioned out in bland revelation by the light she'd turned up herself.

"I'm fine," she said.

Grossmuder Stolis rose to her feet and looked at her daughters. "Esther, Miriam, take Anna Stolis upstairs and get her some dry clothes—though I doubt anything you have will fit, you're both thin as beans."

Anna's eyes widened at the veiled insult and she cleared her throat.

"I'm sorry." Mrs. Stolis laughed. "I've always fancied beans"—she gave Anna's waist a quick pinch—"and fresh bread. Go on now, girls."

Anna grimaced at another stifled laugh from Asa, picked up her bag, and followed the two bewildered sisters out of the room.

The two women, clearly overwhelmed at the abrupt change in events, could do nothing more than lay out clothes for Anna and then they hastily left her alone. She changed quickly, caught up her bag, and went onto the landing to continue up the stairs to the third floor.

She peered down a long narrow hallway of doors and saw the sliver of light from beneath one at the far end. She went and knocked, not knowing what to expect, and a cheerful woman's voice bade her to come in.

Chapter Five

She opened the door and was amazed to see a lovely, fresh-faced woman, gowned and *kapped*, sitting up in a beautiful bed, reading a magazine.

"Mary?"

"*Jah*, are you *Frau* Ruth's niece? She told me about you on my last visit with her. She's very proud of you."

Anna came into the room and closed the door. "*Jah*, I'm Anna. *Danki*. How are you?" She recalled that Aunt Ruth had said Mary proclaimed herself to be "healthy as a horse."

The woman in the bed cast her an easy smile. "I'm wonderful. Do you want to check my pulse and blood pressure? Ruth always does."

Anna nodded, feeling a little dazed. Perhaps she had dragged Asa on a fool's errand, for no woman in labor had ever looked so serene.

Mary's pulse and pressure were excellent. "Any contractions or pain?" she asked, feeling like she already knew the answer. Mrs. Stolis must have been mistaken about the labor.

Mary laid her magazine, which Anna noted was an *Englisch* publication on labor and delivery, on the full mound of her stomach and nodded. "Every five minutes, regular as can be. I should be ready to push soon."

Anna looked around the bedroom, feeling out of her depth. She noted the elaborately carved cradle that stood ready nearby.

"My husband, Luke, carved that at the shop. After we lost our last baby, he wanted to 'make all things new' for this one's arrival."

"It's beautiful," Anna said as she drew out her stethoscope. She didn't want to have to listen for the heartbeat; it was possible that there were no visible signs of pain because the baby had already been lost in utero. Yet she had no choice. She avoided Mary's gentle smile as she moved aside the quilts and bent her head.

She nearly sagged with relief against the bed when she heard the heartbeat, strong and steady, and saw the now visible contractions that tightened Mary's belly.

"Everything's fine," Mary told her before she could say anything, and Anna nodded.

"Forgive me, Mary, please, but how . . . do you know? You should be in some pain at this point, if not a lot."

Mary smiled again and reached beneath the pile of white pillows at her back and drew out a folded piece of paper. "It's simple, really. For this pregnancy, I saw that there were four of us involved, right from the beginning. Luke agreed with me."

"Four?" Anna wondered if it were possible that her patient carried twins and Ruth had missed it.

"*Jah*, Luke, myself, the baby, and *Derr Herr*." She handed Anna the piece of paper.

Anna bent her head to read. "'And he that sat upon the throne said, "Behold, I make all things new."' Revelation 21:5."

Anna lifted her gaze back to Mary's.

"I chose to embrace this verse with Luke and the baby and to make it the theme verse—the quilt pattern, if you will—of this pregnancy. I know that there is newness even in death, of course, but this time I believe that *Derr Herr* has a different plan."

"It's beautiful."

"Our Lord is beautiful. Now it's time to push," Mary said with little ceremony.

Anna drew on her gloves, mask, and gown with haste, but had little time to prepare anything else as Mary urged her to hurry.

Two brief pushes later, a wide-eyed baby boy emerged with perfect breathing and excellent color. Anna had to blink back tears as she laid the baby on his mother's stomach and cut the cord. She'd never felt so humbled by the presence of new life or by the faith of a mother.

She performed her aftercare quietly as she listened to the soft murmurs of love and the prayers of thanksgiving that echoed from mother to child. When both mother and baby were clean and dry, Anna felt enveloped in a peace that would have allowed her to sleep standing upright if she didn't have paperwork to fill out.

She leaned against a bureau and noticed that the sun was beginning to send luminous streaks of light across the window. At some point it had stopped snowing. It was Second Christmas morn.

"What will you call him, Mary?" she asked with pen poised.

"Luke and I decided a long time ago: Christian. Christian Luke Stolis."

Anna nodded and once again felt choked by tears. She

wrote down the time of birth, then glanced once more at her watch, amazed that only forty-five minutes had gone by since she'd first come upstairs. She hoped Mrs. Stolis wouldn't visit soon and disrupt the peace. It seemed as though Mary could read her thoughts when she asked brightly if Anna had met her mother-in-law.

"Yes—for just a few minutes."

Mary laughed. "She's got everyone fooled but me; I know she loves me, though I have tried to encourage her to stop terrorizing everyone else."

Anna gave her a weak smile. "Maybe you'll find you've had some success with that."

With the advent of morning and the new baby in the house—in addition to a cheerful, if not tart, elder Mrs. Stolis—the feeling of Second Christmas permeated the air with warmth and goodwill. Several of the flu victims returned from their beds feeling much better and came to eat an abundant breakfast around the large wooden table. Luke Stolis arrived first and couldn't thank Anna and Asa enough, though he'd yet to see his new son; Anna had given orders that he wait at least twenty-four hours after his symptoms had subsided.

Anna accepted a place at the table, refreshed as always by the new day, though she hadn't slept at all. And though she didn't study him directly, she was conscious that someone had given Asa clean clothes, because the aqua green shirt he now wore so matched his good looks. But it was only when she lifted her head to look at him across her breakfast plate that she noticed the flush on his handsome face. He returned her smile, but his cheeks were red and his dark eyes held the glazed, distant look she'd come to associate with illness in her practice. He coughed once, into his sleeve, then stared with disinterest at his plate of food.

Anna rose from the table. She had no desire to let the household know that there was another case of flu among them until she was quite sure. "Mrs. Stolis, I need to get my midwifery bag back in order, and there are some small chores that Asa might help me with. Do you have an extra room where I can lay all of my supplies out?"

"*Jah,* certainly. Go upstairs to the second floor and turn left. Use any of those rooms; they're all empty. I kept the flu victims on the right wing. If you need to be long, someone can build you a fire."

"I'll do it. *Danki.*"

Anna was sure that only she noticed how abruptly Asa's color changed to pallor when he got to his feet. And by the time they mounted the narrow, darkened back staircase, he leaned on her, and she struggled to get him over the top step and down the hallway.

She chose the first door that she came to and opened it, revealing a large room with a carved bed and pristine patchwork quilt. There was an abundance of pillows, too, she was glad to see. But it was chilly, and she hurried to help Asa to the bed, pulling the quilt and bedclothes down with one hand.

"Asa," she whispered. "Lie down; you'll feel better."

"Just for a minute," he mumbled. "I'll make the fire first."

"But it's already so hot in here." She improvised, knowing

his fever would deter him until she could get the blaze going herself.

"Okay."

She pushed him onto his back and he closed his eyes, sinking against the pillows while she tugged and tucked all the bedclothes tightly around him. He opened his eyes to stare up at her.

"You're so beautiful," he said, then choked on a cough.

"And you're so sick," she returned, ignoring the stabbing emotion that threaded across her chest at his words.

"*Narrisch* for you, Doc," he said as he smiled, then closed his eyes until his breathing deepened and leveled off to a nasty rasp in sleep.

Anna swallowed and went to the fireplace, kindling the heat, while his words warmed her mind.

∽

Asa knew that he was sick, very sick. He couldn't remember feeling this awful since he was a kid. He also knew that whether he was dreaming or not, Anna Stolis was taking care of him. He wanted to believe it was real when she softly urged him to swallow from a spoon or stroked his hair back from his forehead with a damp cloth. He wanted to know that it was her who trailed the coolness down his neck to the width of his shoulders. But he couldn't quite make his way through the haze in his brain to know if she was really there, so he let his mind settle for sweetly tangled, tantalizing dreams.

He cast a line into the deep pool of his favorite fishing spot and relaxed against the tall oak that grew broad enough to support his back. The heat of the summer day had yet to relent, and he reached a long arm down to scoop water from the running creek. He drank with eagerness from his cupped palm. When he lifted his head, he was amazed to see a woman wading in the creek toward him. It was the midwife—Anna—and her bare feet shone slender and white through the clear water as she lifted her dark skirt to her ankles and clambered across the damp rocks. He tried to speak, but his voice caught and he had a hard time managing his breathing as she came closer.

He wanted to tell her a thousand things: about the rock candy he used to make with his *mamm*, and learning to chop firewood, and how his coat itched during Meeting. He wanted to share with her what it was like when he'd found a motherless litter of kittens and took care of them in secret for fear he'd be laughed at by his brothers. And what he thought of her—her beauty and intelligence and strength—and her willingness to risk so much for others. It made his throat ache to think of it, but just then she lost her footing on the stones. He dropped his line and scrambled down the bank as she began to fall forward, reaching to catch her.

Anna's frown deepened as the hours lengthened. She listened through her stethoscope as Asa's chest grew tighter. She knew that the flu this season was especially virulent and that it also showed no predilection for age, affecting both young and old. And she'd been the one to have him outside running around for half the night in the freezing cold when he was probably already getting sick.

Asa pushed fitfully against the mound of covers, but she piled them back on, only to find herself caught against his chest.

"Safe," he slurred, his eyes open and burning with fever and something else. He ran his hands up and down her arms, causing her to shiver through the fabric of her serviceable, borrowed blouse.

"*Jah*, I'm safe. Are you dreaming, Asa?"

"*Mmm-hmm*. About you."

Anna blushed even though she knew he'd probably remember nothing of this.

"Are you dreaming, Doc?" Somehow he'd found her hands and rubbed his hot, callused thumbs over her knuckles in slow, rhythmic circles.

She gazed down at him with renewed wonder. No one had ever touched her hands like this. She felt nurtured and breathless and . . . loved. Her eyes filled with tears. She could never have imagined that *Derr Herr* had such a plan as this waiting for her when she'd arrived yesterday, nor how long and wonderful the night would be. She realized the memory of this man would sustain her through all her earthly life, when suddenly the pressing thought that she might never see him again—like this—intruded.

He lifted his hands to her face and rubbed at the tears, which made slow tracks down the ripe smoothness of her cheeks, and he stared up at her.

"You're crying—are you crying?" he asked, confused.

"No." She shook her head.

"Don't cry," he whispered. "Come here, please."

He tossed restlessly, and she gave in to his pull, laying her head on the quilt that covered his chest. She heard the deep workings of his lungs and bit her lip. She concentrated on praying that he would easily recover from the illness, wanting also to distract herself from being so close to him. "Come here," he said again.

"I'm here."

He lifted her with strong arms despite his fever, until her face hovered inches from his own, and she felt she might drown in the intensity of his dark eyes. His thick lashes lowered as he arched his neck.

"Please—Anna. Please."

She knew instinctively what he wanted and swallowed as she lowered her head to meet his lips, unsure of even what to do. But he knew. He moved his lips tenderly, gently, urging her to kiss him back with a faint lifting of his chin. She forgot to breathe when she finally moved her mouth against his own, and he made a low sound of approval deep in his throat.

A sudden loud knocking at the door bolted her upright as Mrs. Stolis entered without preamble. She raised one eyebrow as Anna made a frantic attempt to adjust her *kapp* and adopt a casual stance by the bed.

"That's a *gut* way to get the flu," the older woman observed dryly.

"I—uh—was—"

"It won't go outside this room. Besides, Asa Mast needs a good kissing. He's needed it for a while."

"Really?" Anna struggled to find her voice. She glanced down and was relieved to see that Asa had fallen back asleep.

"*Jah*, but that's not my story to tell. It's his."

"Oh."

"So, he's sick, is he? Well, he can just stay here until he recovers. I know that you have to go back tonight. One of the boys can drive you into town; the roads should be passable soon. We've heard the snow plows for the last hour."

Anna felt her world dissolving as the reality of her leaving struck with force. It wasn't the two hours' distance that bothered her, nor was it any concern about courting with someone from a different community—her *Aenti* Ruth had left home when she'd married. No, it was something more—an inherent understanding of the man lying in the bed. She felt in her heart that if she ever saw him again, he'd be a polite, distant Amish man, far removed from the wonder and the intimacy of the births and the storm and his fevered kiss. Something else held him, she sensed, and that something would be enough to keep him hidden and reserved and lost from her forever.

Mrs. Stolis cleared her throat. "I wanted to give you something—for helping me and Mary."

"It's not necessary."

"It's necessary to me. Stop your moping and look here."

Anna broke from her thoughts and realized the older woman held a heavy, folded quilt over her thin, outstretched arm.

"Help me spread it out."

"*Ach*, I can't." Anna shook her head.

"Hurry on; it weighs a ton."

They each took one set of the folded ends, and Anna walked backward until the quilt was revealed in all of its glory. Her eyes filled with tears.

"Do you know the pattern?" Mrs. Stolis asked.

Anna swallowed as she gazed at the rich red and green colors against a background of white. The flowers were clustered across the quilt, their wealth of stitchery evident in the outlines of the petals and the double-hued leaves.

"*Jah*, Christmas Roses."

"So it is, and my wedding quilt it was." Mrs. Stolis sniffed once. "It belongs to you now, because you reminded me of what it was like when Henry was alive—of who I was then. And now"—she glanced meaningfully toward the bed—"perhaps it will give you some insight into who you might really be."

Anna chose to ignore the confusing reference. "I can't take it. I mean, I'm so honored, but this belongs to your family—to Mary and Luke and the baby, or to your daughters."

"It's mine and mine to give, so now accept it with good grace as you should from your elder." The older woman walked forward and pushed the quilt into her arms.

Anna gave her a misty smile. "*Danki*. I'll treasure it."

Mrs. Stolis gave a brisk nod. "*Gut*, now I'll leave you to your—nursing care. Come down when you're ready to leave."

Anna hugged the quilt and felt joy fill her, as if she were being embraced by all of the women who'd labored over the beautiful quilt in preparation for a bride. Finally, she laid it in a chair and went upstairs to check on Mary and the baby. She found them dozing in peaceful repose, Christian looking cherubic in the crook of Mary's arm. Anna checked her respirations and did other small chores, then tiptoed from the room.

She went back down to the second floor to check Asa's breathing once more. She secretly wished that he'd wake again, but he slept on. So she sank down into the rocking chair, which held the quilt, and turned sideways toward a window looking out on the snow-laden fields below. Despite the fire in the now warm room, ice crystals splayed in dramatic detail across the windowpane as she felt the first pull of sleep wash over her. She realized that she needed a nap or she'd be crying all the way up the mountains to her home. So, gathering the heavy folds of the cedar-scented quilt about her, she laid her head back and drifted to sleep.

Her training awakened her at Asa's slightest move, and she rubbed her eyes as she realized he was murmuring with fever. She left the quilt in the chair and went to the bed to lay a hand on his brow when his words made her freeze.

"Jennifer," he pleaded. "Jennifer—think . . . our baby . . . please . . ."

Anna drew back as if she'd been struck. She stared down at him as he continued to cry out, and she felt sick to her stomach. She'd lain in his arms less than two hours ago, and now he was crying out for another woman . . . and their baby. A tear escaped and made its way down her cheek as she realized she knew nothing about this man. Nothing but one night. She'd been a fool to be dreaming, she told herself as she stuffed items back into her bag. She could think of nothing but fleeing the room, the house, and going home as soon as possible. She didn't turn to look at him when she grasped the knob of the door because he'd said the name again. Jennifer.

She swiped at her face and fled down the stairs, stopping only for a moment on the bottom step to pinch her cheeks and take a deep breath. There was no reason for any of the Stolises to know of her crying. She did not want anything to be said to Asa Mast when he awoke fully that might make him think he'd gained any interest in her heart. She would leave nothing behind that would allow him to feel he'd had a good joke on a simple, round midwife, and she crushed the tiny voice inside that told her he was not that kind of man.

She lifted her head and stepped into the kitchen area, finding Mrs. Stolis at the stove.

"I want to thank you for everything and to remind you to have Mary and the baby follow up with *Aenti* Ruth tomorrow, but I think, if it's convenient, that I'd better head back to town."

Mrs. Stolis gave her a speculative look. "Hmm . . . if that's what you really want. I thought you might stay for the meal."

"No, ma'am . . . *Danki.*"

"And how is Asa Mast?"

Anna drew a steadying breath. "Stable. I'm sure he'll recover well."

"I've no doubt he will. Did you have a chance to say your good-byes to the man?"

"He . . . was sound asleep."

"Uh-huh. Abel's feeling well enough to drive you in. Abel? Take the midwife back into town to *Frau* Ruth's. She's in a hurry to go."

Anna flushed as the young Amish man put on his coat and hat. "I'll bring the buggy around quick."

Mrs. Stolis surprised Anna by embracing her, and the rest of the family called their thanks and good wishes as she soon found herself being trotted across plowed roads in the blinding glare of sunshine on snow.

Chapter Six

Abel Stolis wasted no time helping Anna down, and she thanked him as he left her, standing alone, on *Aenti* Ruth's porch. She pushed aside the image of Asa's handsome face as he stood in the same spot last night while she felt for the house key in her bag.

Even Bottle's feline greeting did nothing to make her feel less alone as she dropped her bag and wearily went to make up the fire. As she knelt, staring into the low flames, she told herself that *Derr Herr* had a purpose in this, even if it was only to give her memories that, in time, she might be able to reflect on without hurting. She sighed aloud, then curled up on the hearthrug with Bottle beside her and fell into a deep sleep.

She awoke, disoriented, to find that daylight had fled, the windows were darkened, and someone was pounding on the front door. She rose stiffly and glanced at her brooch watch while she hurried to open the door. Six o'clock. She'd slept the day away, and now she prayed that it was *Aenti* Ruth and not another delivery. She swept the door open as she rubbed her eyes, then stopped dead when she saw Asa leaning against the doorjamb in his hat and coat with a brown bag in his arm. He exhaled and coughed when he saw her.

"I was terrified you'd left already; it would have been a long drive to Pine Creek tonight."

"*Jah?*" she queried, her heart pounding. Then unbidden worry for him took over. "You're going to catch pneumonia; come in out of the cold—please." She wrapped her arms around herself and went to poke the fire, trying to ignore his slow steps as he dropped into a chair.

"What do you want?"

He sighed and took his hat off, setting the brown bag on the floor. "You. I want you, Anna Stolis."

She pushed aside the surge of tearful pleasure his words produced and stayed stiff and still away from him.

"And I suppose you want Jennifer too?"

He lifted his fever-flushed face to hers, and she saw absolute pain in his eyes, as if she'd struck him a blow. But he took a deep breath and shook his head.

"No, but I did once—when I was eighteen."

Anna felt as if the floor had fallen out from under her, but she still couldn't move, mesmerized by the raw emotion in his face.

"Jennifer was the most beautiful girl I'd ever seen, *Englisch* or Amish."

Anna's heart sank and she hugged her generous curves more tightly against his words.

"It was my *rumschpringe*, and I saw her at a fall festival in town. It was like . . . like I saw the moon for the first time or a star—so beautiful, but so distant. She was Amish, two years older than me and from a different community, but I didn't care. More than that, she was attracted to me because I was raised conservatively. And she was pulled by the unusual, the things she hadn't experienced."

He looked into the flames of the fire, and Anna saw the taut misery in the lines of his face as he went on.

"I bought a car so I could be with her whenever and wherever I wanted, and I ignored all the warnings from my friends, the little revelations that her exterior beauty might not match who she was inside. I was just so caught up." He looked squarely at Anna. "She became pregnant. It was, for me, a gift—a blessing. I wanted to marry her, and she agreed. But even though I'd drifted so far from how I'd been raised, I wanted to go and confess before the community. I wanted the baby to have security. But Jennifer wanted to leave the Amish. She wanted the *Englisch* world; she always had, and I knew that—" His voice broke. "Weeks went by; things didn't get better."

He swiped his large hand across his eyes. "One night I picked her up and she was wearing *Englisch* clothes. She told me that she'd found someone else who was going to help her, take care of her. She was going to meet him that night. I begged her—it was our baby. She told me to get over it." He swallowed hard. "We were in my car and arguing. I was driving . . . and then a pick-up truck crossed the lane and hit us head-on. Jennifer—the baby—were both killed instantly. I walked away without a scratch." He put his head down into his hands. "The pick-up driver was drunk; he wasn't hurt either."

Anna held her breath, tears slipping down her cheeks as he went on.

"The drunk driver went to prison; I went home. I told only my *mamm* and *daed* about the baby. They . . . forgave me somehow. In time I confessed before our church and her church for my anger in arguing with her while driving, my responsibility for buying and driving a car in the first place, and the way all of that contributed to her death. But I could never speak of the baby, of that incredible loss. And I was"—his voice dripped with irony—"forgiven and baptized and permitted to join the church."

He looked up. "But how could I really go on with a life that included a wife or children, babies, when I was responsible for that baby, that girl, no matter what her choices were? Inside, I've never truly forgiven myself or believed that *Derr Herr* has forgiven me, I guess, until last night."

Anna licked at a tear that crossed the corner of her mouth. "Last night?" she whispered.

He nodded, rising to come and stand before her. "Last night, *Derr Herr* allowed me to experience again, and again, and again, the renewal of life—through you. It was like he was telling me over and over that he forgives me, that I could think of—and dream of—a new life."

Anna could feel the warmth of his body radiating toward her with his nearness, but she had to ask, had to know.

"Do you still love her?"

"No."

"How . . . do you know?"

"Because I was a boy, selfish and blind, who was in love with the idea of her, what I wanted to make her in my mind. I couldn't see past my own self and what I wanted to even know her as a real person, beyond what she looked like."

Anna gave him a steady look. "Well, you'll find no beauty here, no illusion of it either."

He drew a hoarse breath and reached out to lay his hands

on her taut shoulders. "*Ach*, Anna, do you even see yourself? Do you know what you are?"

She lifted her chin. "I know who I am, what I'm capable of with *Derr Herr*'s help."

He nodded, smiling through his tears. "*Jah*, you are strong, like tempered steel. But there are other parts of you—" He bent and pressed his warm mouth near her small ear. "A tender heart, a gentle spirit." She shivered and caught hold of his dark coat as he began to press damp kisses along the line of her neck. "A beloved wife . . . a waiting mother . . . a lifetime of beautiful—"

"*Ach*, Asa." She took a deep breath. He looked down at her, and she lifted her capable hands to his broad shoulders. "I don't know how you can know so much about me. It is as if there are all those women waiting inside of me, but I've never thought, never dreamed—until last night—that it was the Lord's plan for me to become any of them. Not until you."

He bent his head and would have kissed her, but she pressed her hands to his flushed cheeks and wiped at the tears that clung to his thick eyelashes. He turned his head and kissed the inside of her palm.

"Asa, I want you to know—I'm so sorry about Jennifer, about the baby. I know what it's like when *Derr Herr* chooses to take life, when a pregnancy doesn't end like you believe that it should."

He nodded against her hands as she went on.

"But you will be a *gut* father one day."

He gave her a secret, warm glance and she blushed as she realized how she must sound to him.

"Tell me, Anna Stolis." He smiled. "Is that a promise? Or a proposal?"

She pulled from him and covered her hot cheeks with her hands. "That didn't come out like I meant."

He laughed aloud and she thrilled at the rich, full sound. He caught her against him and stepped backward until he dropped into a comfortable chair, with her in his lap. She half-struggled to rise but he held her still.

"Now just a minute, Doc. I've brought you something."

She ceased her playful struggle as he reached down and caught up the brown paper bag from the floor, putting it in her lap.

"Open it."

She looked in the bag, then cried out in glad surprise when she pulled out the heavy Christmas Roses quilt that Mrs. Stolis had given her but she'd left behind in her flight from the house.

Asa reached around her and began to open the folds of the quilt, gently enfolding them both in its warmth and beauty. Bottle jumped up onto Anna's lap and nestled to find a comfortable spot.

"I don't know what Mrs. Stolis must have thought when I ran out of there," Anna said as he found her hand.

"That good lady told me that, apparently, I talk a lot when I have a fever. She figured I'd mentioned Jennifer."

Anna nodded.

"She also said to ask you about a particular nursing style you seem to have perfected to soothe your male fever victims. She said that it might catch you the flu one day."

"*Ach*, that woman!"

He cradled her close. "To tell the truth, I don't really feel all that well just yet. Care to show me?"

And she did.

Reading Group Guide

Guide contains spoilers, so don't read before completing the novellas.

1. Asa and Anna's relationship is formed by a spontaneous meeting that is, in retrospect, clearly arranged by God. What "chance meetings" have you had in your own life that have revealed God's presence to you?
2. Asa's past is redeemed in a unique way through the experiences of the night. How has God turned your past mistakes into healing or wholeness in the present?
3. Anna's character is one of self-reliance and personal resourcefulness until she discovers a love that allows her to lean on another for support. What relationships in your life provide you with the greatest support?
4. How does the symbolism of "new birth" play out in the story on levels beyond the actual deliveries?

Acknowledgments

I'd like to acknowledge my editor, Natalie Hanemann, who continues to be a source of encouragement and strength for me both as a person and as a writer. I also would like to thank my agent, Tamela Hancock Murray, for providing a lot of cheer along the writing process of this work. My love goes out to my critique partner and coconspirator of plotting and love, Brenda Lott, and my deepest thanks goes to Daniel Miller, my Amish consultant for the piece. And lastly but foremost, I want to thank my husband, Scott, for always being there, through all the storms of life—you are my real hero!

A Marriage
of the Heart

For my husband, Scott, the husband of my youth and now, still, twenty-four years later, my love of all time

CHAPTER ONE

"What did he do?"

Abigail Kauffman clutched her hands together and took a deep breath of the cool fall air that drifted in through the open kitchen window. Her father's repeated question and ominous tone had her doubting her actions. But once she began a plan, she usually stuck with it.

"I said . . . he . . . well . . . just made me feel a little uncomfortable with the way he was kissing me . . . and touching . . . and I . . ."

Her father's face turned beet red. "I–I will . . . have words with him."

He clenched and unclenched his heavy hands, and Abigail felt a surge of alarm and deeper indecision.

"Father . . . it was nothing, in truth."

"I will have words with the bishop and that—boy, and then he'll marry you."

Abigail's eyes widened, the swiftness of her impulsive plan ringing in her ears. "Marry me? But I don't love him!"

Her father regarded her with flashing eyes. "Love has nothing to do with marriage. We will go to the bishop and Dr. Knepp, and we will see this solved before morning." He drew a shaky breath. "When I think of that boy, just baptized today, just accepted into the community, and then . . . daring to trespass upon your honor . . . Go upstairs and dress in blue. I will bring the buggy round. Hurry!"

Abigail turned and fled up the steps. *"Dress in blue."* The color for marrying. She gained her small bedroom and slammed the door closed behind her, leaning upon its heavy wooden support. She saw herself in her bureau mirror, her cheeks flushed, her *kapp* askew upon her white-gold hair. She wondered for a strange moment what a mother might say right now, what her mother, whom she'd lost at age five, would say in this situation. Her heart pounded in her chest. This situation . . .

In truth, Joseph Lambert, with his lean, dark good looks and earnest eyes behind glasses, had done little more than speak to her . . . and annoy her. She'd just wanted to pay him back a bit for his casual dismissal of her usually touted beauty . . . and now she was going to have to face his mocking scorn. For she had no doubt he'd laugh outright at the suggestion of any impropriety between the two of them. They'd only been a few dozen feet from where everyone was gathered for the after-service meal, and it would be a bold young man indeed who'd risk anything, let alone steal intimate kisses . . .

But her father had believed her . . . or he'd believed the worst of Joseph Lambert, at any rate. She snatched a blue dress from a nail on the wall and changed with haste. She might as well get it over with, she thought with grim practicality. And yet there was one small part of her that wished things might be different, that wished she might truly be on her way to a marriage that would allow her to escape Solomon Kauffman's rule and cold distance.

She hurried back down the stairs and went outside to where the buggy waited. Her father started the horse before she barely had her seat, and as they gathered speed she tried to marshal her thoughts. She saw her life as it had been ever since she could remember . . . cold, lonely, devoid of love and even simple conversation. Somehow, the *Englisch* world outside seemed so much less austere and confining, so much less full of unspoken pain.

She let herself escape for a moment by imagining marriage to Joseph Lambert. Not only would it get her out from under her father's thumb, but she would be able to keep house, or not keep it, any way she pleased. They wouldn't have to live with her father—at the picnic she'd heard Dr. Knepp, the popular *Englisch* physician, say something about making his barn over into an apartment for Joseph. It would be just as easy to fit two as it would one. She didn't take up that much space. Her possessions were scant. She'd learned how to make two blouses last for a season and the secrets of turning out old dresses to look new again.

No, she'd be little bother to Joseph Lambert. She chewed a delicate fingertip in her nervousness. It might work out well, the more she thought about it . . .

JOSEPH LAMBERT EASED A FINGER IN BETWEEN HIS SUSPENDER and white shirt and drew a breath of satisfaction at the comfort of the simple Amish clothing. He was tired, exhausted from the day and its happenings, but deeply happy. He glanced around the small barn that Dr. and Mrs. Knepp had done over for him and shook his head at the kindly generosity of the couple. To have a bed with clean sheets and a handmade quilt was more than he could have dreamed of in the past years—but to have his own space, his own home, was a gift from the Lord. He lay down in the bed and stared up at the wooden slat ceiling.

The faces of the people he'd been introduced and reintroduced to that day spun in a pleasant blur in his mind. Even the beautiful face of Abigail Kauffman was a delight to recall, though he knew he'd frustrated her—and deliberately so. She was too pretty for her own good, he thought with a smile, remembering their brief conversation near an old oak tree in the orange and red glory of early autumn. He'd had to thread his way through a throng of young admirers to reach the girl as she perched in the refuge of the tree, but the other boys had soon melted away under his penetrating look. But when he'd not shown the apparently expected verbal homage to her beauty, all of her pretense disappeared. He'd been thoroughly charmed by her indignation. But he knew that a girl like Abigail Kauffman was far beyond his reach, especially with a past like his . . .

He sighed and, dismissing the day from his mind, began to pray, thanking *Derr Herr* for all that he'd been given and asking for clarity of direction for the future.

He'd just fallen into the most restful sleep he'd had in days when a furious pounding on the barn door startled him awake. He grabbed for his glasses.

"Kumme!" he cried, scrambling to button his shirt, thinking it must be some urgent matter for the doctor. Instead, once he managed to focus, he saw Bishop Ebersol and another giant of a man crowd into his small living space, followed by the doctor and his wife.

The giant strode toward him, clenching and unclenching ham-like fists. "Scoundrel!" The huge man growled the word.

Who is he? Joseph frantically sifted through the identities of people he'd met that day.

"Now, now, Solomon. Let the boy have a breath." The bishop inserted himself between Joseph and the larger man.

"A breath? A breath is not what he wanted to have today—"

"Everybody ease off!" Dr. Knepp snapped, and there was a brief break in the tension.

"What's wrong?" Joseph asked.

The bishop cleared his throat. "Son, I just welcomed you back into the community this afternoon."

"Yes, sir."

"Well then, what were you doing dallying with Abigail Kauffman not half an hour later?"

"What? Dally—Abigail Kauffman?" Joseph suddenly recognized the strapping man as Abigail's irate father and took an automatic step backward.

"That's right . . . try and run!" Mr. Kauffman roared.

Dr. Knepp snorted. "Solomon, where exactly will the boy go in two feet of space and his back to the wall? Just let him explain."

Joseph knew by instinct that a simple denial of any behavior was not going to satisfy Mr. Kauffman. He'd had to defend himself enough in the past to recognize that there were consequences at stake here, and he didn't like to think where they might lead.

"We talked a little—that's all," he exclaimed.

Mr. Kauffman exploded. "At least be man enough to admit that you dishonored her with your kisses and your hands!"

Joseph's mind whirled. What had the girl been saying? And suddenly, a thought came to him—clear and resonant. Here was a provision from the Lord to have a girl like Abigail Kauffman in his life. It didn't matter that she'd obviously lied; she was young. Perhaps her father had forced her into it . . .

In any case, his impulsive nature took over. To deny the claim would mean the scorn and possible dismissal of his place in the community, something he'd worked too long and too hard to reclaim. And even though the little miss probably had a reputation for being wild, a woman's word, her honor, would always be more valuable than a newcomer's. To admit to the accusations might mean recompense as well, but perhaps not as bad, not in the long run anyway. And he'd have the beautiful Miss Kauffman eating out of his hand for defending her honor.

He lifted his head and met Mr. Kauffman's blazing eyes. "All right. I was wrong. I behaved . . . poorly with Miss Kauffman. I apologize."

"There. He admits to it. I'll get Abigail from the buggy. You can perform the ceremony here."

"What?" Joseph and Mrs. Knepp spoke in unison.

Mr. Kauffman's lips quivered, and for an instant Joseph thought he might burst into tears. "The wedding ceremony. The bishop will do it here, now. When I think of what Abigail must have been feeling . . ." He swiped at his forehead with a rumpled handkerchief.

"Solomon, let Joseph explain," Mrs. Knepp urged.

"*Nee . . . nee* . . . I will see her done right by—" He broke off and tightened his massive jaw. "To think it's come to this for my girl." The big man turned and left the barn.

Joseph resisted the urge to speak. He hadn't expected a marriage . . . a courtship maybe, but a wedding? "Do I have a choice?" he finally asked the bishop.

"Not if you want to stay. *Nee*. Mr. Kauffman will go to the community to defend what he thinks is right."

Joseph nodded and ran his hands through his hair. Things could be worse; he could have been denied a chance to come back. A marriage seemed a worthy price for what he'd received that morning. "All right. Let's get this over with."

Dr. Knepp spoke with low urgency. "Joseph, I know you didn't touch her. You didn't have time, and you were in plain view. Tell the truth—the deacons will vote—"

"*Nee* . . . I'll not take the risk. It means everything to me to be back here, to find and keep a place, a home . . ."

Mr. Kauffman was sliding the barn door back open.

"Seth, do something," Mrs. Knepp begged in a whisper.

Dr. Knepp shrugged his shoulders. "The boy agrees."

"As well he might," Mr. Kauffman growled. He pulled Abigail into the room behind him. She was dressed in blue, and she kept her eyes downward.

Joseph considered the girl as the faces of the deacons flashed behind his eyes. He wondered for a moment how they would vote before he snapped back to awareness as the bishop joined his hands with Abigail's.

She wouldn't look at him. Maybe she was being driven to this. The thought gave him pause; she should have the right to choose.

"Do you want this?" Joseph asked, speaking to the top of her *kapp*.

She gazed up at him then. Her blue eyes were dead-steady calm. He'd seen eyes like those behind the wrong end of a gun, and now he wondered if she'd had a forceful hand in the matter herself.

"*Ya,*" she murmured, dropping her gaze once more.

Her hands were ice cold though, and he rubbed his thumbs around the outside of her fingers as he listened to the bishop speak in High German. It was like a dream, really. The light from the lamp Mrs. Knepp held high threw strange shadows across the corners of the room and made crouching things out of chairs and the table.

He was asked the simple, life-binding questions that would make Abigail Kauffman his wife, and his answers were steady—as were hers. And then it was over.

It seemed anticlimactic. There was no kiss or hug of goodwill between the couple. And once he saw his job done, Mr. Kauffman seemed to shrivel to a shell of a man whom the bishop had to pat on the back for reassurance.

Joseph let go of her hands and finished buttoning his shirt, ignoring the way Abigail's eyes strayed to his chest. He tensed his jaw and walked over to his new father-in-law.

"Mr. Kauffman—it's my plan to be a help and not a hindrance to you all of my days. I know you farm alone with some hired help. You won't need as much help anymore. I need the work, and I'm good at it. Abigail and I will take up living with you in the morning, with your permission, of course."

"*Ya,*" the older man said, clearly surprised. "*Ya,* that would be *gut*; I would miss Abigail about."

Joseph nodded; it was done.

ABIGAIL TRIED TO REGULATE HER BREATHING AS SHE LIS-tened to her dreams of freedom being swept away like a house on a flood plain. It didn't matter at the moment that Joseph had defended her honor and married her out of hand. She opened and closed her mouth like a gasping fish as her father and the others filed out the door, leaving her alone with her new husband.

Joseph pulled an extra quilt and pillow from a shelf near the bed and knelt to lay them on the floor. She watched his strong, long-fingered hands ease each wrinkle until he looked up.

Then she said the first thing she could get out. "Are you *narrisch?*"

"What? For saving you from your lies? You can have a lifetime to thank me properly."

She strode to face him, stepping on his clean quilt. He gazed up at her.

"I don't care about the lies! Are you crazy to have told my father that we'll live with him? You didn't even consult me."

He choked out a laugh. "And you consulted me about this wedding, wife?"

He gave a swift tug to the hem of her skirt, and she lost her balance, landing beside him. He leaned very near to her, and she felt her heart pulse in a curious sensation.

"Just tell me your father forced you into this," he whispered, reaching to brush a stray tendril of white-gold hair behind her ear.

Abigail couldn't bring herself to lie again, not when she was feeling so strange and fluttery inside. She shook her head. "I cannot tell you that."

He ran a finger down her cheek. "I thought not; I just wanted to hear you say it. But why me? I'm genuinely curious."

She looked down at her hands, clenched in her lap. "I—I just thought that you were handsome, and I . . ."

"Please," he sighed, running a hand beneath his glasses and then studying her again. "Just tell me the truth."

"You came over," she burst out, "and then you just talked and mocked me. You treated me like a little girl, and then I thought that if you had to marry me, it might work out well for both of us. You're used to the *Englisch* ways, and I want the *Englisch* ways. We could live here and you could work for Dr. Knepp, and I could—"

"You could do exactly as you pleased, is that it? Without Daddy to interfere? With a husband who was on his knees this afternoon, begging for community, and not likely to make a fuss?" His voice was level but mocking.

"*Ya,*" she whispered in misery.

"Well then, you got more than you bargained for, my sweet." He lifted her chin so that she was forced to meet his dark eyes. "I don't want the *Englisch* ways, Abigail Lambert—that's why I came back. And I will honor this marriage and the responsibilities it entails. And my expectation is for you to do the same."

He didn't wait for her to respond, but dropped his hand and lay down on the quilt, rolling over to his side and clutching the pillow to his middle.

She stared at his broad back.

She wanted to smack him a good one. Instead she sniffed and, with as much dignity as she could muster, rose to go and lie sleepless and chilled on the comfortable bed of her wedding night.

CHAPTER TWO

ABIGAIL WATCHED THE SUNLIGHT BREAK THROUGH THE TWO small windows of the little barn and shifted in silence to stare down at her husband lying on the floor. The quilt was tangled about his lean hips, and one suspender had slipped down in his sleep. His hand was curled under his dark head, and he still held the pillow close to his middle, almost protectively. His glasses lay on the hardwood floor near the edge of the quilt. She let her appraising gaze trace down the fine bones of his face and the firm set of his jaw. He looked younger without his glasses, and she wondered how old he was, exactly. She herself had just turned twenty. She'd have to ask him.

She'd lain awake all night thinking, praying, and discarding plans as to how she might make him agree not to move back to her father's house. The best she could come up with was to try and get Dr. and Mrs. Knepp's support, since they'd gone to all the trouble of making up this place for him. She slipped like a wraith from the bed and tiptoed over Joseph, sliding open the well-oiled door and heading for the main house. She saw a light in the kitchen and knocked on the back screen door.

Mrs. Knepp appeared and cracked the door. "Good morning. Come in."

Abigail stood in the warm kitchen, her eyes tracing the neat shelves and the display of order that permeated the place.

"Are you hungry?"

"*Nee* . . . well, just a little."

"Seth's out on a call. I'll have something ready for you in a minute."

"*Danki.*" Abigail slid onto the bench at the table and watched the older woman's deft movements at the stove. She knew Mrs. Knepp did not especially like her but also knew that the doctor's wife would not be unkind. Abigail ran a small finger around the grain of a knot-hole on the table and bit her lip, for once unsure of what to say.

"How was your sleep?"

"*Ach*, fine. Just fine." Then she flushed as she realized that it was to have been her actual wedding night, and she sounded a bit too casual.

"Joseph's a good man; you're a very fortunate young lady." Mrs. Knepp placed a plate of scrambled eggs, bacon, grilled mushrooms and tomatoes, and toast in front of her.

Abigail's stomach rumbled and she bowed her head over the plate before beginning to eat with pleasure.

"*Ya*, a good man who deserves his own start in life. He's—much too kind to feel he's dishonoring my father by not going to the farm to live. But if we stayed here, he'd have so much more opportunity for independence."

Mrs. Knepp seated herself opposite with a cup of coffee in her hands. "Joseph's had all the independence he could ever want. What he needs now is a good family."

Abigail pursed her lips and wiped daintily at them with her cotton napkin. This wasn't going the way she wanted.

"Children too," Mrs. Knepp said in a casual tone. "They help give a man stability."

Abigail choked on her eggs and flushed scarlet.

"Oh, I'm too forward, I suppose, having been married so long . . . but you'll be more than a blessing to Joseph when you're carrying his baby."

There was a faint irony in the other woman's tone, and Abigail thought that she was being got at.

"I suppose you're right," she remarked airily, recovering her composure. "I'd love to give him twins."

"Now that would be a pleasant surprise," Joseph murmured from behind her, and she jumped.

He leaned close and pressed his mouth to the side of her neck, and she almost slapped him away. She caught herself just in time.

Mrs. Knepp laughed with seeming approval. "Ah, perhaps it is young love."

"Indeed," Joseph agreed, moving to sit next to his wife at the table. But when Abigail met his eyes, she saw the mockery in their dark depths.

"Are you hungry, my love? *Kumme*, share my plate," Abigail offered, pushing it between them and aiming an accurate sideways kick to his shin with one of her small, old-fashioned, hard-soled shoes.

He coughed.

"I do hope you're not unwell," she said with wifely concern.

"I'm fine. Just fine." He was forking up the remainder of her eggs with a set jaw. "Have you packed your things?" he asked. "But then, you had so very little with you last night."

Her pleasure melted away at his words, and she seethed in silence.

"This reminds me . . ." Mrs. Knepp rose. "I have a wedding gift for you." She bustled out of the room despite protests from both of them.

"Are you going to be angry at me for a very long time?" Abigail asked in a whisper.

"Very." He pushed the empty plate away.

"Well, fine. I will await your good grace; I have the gift of patience." She lifted her small, prim nose.

"You're going to need it." He reached a hand up and began to massage the back of her neck just as Mrs. Knepp reentered the room with her arms full.

Abigail tensed at his touch, but he didn't remove his hand. She struggled to concentrate on the beautiful quilt the older woman spread open before them.

"It's a double wedding ring pattern," she said with fond remembrance. "It was given to Seth and me from an Amish woman when we first started out, and I'd like it to be the first gift that you two receive as a married couple."

Abigail felt addled, between the woman's kindness and the warm hand at the nape of her neck. "It's lovely," she squeaked.

"More than that." Joseph dropped his hand and rose to go around the table to embrace Mrs. Knepp, quilt and all. "It's a gift of the heart, and we'll cherish it. Won't we, Abby?"

Abigail blinked at the nickname she hadn't heard since childhood and nodded weakly. She felt sad for some reason. Her mother had called her Abby. To her father she was always the very formal Abigail. But here was her husband speaking to her with endearing words, though she knew he didn't mean a syllable of it. Probably he thought that the shortened version of her name would irritate her. Well, she wouldn't give him any satisfaction on that score.

She rose to help Mrs. Knepp fold the quilt and took it into her arms. *"Danki,"* she said and meant it.

Mrs. Knepp cleared her throat. "All will be well, you will both see."

They thanked her again for breakfast, then Joseph held the door as Abigail passed by him, carrying the quilt outside. She dreaded going back to the little barn where she had so hoped to escape to a new home.

"Best to hurry on," he said. "It will only take a few minutes to gather my things."

Abigail sat down at the little table and watched him pick up the quilt and pillow from the floor.

He raised an eyebrow. "How did you sleep?"

"Not well . . . I was thinking."

"I dread to imagine." He pulled a satchel from a shelf and stuffed a few Amish clothes inside.

"Where are your *Englisch* clothes?" she asked.

"Burned them last night, before I went to sleep—or I guess before I was awakened."

She nodded. Clearly Joseph was determined not to go back to his previous way of life. Well, that could change . . . even though she'd never found the courage within herself to leave the community.

"I'm ready," he announced, and she noticed for the first time the dark stubble on his face.

"Aren't you going to shave?"

He laughed. "I'm married, remember, little wife? It's my wedding ring I wear on my face now, and you'll just have to bear with the roughness on your tender skin until it grows in."

She lifted her chin a notch. "I do not think that it will be an issue."

"Oh no? Just wait until the details of our wedding get around . . . which should be happening right about now. We must present the loving couple to everyone, especially to your father. Although I know that Amish PDA is limited at times."

"PDA?"

He gave her a mocking smile. "Public displays of affection. We're not supposed to make out as obviously as the *Englisch* do, but Daddy is still going to expect to see something in the comfort of our own home."

She flushed at his use of the expression *make out*; she knew it from her secretive *Englisch* magazine reading. But she also realized that he was right. Her father would expect a normal happy couple, or he'd have more than something to say.

"So don't stiffen up like a schoolgirl every time I touch you."

"What else do you expect me to do?"

He leaned over the table and put his face very close to hers.

He smelled clean, like fresh pine soap, and she couldn't help but look into his eyes.

"Relax," he murmured. "Just relax." He leaned closer still and she half closed her eyes, her heart beating in expectation of his kiss.

He laughed and lifted his satchel. "See, you can do it. Just pretend I'm one of those beaus of yours, surrounding you at the tree."

"Indeed," she said in a haughty voice and rose with her arms still full of the quilt.

He slid the barn door open to the full light of day, and she blinked at the sudden brightness.

"Well, Mrs. Lambert, let's go home."

CHAPTER THREE

Joseph turned his horse and buggy out of the Knepps' driveway and started down the highway. He glanced sideways at Abigail. She still held the quilt, clinging to it like a child. He hardened his heart at the thought. Although he'd chosen his own fate to be entangled with hers, it would still probably benefit him to remember that she was no child, but a very stubborn, manipulative woman, who was also his wife. He half smiled at the thought. He'd never imagined himself married to an Amish woman. When he'd lived as an *Englischer* he'd had girlfriends aplenty, and one in particular who was going to regret his leaving the outside world behind. But even Molly, with her riotous red curls and charming freckles, hadn't been enough to keep him from going home.

He glanced at Abigail's heavy white-blonde knot of hair hidden beneath her *kapp* and the thick tilt of her lashes as she appeared to study the passing road beneath the horse's hooves. She was indeed beautiful. But it was a beauty used as a device, and he told himself that it would be good to remember that as well. Still, he had to live with her somehow. He decided to try polite conversation.

"It's a fair day," he offered.

She nodded.

"The horse's name is Carl. Can you drive?"

She glanced at him with a wry twist to her soft lips. "Of course. Can't every Amish girl drive?"

They pulled into the Kauffmans' lane a few minutes later, and he noticed her chest heave with emotion against the outline of the quilt.

"Well, we're home."

"*Ya. My* home."

He pulled up close to the farmhouse and reached a hand to find hers beneath the pile of quilt. "Our home."

She pulled away. "You needn't pretend now; there's no one to see. Father will be in the fields."

"I wasn't pretending. It is our home—for life, as the Lord wills."

She didn't reply, and he jumped down to come around and hold his arms up to help her. She tossed him the folded quilt and leapt neatly down.

Abigail refused to give in to the tears that threatened as she entered the familiar bleak kitchen. There was none of the warmth and order of Mrs. Knepp's home here. Joseph Lambert had a rude awakening coming if he thought she kept house as well as other Amish women. She didn't, or felt that she couldn't, at any rate. No matter how many times she tried to cook or clean, things always ended up worse off somehow.

But Joseph merely glanced around and lifted his satchel. "Where's our room? I'd better head out to the fields as soon as I can."

She blushed at the thought of letting him into her tiny girl's bedroom, but there was no choice. Father slept in the master bedroom, and the other bedrooms were not as well turned out as they might be. She led the way up a narrow staircase and entered the first door on the right. He followed her inside, and they both gazed at the narrow single bed, where her dress from yesterday's picnic lay in careless abandon. The remainder of her clothes hung in a neat row on the common nails beside the bed. The small window gave off a bit of light, illuminating her bureau and the clutter of hairpins and extra *kapps* that lay there.

There was barely enough room for him to lie on the floor beside the bed, she thought, ignoring his gaze. She moved to bundle up the dress and smooth the bright quilt beneath it.

Joseph set Mrs. Knepp's quilt at the foot of the bed. "Is it cold at night up here?"

"Very," she replied. "Look, I'm a lot of things, but I'm not completely selfish. We can take turns sleeping on the bed."

He gave her a wry grin. "Nice of you, but the floor is fine for me. I've slept in much worse places."

"Where?"

"Hmm?" He was unpacking his satchel. "Where? *Ach*, abandoned buildings, strange apartments full of people I didn't know, on the street . . . lots of pleasant memories."

"At least you had a choice."

"A choice? *Ya*, I guess I had a choice, to keep being a fool or to come home. You have that same choice."

She looked at him in alarm. "What do you mean?"

"You know exactly what I mean . . . when do you plan to stop being a fool and come home?"

"You told me yesterday at the tree that this place was never your home—until now. Well, it's never been mine either."

"Fair enough. All right . . . no more chatter. I need to put on work clothes. Do you want to stay?" He reached for the buttons on his shirt, and she glared at him before making for the door and closing it with a slam.

She went down the stairs, feeling breathless and unsure why. She wandered into the kitchen and thought of the endless rounds of meals that were to come. Now she'd have to try harder at cooking, she supposed, and frowned at the thought.

A quick knock on the back screen door broke into her

thoughts, and she went to open it. It was Katie Stahley, one of her school friends, who'd already been married for over a year. She carried a covered dish and had an air of suppressed excitement that let Abigail know the wedding news was out.

"Please, *kumme* in, Katie."

Katie glanced around the kitchen, then gave an urgent whisper. "Is it true, Abigail?"

"Ya." Better to have it out and over with.

"Ach, I knew it. He was looking at you after worship service yesterday. I mean . . . well . . . here. I made bread pudding, extra raisins."

Abigail took it gratefully, thinking that it would help supplement lunch. She heard Joseph's footsteps on the stairs.

Katie giggled.

Abigail rolled her eyes as Joseph entered the kitchen. He came to her and put his arm around her waist, giving her a quick squeeze. "Guests already?" He arched a handsome dark brow, and Katie giggled again.

Honestly, Abigail thought, *the girl has been married for a year already.*

"This is Katie—a friend from school days."

Joseph shook her hand, then turned Abigail to face him. He kissed her full on the mouth, once and hard. "Got to get out to the fields with Father, my love. Katie, a pleasure . . ."

He was out the door, leaving Abigail's cheeks and mouth burning. She bit her soft bottom lip, resisting the urge to touch it. She'd only ever had a beau steal a kiss on her cheek, never full on her mouth. She felt a queer sensation in her knees and turned a fuzzy smile on Katie.

"Ach, Abigail, he's so handsome and still so *Englisch.* I don't think Matthew's ever kissed me like that in front of anyone. Joseph Lambert must really love you."

The fuzziness drifted away, and Abigail almost denied the

other girl's words before she realized how bad that would seem. Fortunately, though, her flushed cheeks must have satisfied Katie, because her friend left with a smile on her face.

Abigail took the cover off the bread pudding and poked a childlike forefinger into the top crusty layer. Delicious. Now if only she could come up with something to complement its goodness. She sighed and went to the back door and out into the sparse kitchen garden.

JOSEPH WALKED PAST THE SMALL HERD OF GRAZING DAIRY cows to where his father-in-law was mending a stone fence. Even from a distance the man looked mammoth as he lifted and balanced the heavy stones. Joseph wished he had work gloves, but there was nothing to be done about that now. He picked up a rock and wordlessly handed it to Mr. Kauffman. The older man accepted it and hefted it into place while Joseph got the next one ready.

"How is Abigail?" Mr. Kauffman grunted.

"Well, sir." Joseph wasn't sure what else to say. He supposed the old man was referring to the wedding night, and he could not offer any more details without lying.

"Looks like her mother, she does."

"I'm sorry that you lost your wife. I remember that time . . . I must have been ten or so."

Mr. Kauffman stared at him a moment, then spoke slowly. "*Ya,* I lost her, in more ways than one . . . But she would have done right by Abigail—the child needed a woman's touch."

The two men lifted and placed the rocks in a steady rhythm as Joseph pondered the words of his father-in-law.

"Can I ask why you never remarried?"

"*Nee.*"

Joseph grinned and nodded. "Sorry."

"No apologies needed."

"You've got a nice operation here. You must work sunup to sundown."

"*Danki*. I . . . appreciate your help. I've not had anyone about the place but Abigail and the hired help since Rachel . . . well, since Rachel's been gone."

The way he said his wife's name was odd, almost as if he feared it somehow, but Joseph decided not to press any more questions.

"You're more than welcome."

They continued to repair the wall in relative companionable silence until Joseph's stomach grumbled, and he noticed that the sun was high overhead.

"You are hungry?" Mr. Kauffman asked.

"*Ya.*"

His father-in-law sighed. "We'll go for lunch, then. Hopefully Abigail will have it prepared." But there was something in his tone that suggested the possibility was doubtful.

Joseph shrugged off the thought and walked in silence beside the older man back to the house.

CHAPTER FOUR

An amazing abundance of well-wishers dropped by with both curiosity and casseroles, and Abigail had her choice of the very best of the community's cookery to set up for lunch. She surveyed the table with satisfaction, admiring the clutch of wild-flowers that resided in the center next to the steaming chicken and dumplings and the broccoli-and-cauliflower cheese bake. Potato salad, plum preserves, and peach jelly sat on heavy plates next to a fresh loaf of bread. A mayonnaise cake with white icing piled high completed the ensemble.

The scrape of heavy footsteps on the back porch broke her reverie, and she swept the kitchen with a hasty eye to double-check that all unfamiliar dishes were out of the way. For once she wanted her father to think that she was succeeding at something domestic. That she didn't want to appear a fool in front of Joseph was not something she'd readily admit, but it wouldn't hurt to give him one less thing to be annoyed over.

Perhaps during the next few days she could take a lesson or two in cooking from some older woman. Maybe Mrs. Knepp might help or even Tillie Smoker, a friend who worked at Yoder's Pantry in town. Abigail's father had never permitted such a thing as cooking instruction before, although she had no idea why. But now she needed to satisfy her husband, and she was sure a few secret lessons might go a long way toward making his stomach happy.

The men entered, and she tried to appear nonchalant as her

father stopped and stared at the table. Joseph sniffed the air with appreciation, then moved to brush his mouth across her cheek before turning away to the pump. She stiffened under his touch but remembered her father. She swallowed when she glanced at Joseph's broad back; he smelled like sunshine and sweat, all mixed in a way that caused her pulse to race. She was glad when her father had washed and they all turned to the table.

She sat down at the foot of the table, her father at the head, and Joseph took a space to her right. The table had always been too large for just two people, but they kept it for when it was their turn to host worship service.

Mr. Kauffman bowed his head for a silent grace and Abigail followed, peeking to see that Joseph did as well. She snapped her gaze down when she caught the dark gleam of his eyes, mocking her for looking.

Her father cleared his throat, and they all looked up together.

"Please, Father," Abigail urged. "Help yourself."

Mr. Kauffman took a tentative scoop of some chicken and dumplings, then breathed a deep sigh of satisfaction when he held the plate close to his large nose.

"I see that I am truly blessed—a beautiful wife and an excellent cook," Joseph announced, savoring a bite of the fresh bread and preserves.

Abigail held her breath, wondering if her father would contradict, but he was too busy enjoying the food.

"*Danki.*" She smiled at Joseph, then noticed his palm as he reached for the potato salad. "What happened to your hand?"

"Moving rocks. I forgot that I don't have work gloves yet. I'll have to pick some up in town."

Abigail was surprised at her fleeting feeling of protectiveness. She stared down at her plate in confusion.

"Plenty of gloves in the barn. Help yourself." Mr. Kauffman spoke between bites. "Should have thought of it earlier."

"Thanks." Joseph smiled, helping himself to a large slice of cake. "Mmm-mmm. Abigail Lambert, what a treasure you are."

He grinned at her, and for once she could sense no mockery in his gaze. *Just wait*, she thought ruefully.

He stretched out his work-worn hand across the table to her, palm up, and she placed her hand in his, not wanting to irritate the blisters. But he squeezed her hand with goodwill, and Abigail glanced down the table to where her father watched as he sipped at his coffee.

She knew the hand-holding was a show and not for her, and something about that sparked irritation in her blue eyes. Joseph must have seen the warning signs, because he withdrew his hand before she might do any damage. She rose to take her plate to the sink.

"I think I'll go get those gloves. Abby, will you show me where in the barn?"

"The barn is the barn. They're hanging up by one of the stalls," she said, a tightness around her mouth.

"Abigail, go along as your husband asks. I've a mind to read *The Budget* and digest a bit before we go back out."

"*Ya*, Father," she replied out of habit, but inside she was contemplating everything from pushing Joseph into the feed trough to dousing him with the sow's water. She stepped out onto the porch and took a deep breath.

"You sure do get riled," he whispered behind her, catching her around the waist and placing a quick kiss on her cheek.

"Let me go," she hissed, starting to struggle.

"I bet Papa's watching," he reminded her and she stilled, her breath coming out in a huff.

"That's better, my dutiful wife. Tell me, how have you lived so long with a man who does not speak more than two words in a whole morning's work?" He slid a stray wisp of gold from her hair covering, and the gentleness brought tears in her throat.

"It's been lonely," she admitted, amazed that someone else might understand how it was to live with her father.

Joseph squeezed her arms in response. "I bet. I see why you want to run, but it's not worth it. Believe me."

He let her go, and she blindly went down the steps toward the barn. She'd never met a man who so had her churning in her emotions from one moment to the next. She eased open the barn door and blinked in the dim interior.

Joseph shut the door behind them, and she whirled around.

"Will you relax?" he asked. "Look, we might rub along better together if we get some things straight."

"Like what?"

"Like, I'm not going to force you to exert any wifely duties, all right?"

"Never?" she asked in surprise.

He sighed aloud. "Never is a long time. Let's just leave it at . . . you decide when you're ready."

"That will be never."

"Are you sure?" He took a step toward her, holding her captive with a certain intensity in his dark eyes that made her think absurdly of warm maple syrup and lazing in the sunshine in the heat of a summer's day.

"No . . . I mean, *ya* . . ." She frowned as she tried to recollect her point.

He laughed. "When was the last time you played, Abigail Lambert?"

"Played . . . Wh–what do you mean?"

He reached down to stroke her cheek and cup it in his large hand. "Played. I don't mean with boys' hearts or people's futures, but just played—for fun."

She tried hard to think of an answer. Play always seemed like a stolen thing to her. Something that she'd had to do away from her father's sight and the endless chores. She was good at getting out of a job, but she always felt guilty about it. To play was an odd notion.

"No idea, right?"

She shook her head.

"Well, in order to improve our—marital relations—we're going to play."

"I don't know what you're talking about."

He gave her a swift swat on her bottom. "Tag! You're it. Now catch me." He darted away while she gasped in outrage.

"How dare you!"

"Catch me, and you can have your own price back." He posed behind a bale of hay. "Come on, Abby. You're not that out of shape, are you?"

"What?" She whirled on him as he danced within hand's reach.

She made an angry grab toward him and almost fell over when she missed. She turned to find him laughing at her and leaning against the gentle family *milch* cow, Rose.

"You need some work, sweet. You couldn't catch a cat."

She lunged for him then, something about his teasing sending tiny electric shocks down her spine. She told herself that she was furious.

She chased him across the hay-strewn floor, stirring up dust motes in a narrow stream of sunlight from the upper window, and then took off up the ladder at his heels to the haymow above. She almost had him at the top and laughed aloud with sudden pleasure.

"What was that? A real laugh . . . oh my!" He was hopping backward and didn't see the pile of feed bags behind him; he went over into the hay, and she grabbed his ankle with a vengeance.

"I got you," she gasped.

He was laughing, the full, rich sound making her shiver. "That you did." He lay in the hay, smiling up at her, his glasses slightly askew. "Now name your price."

She sank to her knees beside him breathlessly. "I want to make you pay."

He folded his arms behind his head, his lean stomach stretched out in easy repose. He wasn't even winded. "Go ahead."

Her blue eyes narrowed like a cat's, and she knew by sudden instinct how to make him pay. "I name a kiss."

"A kiss?"

"*Ya*, and you must keep perfectly still."

"All right." He looked a little bored, and she lowered her gaze to his firm mouth.

Not for nothing had she practiced kissing in the cracked bureau mirror since she was about twelve. She leaned over him and blew softly on his lips as if to awaken them, then she closed her eyes and pretended he was the mirror. She took her time, fitting her lips to the line and contours of his own, until she sensed a tensing in his chest. She drew back and found him staring up at her.

"Done?" he asked in a casual voice, though his tone didn't match the heightened color in his cheeks or his intense gaze.

"*Ya*," she said primly, gathering up her skirts and rising in some confusion. She couldn't tell if he'd been affected or not, and it made her annoyed and . . . hurt somehow. Perhaps the mirror wasn't really a good way to practice. She slipped down the ladder and out of the barn without saying anything more.

Joseph lay in the hay, trying to regulate his breathing. The kiss had thrown him, turned him upside down, in fact. Where had she learned how to kiss like that? He shifted in the hay when he thought of the boys gathered around her at the oak tree, yet he couldn't explain her innocent tenseness at his every touch or look. It was just him, he thought with a sigh. She'd got herself into the marriage with a leap and no look, and if she ever found out the truth about his past, she'd probably despise him.

He got to his feet, brushing himself down from the hay, and

spied a pair of work gloves near the feed bags. He grabbed them and headed down the ladder before his new father-in-law could come looking for him.

He walked across the open field, listening to the stray, gentle mooing of the cows and the busy chirps of sparrows as they sought seed from the autumn's bounty. He resisted the urge to stretch his arms wide and lift his head in praise of *Derr Herr* for such a day. No matter the bonds of his marriage, he felt free. The grass beneath his feet did not seek to hold him, nor did the tree line of pine and oak condemn his every move. The Lord's nature was new and clean and healing, and it was what he remembered most from his time away.

He'd been a fool; he knew that. He'd tried in desperation to fill the void of emptiness with a multitude of the world's things. But nothing had worked, at least nothing that was life-sustaining. But here, even on the borrowed ground of his father-in-law, he felt the potential for peace, and he savored it to his very core.

The unmistakable high-pitched cry of a cat in distress cut into his thoughts. He turned his head to listen again. Then he walked with quick steps across the field to the ribbon of highway that bordered the farm.

CHAPTER FIVE

Abigail washed the last of the lunch dishes in a dreamy fashion. She still couldn't believe her boldness at taking a kiss from her husband. She half smiled at the thought, then frowned again when she wondered what he'd really been thinking. He'd probably kissed a hundred *Englisch* girls during his years away, and maybe she just didn't measure up. The teasing thought that practice makes perfect drifted through her mind, and she snapped the dishcloth to get her thoughts back in focus.

She'd have warm-ups for dinner and bring out a few of the desserts she'd held back, and then she'd worry about tomorrow, tomorrow. She left the kitchen and wandered over to the quilt frame that was permanently set up with the sheet-covered, unfinished quilt her mother had been working on when she died. The quilt pattern was called Abby's Wish, but only fifteen of the eighteen stars had been completed. Abigail often tried to imagine what was in her mother's mind when she'd been quilting and what her wish might have been for the young daughter she left behind.

Father allowed her to dust the frame, but finishing the quilt or packing it away was always out of the question for some reason. And since the frame was "in use," or occupied anyway, Abigail could quilt no new work in her own home. Not that she really knew how.

She sat down in the rocking chair by the front window and gazed out at the sunny day, wondering how Joseph was getting along. Normally at this hour she would sneak upstairs to look at her hidden magazines of the *Englisch* world, but she didn't feel like it today. She longed for the visitors of the morning, even with their gentle nosiness. The house was too quiet, as usual.

Suddenly heavy footsteps sounded from the back porch and Joseph entered, his arms and shirt splattered with blood. Abigail jumped to her feet.

"What happened?"

"It's not me. An old mother cat got hit by a car up by the highway. I tried to do what I could for her, but it didn't make any difference. She was carrying a kitten in her mouth. I can't tell if it's hurt much or not."

He extended his hands, and Abigail took the tiny animal. It, too, was splattered in blood and meowed in pathetic cries. Its eyes were open, but it couldn't have been more than a few weeks old, judging by the slightness of its weight. She took it to the kitchen counter and got a damp cloth and began to swipe at its fur with gentle hands.

The blood came off, revealing no major injuries. "I think she's okay," Abigail said, peering at the animal.

"*Gut.* Well, you can keep her for company, then, if you want."

"My *daed*'s never allowed pets." Her voice was wistful, but then she frowned, not wanting to appear weak in front of him.

Joseph shrugged. "We'll tell him it's a wedding gift, from me to you. There's not a whole lot he can say about that now, is there?"

She gave him a reluctant smile.

"All right. So do you think you can get the blood out of this shirt?"

He started to unbutton his shirt, and Abigail turned her full attention to the kitten, wrapping it in a towel and setting it in a wooden box she pulled from beneath the counter. She wanted to watch Joseph, but she didn't want to give him the satisfaction of knowing her interest.

"*Ya*, I can try to clean it," she said.

"Thanks—I only have this and one other, plus my one for church, so I'd like it to last." He held out the shirt to her, and she took it, darting a quick look at his muscle-toned chest. He turned away and headed for the stairs.

"I'll just grab my other shirt," he called.

She stared down at the shirt in her hands, still warm from his body, and wondered how on earth to get bloodstains out of fabric. She decided she'd better look efficient before he came back, and hurried to pump some water into a basin. Opening the spice cabinet, she stared at its contents. Some of the spice jars were older than she was. She grabbed baking soda and a stray bottle of alcohol and dumped both liberally on top of the shirt. She began scrubbing in haste just as he jogged back down the steps.

He patted her shoulder as he passed by on his way back outside. "*Danki,*" he said, and she heard him walk off the porch.

She frowned and leaned her hip against the counter. The casual touch on her shoulder when no one else was about teased her consciousness with a warm tingle. She supposed he had touched her just to irritate her. It worked. Maybe she should give him a little of his own back. A small smile grew on her lips as she resumed scrubbing, plotting her next move.

THEY MOUNTED THE DARK STEPS TO THEIR ROOM TOGETHER while her father rocked in his after-dinner chair next to the fireplace. Abigail lit the lamp on the bedside table and set the kitten in its box on the floor next to the bed. Then she went down the hall to raid a cedar chest for some extra quilts and a pillow. She returned to find Joseph standing, staring out the dark window with his back to her. She closed the door, then laid the quilts on the floor.

"Will you—will you stay turned, please, while I put on my nightdress?"

"*Ya.*"

She hurried despite his answer, wondering if his idea of "playing" might be to sneak a peek. And despite her resolve of the afternoon to get a little of her own back in teasing him, she found that she couldn't quite bring herself to anything so bold at the moment. So she wriggled into her gown, then grabbed her hairbrush from the bureau and jumped into the bed, pulling the quilt up to her neck and unpinning her *kapp*.

"You may turn."

"*Danki,*" he said with slight irony. He dropped to his knees and started to make his bed, then he reached for the buttons on his shirt. "Only my shirt, dear wife. Do you mind?"

"Of course not," she said, turning her gaze away and concentrating on releasing her braid. She ignored the nagging, innate curiosity that wanted to watch him and ran her fingernails through her scalp. She loved the moment each night when she might take down her hair. It was one of the things that she envied most about *Englisch* girls—their freedom of hairstyle. She had no choice but to let hers grow, as it had done from childhood, and never might she even so much as take shears to create bangs across her fair forehead. Her hair hung past her waist, and now it spilled over the side of the bed as she brushed it with long, even strokes.

A small sound made her turn and glance down at Joseph. He was kneeling on the quilt, shirt off, suspenders around his waist, and he appeared frozen as his dark eyes followed the movement of the brush. Her hand stilled.

"Don't stop."

"Why?"

"It's like a waterfall of gold, all shimmer and shine."

She blushed then, knowing it was only her husband who might view her hair unbound. It seemed he was claiming his right. She finished the remaining count of strokes, then laid the brush before her on the quilt. "There."

He seemed to shake himself as if from a dream and dropped to his back on the floor. She watched him stare up at the wooden slat ceiling as she had so often done herself and wondered if she should say something.

"There're thirty-seven," she remarked. "Boards, I mean—up there."

"Thirty-eight, if you count the half board at the end."

"I never count by halves."

He laughed. "*Nee* . . . for you, it's all or nothing."

"Well, there's nothing wrong with that."

"Maybe not, but it leaves little room for negotiation."

"You mean our marriage, don't you?"

He rolled over and propped his head up on one elbow, reaching to rub a tendril of her hair between his thumb and forefinger. "It's true; there was no room for negotiation. But there's always time."

She felt skittish at his touch and longed to pull her hair free.

"But," he went on, "I'd wager it's you who's been caught in your own web more so than me."

She lifted her chin. "I'm not caught."

"Aren't you?" He wound the white-gold strands around his hand.

She chose to ignore his game, but he only smiled, the dark growth of his beard making him look like a pirate, except for the glasses.

"Abby Lambert—now that's a name I never expected to hear. Time was you probably wouldn't have even looked at a Lambert. My family wasn't the best-regarded in the community before we left."

A sudden, pressing thought intruded on her consciousness as she studied his handsome face and flash of white teeth. "Well, what name did you expect to hear?"

"Hmm?"

She rolled over, inadvertently giving him better access to her hair. "You know what I mean."

He looked up at her. "*Ach*, you mean another girl?"

"*Ya.*"

He wound and unwound the golden strands. "There was no one."

"You're lying!" she declared, yanking on her hair.

"How would you know that?"

"Because you looked down and not at me."

He shrugged his bare shoulders. "So?"

She felt her temper rise at the thought of some unknown *Englisch* girl, though she couldn't understand why. "Let me go."

She pulled free, leaving him with several long strands of hair entwined in his fingers.

"That must have hurt."

"It did not. Now tell me about the girl."

He gathered the hair together and slipped it under his pillow, took off his glasses, and buried his face in the quilted sham.

"No girl," he mumbled, muffled by the pillow.

She watched the lamplight play on the golden muscles of his shoulders and back, and pursed her lips. "Was she very pretty?"

"I'm going to sleep."

"Not until you tell me the truth, you're not."

"You'd be amazed at what I can sleep through." He nestled against the pillow.

She grabbed her own pillow without thinking and threw it at his head as hard as she could.

He lifted his face with his hair standing a bit on end and arched one dark eyebrow at her. "So you want to have a pillow fight?"

She shrank back in the bed. "No," she squeaked.

There was a glimmer of mischief in his eyes. He sat up, the quilt sliding from him as he lifted his pillow.

She scrambled out of her bed toward the door. "My father will hear."

"That's *gut*, for your father to hear."

He stood up, and she leapt back onto the bed and then dived over the side, snatching up her pillow. She faced him, heart pounding and bare toes digging into the wooden floor.

"Ladies first." He bowed.

She raised the pillow.

"Wait," he said. "My glasses." He bent to retrieve the lenses, and she smacked him across the back of the head and then jumped back on the bed.

He set the glasses on the bureau and grinned up at her. "Mrs. Lambert, I believe that you don't quite fight fair."

She swung her pillow fiercely. "Tell me about the girl."

He dived at her feet, and she would have gone backward off the bed if he hadn't hoisted her over his broad shoulder.

"Let me go," she hissed, whacking the pillow against his lower back.

He dumped her without ceremony on the bed, then gave her a swift pat with the pillow.

She scrambled to rise and he sat on the edge of the bed, holding her down with one hand on her shoulder.

She realized she was trapped, so she sucked in a deep breath and regarded him through venomous blue eyes.

"If this is how far you're going to keep from telling me, I'll just have to imagine the worst." She closed her eyes, ignoring his nearness. "Green eyes . . . a fine figure, brown hair . . . no, maybe red . . ." She peeked up at him.

There was a sudden tenseness to his firm mouth that bothered her.

"I'm right, aren't I . . . red hair?"

He rose and pulled her quilt up around her, tucking it in at her shoulders. "Good night, Mrs. Lambert," he said in a sober tone.

She watched him pick up his pillow and return to the bed on the floor. She felt lost somehow, adrift, and she admonished herself for the feelings. Of course there was another girl, an *Englisch* girl. Perhaps he'd been in love even, and she had stolen all of that with her careless plotting.

But then, he had been the one to rejoin the community and end any possibility of a life outside. Still, she swallowed and grasped a handful of her own hair. How completely opposite it was to red— he must despise her. She stifled a sniff and turned over, refusing to allow any tears to fall as she drifted into a fitful sleep.

CHAPTER SEVEN

HE WAS DREAMING. HE KNEW IT AND DIDN'T REALLY WANT to wake. Molly was smiling down at him, her hands on his chest. They were sprawled on a picnic blanket in the summer sun in the middle of a park. He felt happy, sated. She bent to kiss him, and he could count the freckles on the bridge of her nose. He returned the kiss with ease, his hands threading through her wild red curls. But suddenly everything was being swept away by rushing water. He tried to hang on to Molly, but she was gone from him and he was drowning. He finally caught hold of a stand of honey wheat protruding from a creek bank and held on until the water slowed, then drifted to a lazy trickle. Shivering, he pulled himself up against the wheat and it turned into long blonde hair that wrapped around him with an intense warmth, making his chest feel tight. He clung to the hair and breathed in its sweet fragrance, like melting mint, and smiled as he buried his face in the hot strands.

He awoke with an uncomfortable gasp, hiking up to a sitting position and glancing over in the near morning light to the lump of covers that was his wife in her little-girl's bed. He stretched his fingers to touch her hair, which still spilled over the mattress and to the floor. Then he half laughed at himself for the dream; he was clearly a fool when it came to women and their wiles. He let her hair go and hugged the quilt against his chest, realizing that he was cold. He considered rising before the sun came up to start the chores when Abby rolled over and sat straight up in the bed.

"Wh—what are you doing here?" She was still half asleep.

He put his glasses on and smiled at her. "Just me, Abby—your husband, remember?" He watched her curl up.

"*Ya,*" she murmured. "I did that to you."

"Did what?"

"The marriage . . . sorry," she murmured, still half asleep.

"Now, now—no time for regrets. Why don't you go start breakfast?"

She opened her eyes then, peering down at him with an annoyed look in the half-light. "Joseph?"

He was feeling for his shirt. "Mmm-hmm?"

"I might as well tell you something, a secret. It's really bad."

His hands stilled. With Abby, he should be prepared for anything: She only married him to make another man jealous? She knew where a body was buried?

"I can't cook."

"What?"

"I can't cook," she whispered, her tone taut. "All that food yesterday—it was from neighbors who wanted to know about us. I can't cook."

"So you're a bad cook, so what?" He resumed looking for his shirt.

"You don't understand, but you will. I make a mess of everything that an Amish housewife is supposed to do."

"And what is an Amish housewife supposed to do?"

"Everything right," she mumbled with sarcasm.

"Sounds boring."

She let out a huff of frustration, then began braiding her hair. "You're going to see—I don't know what my father thought. It was probably the first time he wasn't disappointed in me. Now you're going to be disappointed, too, but it's just going to have to be the way it is, because I am not going to try and change for you."

He considered her words as he hitched up his suspenders and folded the quilts.

"I'll help you cook," he said.

"What?"

He'd taken his glasses off and was splashing water on his face from the bowl and pitcher on her bureau.

"I know how to cook. We'll just get up a little earlier every day and go down and do it together. I can give you tips for lunch and dinner too."

He dried his face on a towel that smelled like fresh mint and put it down with haste, recalling his dream. He turned to the bed.

She was staring at him, her fingers poised on her braid. "You'd help me? Why?"

He shrugged. "I'm your husband."

"*Ach* . . ." she whispered. She finished her braid and rose from the bed, careless of her nightgown this morning.

He turned to look out the window. "Do you want me out of here so you can dress?"

"*Ya* . . . I mean . . . *nee*, it's all right. I guess I'll hurry up."

He felt the back of his neck grow warm as he listened to the various sounds behind him. The slide of her gown coming up her body, the pulling on of another. He closed his eyes against the wash of images going through his mind. His wife. She was his wife.

"All right," she said, snapping him out of his reverie. He turned, feeling awkward, to watch her adjust her *kapp*. "I'm ready."

He nodded. "Let's go, then."

He waited until she'd scooped up the kitten in its box, then followed her down the stairs to enter the still-dark rooms below. She went about turning up the lamps while he peered into cabinets in the kitchen. He found a frying pan but no spatula, then went to light the woodstove.

Lighting a woodstove was like riding a bicycle, he thought; you never forgot how to do it. There was always a firebox in the left-hand corner that contained shredded paper, wood chips, and small pieces of wood. He knew that the type and amount of fuel used were one of the easiest ways to control the heat. Good cooking required a low, slow burn and no raging fire. The woodstove also had two dampers, which he fooled around with for a minute to get them just right. The chimney damper controlled the amount of smoke moving out of the woodstove into the chimney, while the oven damper regulated the amount of heat moving between the firebox and the oven.

When he'd adjusted the dampers to his satisfaction, Joseph rose and put the frying pan on top of the stove. The entire surface of the stove could be used for cooking, but you had to spend some time getting to know a stove's quirks to get adept at moving pots and pans around to capitalize on the hot spots. When he was done, he turned back to Abby.

"All right. When you say you can't cook, how bad do you mean?"

She frowned. "I can't even scramble eggs without them being watery."

"Why?" he asked.

"What?"

"Why can't you cook—I mean, really?"

She scuffed her small shoe on the wooden floor. "My *mamm* died . . . you know that. Father never taught me anything . . . and there's never been other womenfolk around. He wouldn't allow it. So I've just tried to figure it out, and I haven't been very good at it."

"You mean to tell me that your father let you try and run this house from the time you were little?"

She nodded. "I know . . . I should have it figured out by now."

"No, that's not what I mean. You were a baby girl—five years old. You could have been badly injured in the kitchen or even filling the lamps."

"Well, I have been burned a few times." She absently rubbed at her left arm under its long sleeve. "But *Mamm* taught me a few things before she died—how to peel vegetables, just not how to grow them . . . and how to make up the beds and do the laundry."

"You were five years old," he repeated, his heart aching for the image of a blonde, tumble-curled little girl trying to cook breakfast all alone.

"*Ya*, but I'm not anymore, and I . . ." She grimaced. "I thank you for helping me."

He looked carefully at her face, recalling the circumstances of their marriage, and hardened his heart; she could be lying even now. He turned to the stove, then glanced at her over his shoulder.

"I hope that you can at least gather eggs," he remarked with sarcasm, ignoring the sudden flash of hurt on her pretty face.

"*Ya*." She nodded. "It's the least that I can do."

She marched out the back door, leaving him alone in the cold kitchen.

CHAPTER EIGHT

SHE STOMPED TO THE HENHOUSE, WIPING WITH THE BACK of her hand at the unbidden tears of frustration that stung her cheeks. He'd seemed so kind, yet she forced herself to admit that she knew next to nothing about him, really. And just because he'd been amiable the day before didn't mean that he was in any way over his anger about her deception in their forced marriage. She sighed as she felt for the eggs beneath the warm, feathered hens that clucked at her in disapproval. She had no right to expect anything from him except anger . . . but she'd had enough of that from her father.

Yet she had patience on her side. One of the few times she'd received positive affirmation from a female in the community had been from her seventh-grade teacher. Miss Stahley had noticed her persistent efforts at the more difficult math problems and had touched her shoulder. "I do believe that *Derr Herr* has gifted you with patience, Abigail. You'll wear down those sums yet."

It was funny how she'd kept that stray observation tucked away in her heart through the years, probably because such encouraging remarks were so few and far between in her young life. But as she gathered the last egg, she found herself praying that the gift of patience would continue to bless her as she puzzled out her new husband.

She returned to the house with the egg basket and a much refreshed attitude. Joseph had found the bacon and had a good portion frying in a pan. She always managed to either overcook it to charred crispness or leave part of it underdone.

246

He glanced up. "Abby . . . look . . . I'm sorry for snapping at you. I'm just as new as you to this idea of marriage."

She nodded, feeling a strange surge of relief in her chest. "*Ach*, that's all right. I'd want to snap, too, if I were you. Here are the eggs."

"All right, let me show you the perfect way to scramble them."

"How did you learn to cook?"

He was cracking the eggs into a blue mixing bowl with a large chip out of its rim. "Well, first when I was a kid, I guess. My mom and dad, after they left the community, drifted from here to there and kind of drank—a lot. It was either learn how to cook or go hungry. My kid sister needed me, too, so I suppose that helped."

"Your sister?" Abigail was surprised. She didn't recall a little sister.

"Yep. She's twenty now, five years younger than me. She got a full ride—a full scholarship—to NYU. That's New York University. She's going to be an artist." He laughed. "She'll really be surprised that I'm married. We write to each other a lot."

So he's twenty-five, she thought, ignoring his comment about his sister's surprise at their marriage. He looked younger, except when he was serious, like now.

"And your *mamm* and *daed*?"

He shrugged his broad shoulders. "Don't know. I ran away when I was about seventeen. I'd send money back to Angel, my sister. She stayed with an aunt of ours. But I haven't seen my folks in years."

"Don't you—want to?"

He whisked the eggs with a fork. "*Nee*, not really. I don't know if I'm ready for that yet. I guess the Lord will let it happen when it's time. Now here's the trick with the eggs—instead of a little milk, add some cold water, about three tablespoons for every six eggs. The water makes them fluffy and light without the runniness." He poured the bright yellow mixture into a sizzling pan. "And watch the heat after the first minute or so. Move the pan around so things don't burn." He plunked the perfectly done bacon onto a towel while Abigail watched his every move.

Just then they heard her father's footsteps on the stairs. Joseph thrust a spoon into her hand and quickly sat down at the table. She turned and began to shift the eggs back and forth, wondering anew at his quicksilver kindness.

"It smells good in here," her father remarked suspiciously as he took a seat at the table.

"*Ya*, so it does," Joseph agreed as Abigail turned her first perfectly scrambled eggs out onto a platter. She brought plates and tableware and served the bacon and eggs with the bread pudding left from yesterday. Once more she watched her father's face relax from disbelief to enjoyment as he forked up his food.

She felt a sudden rush of gratitude and looked at Joseph with a quick smile, surprised to find him return her gaze with a wink of his dark eyelashes. She felt good inside, like she had a secret friend. Her heart softened toward him, and she uttered a silent prayer of thanks to *Derr Herr* and began to eat her eggs.

Joseph watched her from the corner of his eye as he ate. How pretty she was with the slight flush of pleasure on her cheeks. He wanted to remind himself that she was manipulative, but he couldn't bring himself to do so at the moment. He just knew that he felt content. His belly was full, he had work to attend to, and he happened to be married to a very beautiful woman.

A sudden mewing sound broke the silence in the kitchen.

Mr. Kauffman looked up. "What's that, then?" he asked.

Joseph smiled. "A wedding gift from me to your daughter, sir. A kitten to keep her company. Do you want to see it?"

Mr. Kauffman frowned. "*Nee*, I've work to be about. As do

you, if you've a mind to." The older man pushed back his chair and rose from the table. "I've got a small harvest of corn to get in."

"Do you can it?" Joseph asked, then realized his mistake when he saw his father-in-law's frown deepen. Obviously Abby didn't know how to can. "I mean, we'll can some of it, *ya*? I've missed canned sweet corn."

"I've just been storing it for stock feed the past years."

Abigail spoke up. "Well, this year, Father, please bring a few bushels to the house. I—I'll can it up right."

She glanced at Joseph, and he felt pleasure in giving her a faint nod. Maybe he could work in a late-night canning session. The tendrils of hair at her temples might curl in the steam, and her cheeks would be flushed . . .

He drew himself up sharply when he realized Mr. Kauffman had repeated himself.

"*Ya*, I'm coming now." Joseph rose, then bent to brush his lips across her temple before depositing his plate in the sink. He followed his silent father-in-law out the door and left Abby alone with the kitten.

CHAPTER NINE

ABIGAIL DECIDED THE MOMENT THEY'D LEFT THE KITCHEN
that she would surprise Joseph with at least a basic knowledge of
canning. It was the least she could do to return his kindness about
the cooking. She ignored the warm rush of feeling that she had
when she thought about her new husband.

She would need basic supplies, like canning jars. She'd go
into town and get some information first, from the best source she
knew, Yoder's Pantry. Tillie might be able to help. She saw to the
kitten's small needs, then she raced upstairs to change her blouse,
thinking how funny it was that she was getting so excited over
something domestic.

Still, she considered, as she left the house a few minutes later
to hitch Carl up to the buggy, her interest truly lay in surprising
her husband and in wanting to see his face light up with pride.
It was a curious sensation for her, this desire to please someone
besides herself. If she'd felt it with her father, it had long ago been
squashed by too many failed attempts.

Joseph was different. Although he could be angry and cutting,
he was also infinitely kind—like with the kitten. He'd wrangled
her father into a pet without so much as a cross word, something
she had never been able to do. And he was willing to talk about his
past and his family, willing to be open with her when most people
kept their distance. *And probably for good reason*, she thought ruefully as she navigated the buggy into town. She had always been
one to gossip, especially about other girls, and she didn't feel

particularly good when she considered this aspect of her personality. Could it be that a few simple days of marriage were revealing her most intimate characteristics to herself? She wasn't too sure she liked the idea.

As she climbed down from the buggy to hitch up in front of Yoder's, a passing pair of *Englisch* girls caught her eye, and the old, familiar pull of interest in the outside world made her stand still on the sidewalk. She admired their clothes, the bright colors and cut of their skirts, as well as their free-flowing hair. But it was more than that. She felt like they walked unencumbered by the social boundaries so imposed by her own people—the role of women and the expectations of their duties in life. She mentally shook herself. For someone who had so longed after the *Englisch* way of life, it was a funny thing to be seeking out the best way to can sweet corn.

She entered the restaurant, enjoying the rush of air-conditioned coolness that met her arrival. Her friend Tillie was waitressing, just as she had hoped. She came over and greeted Abigail with a large menu.

"Abigail, I'm so glad to see you. We're still doing breakfast, if you like."

Abigail returned the smile. At one time she'd wanted to be a waitress. It would have allowed her a closer brush with the *Englisch*, but her father never permitted it. And now, her mind whispered, she had her own former *Englisch* man at home.

Tillie leaned close and spoke behind the menu. "How is it to be married to Joseph Lambert?"

Again Abigail smiled; it was nice to be the center of attention, even for a short time. And she found, to her surprise, that she could respond with honesty to the other girl's question.

"It's *gut*—really."

Tillie's eyes twinkled. "It should be. He's hot."

Abigail giggled at the use of the *Englisch* word, but she had to agree. Joseph was hot—the idea made her face flame.

Tillie laughed. "Come on, let me seat you."

Abigail caught her arm. "Tillie, wait . . . um . . . this may sound funny, but actually I came in today because I was hoping I could take a peek in the kitchen. Maybe talk to one of the cooks or to you for a few minutes—about canning."

Tillie looked at her blankly. "Canning?"

"*Ya* . . . you know, how to do it?"

"That's what you're thinking of during the first week of marriage?"

Abigail flushed. "Well, Joseph likes sweet corn, and I . . ."

"Just want to make him happy." Tillie beamed. "It must be true love if it brings *you* to the idea of canning corn. Come on in the back. I'll introduce you to Judith. She's Amish and a great cook. And I happen to know that she's putting up carrots today and could probably use some help. You can learn firsthand."

Abigail followed her friend through a door into a large, modernized kitchen. She was amazed at the amount of stainless steel and all of the electric appliances and mysterious gadgets. She also recognized at once the precision and order of the busy place as four Amish women worked together to get orders met.

"We've got four wonderful cooks," Tillie explained. "Martha, Mary, Judith, and Ruth—this is Abigail. She wants to learn some canning tips; she just got married."

The older women laughed as Tillie continued. "Ruth mainly does desserts. Martha and Mary work the main dishes, and Judith processes all the produce that comes through. Judith, I told Abigail that you might be doing some canning of your own today."

The cheerful, round-faced woman nodded, her blue eyes twinkling. "*Ya*, and I could use a pair of young hands to help."

"Oh, *danki*," Abigail said, glad she'd changed into a spotless apron before she'd left home.

"I'll leave you to it, then." Tillie smiled and waved, leaving the kitchen.

"You need a hair net first, Abigail," Judith said, handing her a folded packet.

Abigail opened it awkwardly, withdrawing a white net and slipping it over her *kapp*.

"And plastic gloves. I think you'll take a small pair."

Abigail stood awkwardly but eagerly next to a shiny counter.

"It's *gut* for a young wife to have a cellar full of the colors of canning—the vegetables, fruits, and jellies, *ya?* Do you remember your *mamm's* pantry?"

Abigail shook her head and spoke low. "She died when I was five."

"*Ach*, I'm sorry." Judith regarded her with compassion. "So perhaps you've never had the chance to learn canning properly?"

Abigail shook her head.

"Well, I will teach you today, and someday you'll show your own daughter. Come, let's begin."

Abigail's mind caught on the image of a dark-haired, blue-eyed baby. Any daughter of Joseph's would be good-natured and beautiful, like her father . . . She snapped back to attention at Judith's brisk movements.

The older woman was lifting quart-sized glass jars from a sectioned box on the floor. Abigail bent to help her. Then she gathered up two parts of a brass lid for each jar: a flat lid and a screw band.

"To can fruits, vegetables, sauces, and the like, you use jars like these, with the wide mouths. The regular-size jars are better for jams and jellies."

Abigail nodded, almost feeling like she should be taking notes. But she was a quick study when she wanted to be, and she wanted to be now.

"What are you planning on canning?" Judith asked as she hefted a wooden box overflowing with carrots with green, leafy tops onto the counter.

"Sweet corn first, but we only have a small harvest."

"It doesn't matter; it's all provided by *Derr Herr* and is His bounty, *ya?*"

"Yes."

"All right. We're doing carrots today, but I'll write down the steps for sweet corn for you later. Much of the processing is the same. To begin, you wash your carrots very well, then you cut off the tops and peel them. There's a knack to peeling with a knife and getting it just right. You want to keep your peelings as thin as possible, so you've got to have a sharp knife and a steady hand." She gave an example, slicing fast and neat down a carrot. "Now you try."

Abigail took the knife and attempted to imitate the other woman, but ended up digging unevenly into the carrot.

Judith laughed good-naturedly. "You'll get better. In fact, you'll be an expert by the end of the day."

She was right. Abigail gained more confidence as her peelings began to resemble the neat piles that Judith made. And though she was slower, she became accurate and surprisingly interested in what she was learning.

"Carrots, like sweet corn, need to be cold-packed," Judith explained. "This means a lot of *gut* things for the cook. First, it is easy and doesn't require standing next to a hot stove for the whole day. And you can be fairly sure that all of the bacteria are killed with this method. There's nothing worse-smelling than a poorly canned jar of vegetables."

Abigail helped to blanch the peeled and sliced carrots, then she watched how Judith dipped the vegetables into cold water before beginning to pack them into clean, hot jars. She added a bit of hot water and some sugar to the top of each jar, and then she showed Abigail how to adjust the seals and lids before placing them into boiling water for a short amount of time.

"And that's it," she announced, removing the jars with long

tongs. "Now we'll do the next batch, and you'll be more than ready to do your own canning—if you're not too tired."

Abigail laughed with the other women, feeling included and part of the group. It was an unusual sensation. There was more to this than just drudgery or the perfecting of a recipe, she could see. There was a legitimate science and method. She knew in that moment that *Englisch* or Amish, people had to cook to eat. She had a sudden desire to experiment in her kitchen, and she knew she would never be able to explain to Judith how much her friendly instruction had meant to her.

She settled for a quick thank-you and was surprised when Judith pressed a covered basket into her hands.

"Here're some of the carrots that you did and directions for the sweet corn. And there's something else so you needn't worry over supper. I also put in a *gut* box of Amish recipe cards. You can be a good cook, Abigail, if you'll have the patience for it."

"I will. *Danki*." And she knew it was a promise that she meant to keep.

CHAPTER TEN

THE SUN WAS BEGINNING TO SET, FRAMING THE GENTLE curves of the landscape with pink and amber light when Joseph left the fields, tired but fulfilled. He walked back toward the house alone; his father-in-law had waved him on ahead. He was hot enough from the warm September weather that a good long soak in a tub sounded like heaven. But since he knew that Abby would probably be unnerved by the whole process, he decided instead to jump into the rather secluded creek that ran through the Kauffmans' property.

Ducking through some overgrowth, he eyed a fairly deep spot in the moving water and stripped down with pleasure, tossing his clothes over a bush. The water was icy cold but felt wonderful, and he wished that he had a bar of soap. He scooped up a handful of sand from the creek bottom instead and scrubbed with abrasive enthusiasm. Then he sat down on a convenient, flat, underwater rock and let the current swirl past his chest while his mind drifted into pleasant abeyance.

ABIGAIL WAS HOT AND TIRED BY THE TIME SHE PULLED THE buggy up to the hitch at home. She knew that she should have been there a lot sooner to get supper ready, but she just felt like she had to get the canning supplies to apply her newfound knowledge. And, she admitted to herself, to make Joseph proud.

When she entered the house, she found everything quiet as usual except for the kitten, which wanted to be fed. She washed her hands, then poured a saucer of milk for the small creature and set it inside the box, blowing at the hair that clung damply to her forehead. She glanced around the kitchen with one eye on the setting sun. Joseph and her father were apparently working late in the fields. She decided she'd indulge in one of her favorite secret pursuits before attempting supper. Besides *Englisch* magazines, she loved dipping her feet in the local stream.

She stole out the back door and skirted the property to the creek that cut through the area. She slipped off her heavy black shoes and thick kneesocks, then she caught up her skirt above her ankles and went to perch on her favorite log, dangling her toes in the refreshing water.

"I see we're of a similar mind today."

Joseph's cheerful voice almost made her tilt backward off the log as she glanced down the creek and saw him sitting no more than ten feet away. Her gaze skittered to his clothes on the bush and then back to his bare chest. He grinned at her.

She said the first thing that came to mind. "Where are your glasses?"

"Safe on the bank." He started to tread water with his arms, as if preparing to come closer, and she jumped to her feet, her bare toes digging into the rough bark of the log.

"Uh . . . just stay there, please . . . I've got to go back and start supper."

"Nervous, Mrs. Lambert?" he asked.

"*Nee,* " she snapped, though her face flushed.

He laughed aloud, the sound causing chills to run in delicious tingles across the back of her neck and down her spine. She pushed the intriguing sensations away and lifted her chin.

"Maybe you're the one who's nervous."

His smile deepened, and he held her captive with the intensity of his dark eyes. "Maybe. This is all new to me, too—having a wife share my bath."

She stuttered on her reply. "I am not sharing your bath. And why aren't you bathing at home in the hip bath, like everyone else?"

He splashed at a stray dragonfly. "I don't know. I guess I thought I'd preserve your maidenly dignity."

Another thought crossed her mind and caused her to frown in irritation. "You do realize that anyone could come along here and see you?"

"*Ach.* You mean another girl, right?"

She nodded in spite of herself. "That is exactly what I mean."

"Well then, I'd best get out, don't you think?" He moved as if to rise and she turned and fled barefoot, his laughter ringing in her ears.

JOSEPH BROUGHT HER SHOES AND SOCKS TO HER WHILE HER father looked on askance.

Abigail stood next to the stove, heating up the bean and bacon soup Judith had given her so she didn't have to worry about supper.

"You seem to have forgotten something," Joseph teased in a low tone.

Abigail ducked her head, then lifted it again, only to wish she hadn't when she caught the clean, masculine scent of him. His hair was damp, too, and clung to his neck overlong in places.

"You need a haircut."

"Can I trust you with a pair of scissors?"

"I cut Father's hair," she replied in an injured tone.

They both turned to look at Solomon Kauffman's hair, which was actually layered neatly and fell with some style to complement his long beard.

"What is it?" he asked, frowning at them.

"Just debating the merits of a haircut at home," Joseph answered.

"*Ach*, well, Abigail is a fair hand with the shears."

"Well, *gut*, then."

After supper Joseph found himself seated on the back porch. A large white sheet was draped around his neck and flowed down over his chest and arms. Abigail stood considering him while he chafed under her perusal.

"Just cut it already."

"Take off your glasses. I need to see the true shape of your face."

"Honestly, Abby, there's no style with the Amish—just saw away."

He knew she was ignoring him and he closed his eyes, holding his glasses under the sheet. When she first touched the back of his neck, he started with a little jump.

"You are nervous, Mr. Lambert," she teased.

He laughed. "Again, maybe—this is new to me too."

She ran her fingers through his hair, sending exquisite chills down his back. When was the last time someone had touched him with such gentleness? Her delicate, tentative fingers were playing havoc with his insides, and all she was doing was cutting his hair. He blew out a breath of disgust. Still, there was something to be said for being attracted to one's own wife, no matter the circumstances of the marriage.

She diligently combed and cut, and he began to relax beneath her touch. She had the persistence of an artist, and he knew no one had ever taken so much time with his hair. He let his hands rest on his knees and almost dropped his glasses when she spoke.

"There!" she said with satisfaction. She held up a small hand mirror. "Father always wants to see the back. What do you think?"

He slipped his glasses back on and peered at the mirror behind his shoulder. His dark hair fell neat and even, and she'd done something to make it curl at his nape.

"It's great, Abby. Thank you."

She trailed the mirror around to his front and he poked self-consciously beneath her gaze at his bangs. "Really great."

She smiled at him, clearly pleased, but there was also an air of suppressed excitement about her that made him just a little nervous.

"What?" he asked.

She clutched the mirror to her chest. "I learned how to can today . . . carrots and sweet corn. For you."

He smiled up at her. "Where did you go?"

"In town, to Yoder's Pantry. Do you remember? It's a restaurant—one of the cooks was really nice and taught me about canning. I helped all morning and afternoon."

He felt a funny feeling in his stomach as he watched her. A surge of protectiveness and caring for her fragile excitement. For him. She said she'd learned for him. It humbled his heart somehow in the way that a hundred other gifts might not have done. He reached his hand out from beneath the sheet and caught her own smaller one in his palm.

"Thank you, Abby. I think that's one of the nicest things anyone's ever done for me."

She blushed, and he had to suppress the urge to rise and take her in his arms. It was one thing to tease, but quite another to kiss her with intent. And the way he was feeling at the moment didn't allow for any casual contact.

"I'd better go in and clean up the dishes. Will you—bring me some corn tomorrow from the field?"

"First thing, I promise."

"*Danki.*" She gathered up the scissors and the mirror and whisked the sheet from around his neck with one hand, shaking the dark clippings out onto the ground.

"The birds like the hair to feather their nests for winter."

He nodded. "I remember."

"All right, well, *gut*."

She went in through the screen door, leaving him sitting in the falling darkness, alone with his thoughts.

CHAPTER ELEVEN

IN THE TWO WEEKS FOLLOWING THE HAIRCUT, AN UNEASY tenseness settled on Abigail whenever Joseph was around. When she'd been touching him, she had felt overwhelmed by the feelings of tenderness and attraction that had caused her heart to race and her hands to be not quite as steady as she would have liked.

She tried to evaluate her feelings objectively as she lay on her bed one afternoon, snatching a few minutes of time for herself. Was he handsome? *Hot*, as Tillie had said? Yes. Was he intelligent, kind to the kitten and to her father as well as to herself? Yes.

But so what? There were plenty of kind, handsome men about. Why should she find herself becoming entangled with the man she'd married out of convenience? She turned over and thumped her pillow, groaning aloud. She hated now what she'd done to him, how she'd trapped him, but he never seemed to give her an opportunity to talk about it. And half the time, she had no idea what he was thinking behind those deep, dark eyes of his.

She laid her head down on her pillow for a moment, then she reached her hand down between the mattress and bedspring, sliding out one of the teen magazines she hadn't looked at in a while. Today the glossy *Englisch* girls and boys annoyed her with their perfect smiles and posed looks. Somehow they'd lost their appeal, and she wasn't sure exactly how it had happened. She sighed and was about to thrust the magazine back into its hiding place when the door opened and Joseph walked in.

"Hey, what are you doing?" He smiled, then caught sight of the magazine.

Abigail flushed and ignored the urge to stuff it under her belly. "Just relaxing for a minute," she replied with as much casualness as she could muster. "What are you doing?"

"I need a clean shirt. I have to run into town to get a blade for the harvester for your father. What are you reading?"

He came close and sank down on the edge of the bed. She tried to ignore the pull of his handsomeness and the smell of the outdoors that clung to his skin and sweat-dampened hair.

"Nothing—it's just silly, really."

"Let me see."

"No, I'd rather not." She moved the magazine to her far hand and turned her head away from him. He reached across her back and snatched it from her, as she'd expected he would. She waited for his recriminations to fall on her head.

She heard the pages turning, and her face burned when she thought about all of the feminine details contained within. Then she felt a light tap on the back of her cap.

"Hmm . . . here you are. I've got to get moving or your *daed* will have a fit. Do you want to come?"

She rolled over and looked up at him, taking the magazine back with suspicion. "That's it?"

"What?" He paused in easing down his suspenders.

"The magazine? You're not going to say anything?"

"What do you want me to say?"

She bounced upward to sit, unsure of why she was irritated. "I don't know—something."

He laughed as he grabbed his extra shirt. "I will never understand women."

"What do you mean, *women*? Shouldn't you say *woman*? I am your only wife, right?"

"Look, do you want to go or not?"

"No," she pouted, feeling foolish.

"Suit yourself."

263

He whistled as he buttoned the shirt, and she glared at him. For some reason she wanted to fight, to break his easy calm. Even as she thought it, though, her heart convicted her. He was her husband. She'd made him sweet corn, cut his hair, and thought about him more than she ever had any other man . . . so what was wrong with her?

He had his hand on the doorknob when she cried out, "Wait!"

"What?"

"I'll go."

"Great, let's move."

Abigail slipped off the bed and grabbed up her change purse, where she kept the household money her father gave her each month. She followed Joseph down the steps, pleased that she could go with him without worrying about supper. She'd been using the valuable recipe cards from Judith to a distinct advantage and had made great strides in the kitchen. She'd also found that she enjoyed both her own endeavors and the smiles of pleasure on Joseph's face when he tried something new. Today she left ham and green beans and a fresh huckleberry pie warming on the stovetop as she hurried out the door.

Joseph brought Carl around, and she climbed into the buggy without assistance. They set off at a good trot.

"I've got to get that blade back to your *daed*, but I think we can squeeze in a bit of lunch if you'd like." He slanted her a glance from his dark eyes, and she nodded in agreement.

It would be the first time they'd gone out together anywhere but church, and she thought it was both ironic and sad that they were having their first date weeks into their marriage. But she refused to be glum and set about chattering in the way she was used to doing to entertain a man. When she'd covered everything from the crops to the weather, Joseph laughed out loud and held up a placating hand.

"Whoa . . . please, Abby . . . you don't have to talk just to entertain me."

"I wasn't," she snapped, feeling embarrassed.

"Okay . . . let's just say that I like your normal way of talking."

"Which is what?"

"To the point."

She huffed aloud. "I should not have come."

He reached out a large hand and covered her own where they rested in her lap. "I'm sorry. I just want you to feel comfortable around me."

"I do," she lied, then thought better of it. "At least—sometimes I do."

He laughed, squeezing her hands, then letting go. "That's better. I can see that we're going to have to do more courting and playing until you feel more comfortable."

"Well," she admitted, "I do like to go out for lunch."

"And where should we go?"

"Yoder's Pantry," she answered promptly.

"All right. Yoder's it is." He clucked to Carl to pick up the pace.

Abigail tried to avoid glancing in his direction and looked at the passing farms instead. The land was alive with the harvest; crops coming in, butchering time, work from sunup till sundown. But soon it would be over, and the time for the county fair would come around. She wondered if Joseph would take her and realized that it was the first time she'd have a canned vegetable to enter. The thought made her smile to herself, and the day suddenly became more than promising.

JOSEPH CAUGHT THE SMELL OF FRESH MINT THAT DRIFTED to him from her hair and tried to concentrate on his driving. In truth, he knew that her father wouldn't like it if he'd known Joseph was planning to spend lunch in town. But time with one's wife somehow outweighed a blade for the harvester, and he decided it was worth the possible irritation on the part of his father-in-law.

"So, you're looking well today. That wine-colored blouse is becoming." He sounded like a stilted old man, he thought ruefully. Why was he being so formal? She'd kept him at an effective distance of late, and he made a sudden decision to change that over lunch.

"Thank you," she murmured. "You look well too."

"Fresh from the field?"

"Well . . ." She turned appraising blue eyes upon him. "*Ya.*"

It was something, he considered.

They arrived in town in good time, and Joseph hitched Carl to the post outside Yoder's. He came around and made a point to help Abby down, letting her slide against the warmth of his body for a brief moment. He was pleased to see a blush on her cheeks and caught her hand with goodwill as they entered the restaurant. Joseph noticed that there seemed to be some secret between his wife and the waitress who greeted them, as they both smiled and looked at him appraisingly.

"Joseph," Abby said. "This is Tillie, a *gut* friend of mine. She helped get me my canning lessons."

Joseph smiled. "Then I hope that you will be a good friend of mine too. I really appreciate your helping Abby. Her sweet corn was great."

Tillie nodded with a happy smile and led them to a table near the window looking out onto the street.

"What would you like to drink?" she asked.

Joseph darted a look at Abby and thought how funny it was that he was having an actual first date with his wife. In his old life, the situation would have called for champagne, but he was more than happy to ask for hot tea. Abby did the same.

"So, this is a nice place," Joseph remarked.

"*Ya.*" Abby giggled. "Father had many a meal here before you came along."

Joseph gave her his best smile. "Your cooking has really improved."

"Thanks to you."

"It's been my pleasure," he said, reaching across the table to catch her slender fingers in his hand. "It's funny," he said. "I forgot that the Amish don't wear wedding bands or jewelry. I'd have liked to have given you an engagement ring."

"For our very short engagement?"

"Why don't we try to let that go?" he suggested. "You know, you've never considered that I might have been interested in marriage . . . and in you."

"Really?" She blinked wide blue eyes.

"Really. Now let's just concentrate on tea. Here it is."

"What will you have?" Tillie asked. "The specials today are potato soup, stuffed peppers, and Ruth's own sour cherry pie."

"That all sounds good to me," Joseph said, closing the menu, which he had yet to even glance at. He ignored Abby's startled look. "I'm hungry," he confessed.

"I'll just have the soup and the pie."

"Great. I'll get that right out to you two newlyweds."

Joseph saw Abby shoot a surprised look at her friend and smiled to himself. He lifted her fingertips to his lips and felt her try to pull away.

"Joseph! We're in a public place, and my father is not around. You don't have to pretend."

He smiled at her. "I think we're past pretending, Abby, don't you?" He let her go, and she tucked her hands into the safety of her lap.

"I don't know what you mean."

He took a long sip of his tea and watched her until she looked away out the window. Their food soon arrived, and he took pleasure in everything, but especially in watching Abby wriggle under his obvious attentions. It occurred to him that he'd never had such fun going out for lunch before.

IT WAS MID-OCTOBER AND A BRIGHT, BEAUTIFUL MORNING. But Abigail had seen the sun far too early for her liking, having been up half the night with a laboring sow. She had always felt more competent in working with the farm animals than she'd ever felt in the house, and the past night had been no exception.

The kitten, now a spry, streaking little thing that she'd named George, had kept her company while she'd let Joseph sleep. Now she came out of the barn, having finished tending to the mother and piglets. She wiped her filthy hands on her apron and blinked in the sunlight—then stopped dead, staring at the apparition of a low-slung blue convertible and a tousled red-haired *Englisch* girl with a devastating white smile. She was talking to Joseph, who leaned against the car door with familiarity, looking down into her face.

Abigail straightened her spine and walked toward her husband.

"Oh, here's Abby now. Abby, this is Molly, a—friend from the past."

Molly scooted her charming figure forward on the front seat and leaned to extend a hand to Abigail. "Hi," she said with a bright smile.

"Hello," Abigail returned, catching Joseph's eye. "Joseph has mentioned you . . . your hair . . . It's lovely."

Molly giggled and looked at Joseph. "Thanks. It was always his favorite, but I guess he went and chose a blonde anyway. I can't believe you're married."

Abigail was working herself up to a boil, and Joseph must have sensed it, because he straightened from the car and looped an arm around her waist.

"Married as can be," he said with cheerful vigor.

"Well, I just was out this way and asked around for you. I'm staying at a bed-and-breakfast in town. I thought I'd stop for a few minutes," Molly offered, clearly wanting an invitation to stay and visit.

Abigail tried to ignore the girl's desire for hospitality, but her heart convicted her. "Would . . . you like to come in, then?" She felt Joseph's surprise.

Molly smiled. "Of course. Thanks." She reached out her slender arms to Joseph, who moved away from Abigail to swing her out of the car.

"I'll just go on in and change my apron and leave you two— friends—alone for a moment," Abigail said sweetly, though her heart was pounding. She marched past them and entered the kitchen, where she stood frozen for a moment. Then she found herself beginning to pray. "Please, Lord, give me patience, an extra measure, in this situation. Please bless this girl, Molly. Oh, Lord, please guard Joseph's heart. Help him not to remember too much of his time with her."

She realized that they were on the porch and rushed to change her apron. She was slicing apple bread when they came in and was grateful for something to focus on.

"Mmm . . . a real Amish kitchen . . ." Molly looked around her like she was in a museum. "I'd like to paint it, Joseph."

"We like the light blue," Abigail said.

Molly laughed. "No, I mean paint it . . . like a scene, honey. I'm an artist."

"Oh." Abigail blushed, feeling foolish. "Would you like a drink?"

"What do you have?"

She was about to reply when Joseph interrupted, for some reason in a dry tone. "Lemonade, tea, or springwater, Molly."

The girl laughed again, tossing her curls. "Things sure have changed, haven't they? I'll have tea, honey. If it's cold . . ."

Abigail nodded. "Of course. Please sit down. Joseph, what would you like?"

She kept her expression placid, though she felt furious with him for some reason. After all, he had no idea that the girl was going to come looking for him . . . did he?

"*Nee*, you sit. I'll get the drinks. Do you want lemonade?" Joseph asked.

Abigail could tell that something was bothering him by the tense set of his jaw, but she wasn't sure whether she was the cause, or Molly. After all, her conscience pricked her, she was the interloper here in a way. She'd forced this marriage upon him when maybe he'd been wanting to marry this beautiful *Englisch* girl instead. But if that were so, why had he come back? She stopped trying to puzzle it out when she realized Molly had asked her a question.

"I'm sorry. I was thinking . . . Please, what did you say?"

"I asked how long you've been married . . . It can't be long. I was seeing Joseph as recently as a year ago."

Abigail flushed and met her husband's eye. He returned her gaze with an expressionless face. She pursed her lips, then smiled with sweetness, moving to slide an arm around Joseph's lean waist.

"Actually," she murmured, batting her eyelashes with a coy effect, "we're still newlyweds. Isn't that right, my love?"

Joseph half turned toward her body and stared down into her eyes. "Indeed. And I hope that we'll always feel like newlyweds, even when we're old and gray."

Abigail flushed beneath his intense eyes and at his unexpected words. She also noticed that Molly looked none too pleased with his response.

"Well," their visitor said with a toss of her curls, "I suppose that's nice, but what is it that they say—'Young marriages are the most fragile'?"

"I've never heard that saying," Joseph remarked. "Now let's finish our drinks. I've got work to get back to, as does Abby."

Molly quickly recovered her composure. Indeed, if Abigail didn't know any better, she would have believed the girl's sincerity and goodwill. But to someone who'd led boys on in the past herself, it was obvious to Abigail just exactly what Molly was up to.

She sighed within herself, kept up a silent running stream of petition to the Lord, and was glad when Joseph finally escorted the girl to the back porch and out of their lives for good.

CHAPTER THIRTEEN

JOSEPH WATCHED THE CAR DRIVE AWAY AND FELT THE PULL of desire so badly that he could taste it. As she said good-bye, Molly had offered him a bottle of pain pills with the same non-chalance that she always had. He'd wanted to say no, had heard himself say no in his head, but everything that was flesh in him was crying out yes. And he'd taken them. His eyes burned as he thought about the good feeling, the elation the pills had always given him. He'd felt more confident, productive, and kind. He'd asked himself a million times when he was with the *Englisch* why painkillers couldn't just be legal for everyone—especially when he'd believed they made people not just feel better but *be* better people. He was amazed now that he ever could have thought like that, but that was part of true addiction. And so was the fact that he now clutched the white-capped bottle until it imprinted his palm.

He swallowed hard and shivered as he looked at the dust rising from the lane as Molly's car turned onto the highway. He started to pray, just as he'd done the first time he'd said no, when it had nearly killed him to do so. Withdrawal, done alone in an empty apartment, with no support or food, had been a nightmare. He hadn't emerged victorious, just alive, and barely at that. God had been the only One with him, and it was then that he first felt the incredible desire to return home to his Amish roots. So then why had he taken the bottle? He stared down at it in his hand. Was he crazy? He had peace, freedom, a new way of life, and he was standing there willing to throw it all away.

The creak of the screen door brought him to his senses, and he turned to face Abby, who stood uncertainly on the porch.

"So that was Molly—the redhead," she said in a small voice.

He thrust the bottle into the pocket of his pants, mounted the wooden steps, and caught her unyielding figure in his arms.

"What are you doing?" she asked.

"Holding you."

"Why?" She tried to shrug him off.

"Because I need to right now. Hold me back, Abby—please." He rubbed his hands up and down her back and nuzzled his chin against her soft neck.

"I will not," she snapped. "Not when you're just pretending that I'm her."

He pulled away from her then and stared down into her hurt blue eyes. "Don't think that. It's not true."

"Then why do you want me?"

The question hung in the air between them.

He moved to thumb her delicate jaw. "You're my wife," he whispered. "Not her."

He ignored the sudden parting of her lips, the yielding of her thick eyelashes against the cream of her cheeks, and began to feather kisses along her temple and down her jaw. He felt rather than heard the small sigh escape her as the tension unwound in her body, and she lifted her chin to give him better access to the line of her throat. He made a choked sound of pleasure and let his mouth trail along her sweet-smelling skin. He stopped and stared down at her; her hair was coming undone, and a few hairpins pattered to the porch below.

He gently lowered his mouth to hers, and she began to kiss him back. He closed his eyes against the wash of sensation, drowning in the honeybee-light touch of her lips. She lifted her hands to touch each side of his face and rub the soft lay of his beard.

"I'll hold you," she breathed. She lifted her slender arms and encircled his shoulders, and he gave in to the gentle touch, rocking his weight forward.

His eyes filled with tears as the thought came to him that perhaps the Lord Himself had had His hand in their marriage.

A sudden clearing of a masculine throat startled him and he pulled back, glancing over his shoulder. His father-in-law stood on the steps of the porch.

"It's lunchtime," Mr. Kauffman announced in a gruff voice.

"Right," Joseph agreed, turning fully to shield Abby's disheveled appearance. He felt her press against his back.

"I've a few chores to take care of in the barn. I'll be in directly." He stomped down the steps and walked away while Joseph turned back to his wife.

"Thank you," he murmured.

She nodded, clearly flustered, and bent to retrieve her hairpins. He stooped to help her at the same time and they knocked heads.

"I'm sorry." He laughed. "Are you all right?"

"*Ya,*" she said, smiling. "I'm fine."

He handed her the pins and she rose to hurry inside, her hands at her hair, leaving him to stare after her.

CHAPTER FOURTEEN

THE BOTTLE OF PILLS STOOD AMONG THE CASUAL CLUTTER on Abby's bureau with deceptive innocence. Part of the everyday landscape to someone else, the bottle screamed to him with a chilling audibleness that reached to the edge of the bed where he sat and into his very soul. Abby was downstairs, cleaning up after supper, and he was wrestling a demon he thought he'd defeated. He rose and walked to the window, staring out at the moonlit fields. But out of the corner of his eye, the bottle called. Maybe just one . . . just one and he'd feel beyond good. He might even get up enough nerve to press Abby into a few kisses . . .

He shook his head, amazed at the pulse of addiction that riveted through his veins. Then he thought of Molly. She'd been the one to first introduce him to the drug, to drugs in general, but specifically to the pain pills. And he'd been in pain when he'd first met her, hurting deep inside for want of a family, a future. Now he had those very things, but he was still willing to pick up the drug.

He touched the lid with his fingertips, then gave the bottle an experimental shake. He clenched his jaw and unscrewed the lid, automatically doing a visual count of the white pills inside. A good twenty or so. He hadn't had anything in over a year, so just one would probably be enough to produce the familiar feeling. At the end, before, he'd had to take four at a time to get there. He spilled a single pill out into his hand, and a roaring like wind in a train tunnel filled his ears. His eyes watered; his mouth burned. But then it came to him—peace. The peace of *Derr Herr*. It crept softly in on the breeze of the dark air, swirling around him, touching his fevered head and heart. He drew a shaky breath and put the pill back in the bottle. He knew for sure that he could lean on the Lord, that Christ in him could defeat this unholy desire over and over again, if need be.

As he moved to replace the lid on the bottle, the door opened and Abby walked in. He started and spilled the bottle, the pills falling in a splatter on the hardwood floor. She stared at him, confusion on her pretty brow.

"Joseph, are you ill? Have you been to the doctor?"

He wet his lips, uncertain of what to say. But then his heart convicted him, and he began to speak in measured tones. "No, Abby—I–I'm not sick, at least not in the way you're thinking."

"What do you mean?" she asked, bending to pick up a pill.

"Don't . . ." He broke off, and she rose to her feet, extending her hand to him. He shook his head. "Abby, when I came back here, I told you, or the community, only part of my story."

She dropped her arm and walked into the room, closing the door behind her. She sat down on the bed and looked up at him.

"Well then, tell me the whole story."

He gave her a wry smile. "You'll hate it—and maybe me. You won't understand."

Her bosom heaved indignantly. "You can try at least—does Molly know the whole story?"

He sank to the floor, his back against the wall. "Here." He stretched out a long arm. "Read the prescription on the bottle."

She leaned forward and took it from him, and he watched her face as she processed the name.

"Molly Harding? Why do you have her medicine?"

He waited while she clutched the bottle against her apron.

"I took it from her."

"You—stole it?"

"*Nee* . . . She offered, and I took it."

Abby shook her head in confusion. "What are you trying to say?"

"I'm a drug addict, Abby. Those are pain pills. I used to take them all the time, just to feel good."

She bowed her head, staring at the bottle in her hand. "You say 'used to.' Do you still?"

"No. But I wanted to—tonight, today. And I'll probably want to again. But for now, right before you came in, I felt like *Derr Herr* was with me, and I was able to stop. I believe that as long as I cling to Him, hide in Him, that I'll be able to stop."

She took a deep breath. "And Molly. Are you—addicted to her?"

He frowned, not understanding her trail of thought. "Molly . . . No, she means nothing to me." It was true, he realized, deep inside. There wasn't anything left for Molly.

"So whatever you had with her, with the pills—it's over?"

"Yes."

"Do you want it to be?" She looked him square in the eye. "I mean . . . You know what I did, we both know—how I got you to marry me."

"We're a *gut* pair, aren't we? Both of us thinking we're not worth the other . . . but maybe the Lord has a plan in all of this."

She placed her heavy shoe lightly atop a pill beneath her foot and pressed. "I want these pills gone. I want her gone. Will you let me help you?"

It was not what he had expected—her calmness, her steadiness. Where was the petulant, demanding girl who'd had the boys dangling after her barely two months ago?

"Well?"

"What?"

"Will you let me help you—do something, anything?"

Anything. The word echoed across his mind. When had someone last offered selflessly to do anything for him?

"Pray for me," he choked finally.

"I'll pray for you, for us."

"Me too."

"*Gut.*" She pressed her foot fully to the floor, leveling the pill into fine powder. "I'll get rid of the pills?"

It was a question. He nodded in agreement, then spoke the truth.

"But it would be easy for me to get more."

"From Molly?"

"Not just her. Anywhere, really . . ."

"Are you going to get more?"

"I can only promise you moment by moment, day by day, Abby. If I say no forever and then fall, I'd be lying to you, and I don't want that. Not for you. Not for us."

It was the closest he'd come to admitting his feelings for her, but as he watched her beautiful face, he knew she was already on to another thought.

"Dr. Knepp . . . and his wife . . . they know about all of this, don't they?" She gestured with the pill bottle.

"*Ya.*"

"How?"

He sighed deeply. "Dr. Knepp was at a conference in Philadelphia. He—found me, on the streets. I had pneumonia and was out of it with a fever. I was speaking Pennsylvania *Deitsch*. He heard it and brought me back to the home of some friends there. He and Mrs. Knepp nursed me back to health, then they asked if I wanted to come here. It was the Lord who made it coincidence that he practiced in the same community where I was born."

"So he got you to stop the pills, then?"

"*Nee*, I did that alone . . . or with *Derr Herr*, I should say. It was before I got sick. I left Molly, all of our so-called friends, and went to an empty apartment and battled it out. But then I had no money, no food. I got sick—but I told Dr. Knepp the truth. He said—he said that he believed in second chances and persuaded me to come back, so I did."

"But, Joseph, how could you let Molly here then today? How could you even have her around?" Her voice rose in confusion, in accusation.

He hung his head. "How could I take the pills then too? I can't explain it to you . . ."

"Then you kissed me like that, on the back porch . . ." Her voice trailed off. "I thought—I thought that you . . ."

He looked at her. "I meant that kiss, Abby, every second of it."

"I don't know if you did or if you didn't, Joseph." Her shoulders sagged then straightened. "Please go, leave the room. I want to deal with these pills."

He slid back up the wall, needing to touch her, but he felt the barrier of her hurt, her confusion. Yet what did he want? It was enough that she'd said she'd pray—he didn't expect her to love him.

CHAPTER FIFTEEN

Abigail methodically began to gather up the pills from the floor. She got down on her hands and knees, looking under the bed and peering beneath the bureau. Then she realized that she could look at the bottle and tell how many were supposed to be there—if no one had taken any, that was. If Joseph hadn't . . .

She pulled her mind and heart together in support of him. He said he hadn't, so he hadn't.

But her mind whirled when she thought about his revelation. She had read things in her magazines about teenage addiction and drugs, but it all seemed so far away from her way of everyday life. Yet it was real, very real, and it threatened the one person who had gone out of his way to help her, despite how she had treated him in the beginning.

She sat back on her heels, deep in thought. And what of Molly? Abigail clutched a white pill in her hand and wished she could bring back the scene, turn away the red-haired girl who'd mocked her in her own house and brought this turmoil back into Joseph's life. Yet he had said it was a choice.

Still, she rose with determination. She may not be able to keep him from other drugs in the future, but she could keep one girl from her husband; she was sure of it.

She grabbed up a dark cloak and put the last of the pills into the bottle. Then she slipped down the stairs and out the front door before anyone could see her. Her father had gone to bed, and Joseph must have gone into the living room. She moved steadily in the dark, going into the barn. Once there, she emptied the pills out onto her father's workbench, took a mallet, and pulverized them into a pile of white powder. Then she scraped the stuff back into the bottle, being careful to wipe the bench clean of every trace of whiteness. She peeled off the label on the bottle and tore it to tiny shreds, adding it to the bottle, then left the barn, moving into the cold night air. Whispering a prayer, she stood behind the barn, where she opened and tilted the medicine bottle, holding her hand aloft. An autumn wind caught the contents and sent them blowing away into nothingness. She drew a deep breath of peace. She walked calmly back to the house and threw the bottle into the garbage, being careful to press it down under several items.

"That was the easy part," she murmured aloud as she made her way back outside. "Now for the true battle."

She prayed as she hitched up Carl to the buggy. She felt as though she was driving to meet not just another woman, but a direct threat to her marriage and way of life. If Molly so carelessly thought to hurt Joseph, what else might she do if she stayed in town for a few days? And though she believed him when he said the girl didn't matter, she wasn't sure where Molly stood, especially since she'd gone to the trouble to find him.

She caught a firmer grip on the reins as a car whizzed past, honking at the buggy. She didn't especially like to drive at night, but it was something she'd learned to do well nonetheless. And Carl was a steady horse.

She soon gained the town, and though there were numerous bed-and-breakfasts throughout the streets and outlying areas, she'd prayed that she might be able to recognize Molly's blue convertible easily from the street. And sure enough, by the time she'd come to the third business, Bender's Bed-and-Breakfast, she saw the metallic gleam of the blue convertible reflected in the streetlamps. She pulled Carl in and slipped out of the buggy to hitch him up to the convenient post. The place was Amish owned and run; she knew the Benders vaguely, though they attended a different service.

She saw that lights still burned in the downstairs windows, and she marched up the steps and knocked. Her heart pounded, but she still prayed beneath her breath. *Derr Herr* would give her the words that she needed to say. The door opened, and Mrs. Bender peered out into the relative dark of the porch.

"*Ya?*"

"Mrs. Bender, it's Abigail—Kauffman. But I've recently married. I'm Abigail Lambert now."

Mrs. Bender smiled and the door widened. "*Kumme* in out of the chilly night."

Abigail stepped inside and darted a look into the adjoining sitting room. She was relieved to see only Mr. Bender, reading *The Budget*. He nodded to her, then went back to his paper.

"I'm sorry for the late hour, Mrs. Bender." In truth, Abigail wasn't entirely certain of the time.

"It doesn't matter. Do you want some tea? What can I do for you?"

"Tea would be nice."

Abigail followed her into the kitchen and sat down at the wooden table. She glanced around at the beautifully carved wooden cupboards with their intricate scrolling.

Mrs. Bender followed her gaze. "My Luke does cabinetry on the side," she said with pride.

"It's beautiful."

"*Danki*. And your husband?"

"He works with my father."

"*Gut*. It's good to keep work in the family."

Abigail nodded, unsure how to broach the subject she'd come about.

"So you're Abigail Lambert now, hmm? It seems your husband is a bit popular around here lately."

Abigail lifted her gaze to Mrs. Bender's twinkling eyes.

"*Ach* . . . that's what I've come about."

"I'm sorry, my dear, for telling the *Englisch* girl that I knew of him."

"That's all right. And I . . . I don't want to disturb your guests, but . . ."

"You need to talk with her?"

"*Ya.*"

"Second door on the right at the top of the steps. I'll keep your tea warm for you."

Abigail got to her feet. "*Danki*, Mrs. Bender. I won't be long."

She went out of the kitchen and up the carved staircase, sliding her hand along the patina of the balustrade. She continued to pray beneath her breath until she came to the door. She knocked on the wood, and a moment later Molly stood in the doorway, considering her with an insolent smile.

"I think I rather expected you, little Amish wife. Or maybe not. Aren't your kind supposed to avoid confrontation?"

Abigail spoke in a quiet voice, though her ire was pricked by the other girl's words. "May I come in, please?"

"Sure, honey."

Abigail entered the room and closed the door behind her. She noted the heavy smell of perfume and the abundance of clothes thrown about. A half-painted scene of the countryside stood on an easel near the window, and fresh paint stained a palette. The bed was unmade, and a cigarette smoldered in an ashtray on the nightstand. It was a room of chaos for Abigail's senses despite the beautiful carved furniture and rumpled Nine Patch quilt, and for a moment she felt out of her depth. But then she remembered why she'd come.

Molly lounged with her denim-clad hip against a bureau while Abigail collected her thoughts.

"I can't believe that Joseph's got a girl fighting his battles for him."

"I'm his wife."

"Are you? I've heard it nosed about that yours was a rather hasty marriage. Maybe you're not as pure as you'd like to present—all lemonade and apple spice . . . But then, Joseph is a very persuasive man."

Abigail smiled. "It might interest you to know that my character is exactly as you say, but his is not. You see, despite the Amish dress, I think I've been like you in some ways. So I understand what's in your heart."

Molly snorted and crossed her arms. "You're a child, for all you know of the real world."

"Maybe . . . but maybe not. Maybe you came looking for Joseph because you saw that potential for good in him and you hungered for it. Or perhaps you wanted to destroy it, because it's something you can't truly understand."

"Oh, I understand a lot more about Joseph than you ever will."

Abigail lifted her chin. "And I understand that you're hurt and lonely and despise who and what you are deep inside."

"Shut up," Molly hissed. "Do you think that I'm going to stand here and take this from some little girl? Some stupid, isolated, insular little girl. So you know about the drugs, hmm? But do you know everything?"

"I know what my husband told me, that's enough."

Molly laughed as she turned her back and picked up a paintbrush. She gave the canvas a few experimental strokes, then looked over her shoulder.

"Do you know that you can never trust a drug addict? That they lie, out of habit. Do you know that it's a fact that 'once an addict, always an addict'?" She stepped back to consider the painting, then began to walk around Abigail. "Do you know how easily he took those pills from me, at the very beginning of his so-called new life? What do you think he's going to do when things get hard? When boredom sets in? And it will. Joseph is too smart to be occupied by cows and bonnets for very long. How are you ever going to trust him fully? Can you answer that?"

Abigail felt as though it was a hungry wolf that prowled around her . . . but then a word of Scripture came to her mind. *"No weapon that is formed against thee shall prosper."* This girl was using all she had because she was intimidated, scared inside, and so very, very lost.

"I can't answer that, and that answer doesn't belong to you anyway. It belongs to Joseph. So listen well to what I say . . ."

Molly stood still and cocked one hip. "Go ahead, honey."

"If you come near my husband again, in any way, it will not go well with you."

"Aren't the Amish against violence?" Molly reached and flicked at one of Abigail's *kapp* strings.

"Yes, but you see, I'm not very good at being Amish . . . so remember what I say."

She stared with intent into the other girl's eyes until Molly looked away. It was enough for Abigail.

She turned and left the room without looking back.

CHAPTER SIXTEEN

JOSEPH PACED THE TINY BEDROOM. IT WAS AFTER TEN o'clock, and Abby was nowhere to be found on the property. He hadn't told her father, but he'd found Carl and the buggy gone. He also knew, without a doubt, where she had gone. One aspect of his masculine pride was affronted at letting it seem like he'd sent his wife to fight his battles. But another part of him was touched to the depths that she would so want to defend him.

It was not that he couldn't go after her; there were three other horses in the barn. Yet something held him in check, some instinct or feeling from the Lord that he should wait.

But he wasn't good at waiting.

Finally he heard the sound of hoofbeats on the lane. He resisted the urge to run down and help her unhitch. Maybe she needed some time alone. But soon enough he heard her quiet movements as she entered the house and came up the stairs. He leaned against the windowsill, trying not to appear anxious when she walked in.

The first thing he noticed was that she looked very pale and distracted. She barely seemed aware that he was there as she slipped off her dark cape and missed the nail as she went to hang it up. She sat down on the edge of the bed, and he saw that her hands were shaking.

"Abby?" he said, coming to kneel in front of her. "What's wrong?" He caught her hands together in his own and felt their icy coldness.

She looked at him. "I saw Molly."

He nodded. "I thought that's where you were. You didn't have to do that."

"I know . . . and I felt all right when I was there, but then—coming home, I just started to shake."

He put his arms around her, rocking her forward until he felt her hands slide up tentatively along his shoulders.

"It's all right, Abby. I'm here, and you need never again deal with Molly. I promise." He felt her stiffen and drew back to study her face. "What is it?"

She wet her lips, and he was hard-pressed not to be distracted by the motion of her tongue, but he dragged his gaze back up to her blue eyes.

"It's—nothing. I'm all right now, just tired. I think I'll go to bed."

He didn't let her go. "Abby—I know you. At least, I think I do. What did she say?"

Abby wouldn't meet his eyes. "You said—you promised. And she said . . ."

"That you can never trust the word of a drug addict?"

She nodded.

He slid his hands back to rest on his thighs and looked at her. "Well, maybe she's right. That's up to you to decide. But I've been honest with you this far. It's my plan to keep on telling the truth, inasmuch as I know it about myself. But I can't spend a lifetime trying to prove something to you; that would be cheating both of us."

"I don't want to hurt you."

"You haven't. At least, the truth may hurt, but it's a clean cut. I'm fine." He paused, then touched her hand once more. "How are you?"

"Better."

"*Gut,*" he whispered.

He rose up on his knees and bent forward to press his lips against her own. *Light,* he told himself. *Keep it light. A good-night kiss . . . that's all . . .*

But she was suddenly kissing him back with a fervor, her arms around him, her hands doing small things with the back of his hair that made him catch his breath.

"Abby . . ." he managed. "What are you—"

"I just want to forget tonight. Help me forget, Joseph, please."

It would have been easy just then to give in to the pull of her words, to help her forget, but he caught an iron grip on his emotions and pushed her gently away from him. He didn't want her responsiveness when it was based on fear or worry. He shook his head, swallowing hard.

"Abby, no . . . I can't . . . not like this. You'd resent it later."

"But you're my husband." Her voice took on a shrill note.

"I know, but . . ."

"Never mind. I'm going to bed." She yanked herself away from him.

"Abby, please . . ."

"Good night!" She climbed into bed, not bothering to change into a nightdress, and yanked the quilt up and over her shoulder.

Joseph slid in misery to his own cold place on the floor.

ABIGAIL FELT SO CONFUSED AND ANGRY, SHE COULD SPIT. She tried to regulate her breathing beneath the cocoon of the quilt and to ignore Joseph's rustlings on the floor. She couldn't believe that she'd just been kissing him like that and he'd rejected her! She squirmed in embarrassment. And then that awful girl and her poisonous words . . . Why did she, his wife, repeat them to Joseph? She'd been so confident at the bed-and-breakfast, but in the reality of her own room, things seemed less clear. Her mind swirled and her stomach churned as she finally fell into an uneasy sleep.

All too soon it was morning, and she dragged herself from bed, wanting to get downstairs ahead of Joseph. She felt like a mess after having slept in her clothes, but she didn't take time to repair her *kapp* and hair. She had no idea what to say to him. She had her hand on the doorknob when his voice halted her.

"Running away?"

She turned, staring at him in the half-light as he leaned up on one elbow.

"*Ya.*" It didn't occur to her to do anything but to tell the truth.

"Come here."

She shook her head, biting her lip. "*Nee*, I've had enough of—everything last night."

He got to his feet easily, his torso half in shadow as he reached for her brush from the bureau. "Come here, Abby. Please. Let me help you with your hair."

Just the thought of him touching her hair made her mind tingle with delight, but she clung with stubbornness to the doorknob.

"Why should I?"

He smiled. "Because I'm a fool. Because I don't deserve it. Because you want to."

She glared at him. Why did he have to be so right all the time? She took one step forward and he was across the floor to meet her, his bare feet moving in silence.

"Come on. Sit down on the bed."

Reluctantly she let herself be led to sit on the edge of the bed while Joseph moved to kneel behind her on the mattress. She felt him put the brush down. His clever fingers found the hairpins with no problem. He lifted her *kapp* off and set it somewhere behind her. Then he began to unwind the complicated braid.

He took his time, separating the long strands with his fingers, reaching up to massage her scalp tenderly. She felt a constant ripple of chills play up and down her arms. Then he began to brush her hair, starting at her scalp and then arching his body to reach the very ends. He was so gentle, so thorough. She found it difficult to sit still.

"You're beautiful," he murmured, and she responded to the husky pull of his voice, though she shook her head at his words. She wished he'd kiss her, touch her somehow beyond the brush, but he kept stroking. And she soon thought she'd die with the sensuous tension spinning sparks inside of her.

"There," he said finally, leaning down over her shoulder so that their eyes could meet. "How's that feel?"

"Wonderful," she breathed.

He smiled at her, a warm, rich smile that touched his eyes and made her think of sunshine and shadows and enchanting forest glens. *He is the one who is beautiful,* she thought. And then he bent his head, and she saw the dark fall of his hair while his mouth found the warmth of her shoulder through her blouse. And then he stopped. She nearly fell backward at the sudden withdrawal of his body from behind hers. He got off the bed, replaced the brush, and leaned his hip against the bureau.

"That's the best I can do. I can't braid."

She stared at him. "I can't braid."

He arched one dark eyebrow. "What?"

"Nothing . . . I mean, nothing. Of course I can braid." She reached shaking hands up to work at her plait while he pulled his shirt on. She had to turn her head to ignore the movements of his fingers, and once more felt torn between a restlessness and a desire to wring his neck.

He pulled on his glasses and dropped a quick kiss on her cheek. "All right, sweetheart. I'll see you downstairs. I'm really hungry this morning."

He was out the door before she could speak, and she wondered for the second time in as many days whether she was losing her mind—or her heart.

CHAPTER SEVENTEEN

IT WAS A SATURDAY IN LATE OCTOBER AND THE FIRST DAY OF
the county fair when Abigail awoke with the beginnings of a bad
cold. She sneezed and sniffled and roused Joseph, who peered up
at her from his bed on the floor.

"Are you sick?"

"*Nee.*"

"You're sick. You're staying home today." He rose to stand
next to the bed, considering her with a frown as he adjusted his
glasses.

She set her lips in a firm line. "I am not staying home. I want
to go . . . with you."

He sat down on the edge of the bed and reached a firm hand
to press against her forehead. "You've got a fever. You're staying
home. I'll stay with you."

She flopped back against the pillows. "No, you can't do that.
Father is expecting you to look at the stock with him. I just wanted
to see how my sweet corn does."

And spend the day with you, she thought.

She loved the fair and the freedom it had always brought in the
past. Her father had always been too involved in his own manly
pursuits, so she'd been able to roam as she liked. And she liked the
idea of tasting treats with Joseph, walking beside him, and maybe
winning a prize. But she did feel like a day of rest would probably
do her good, so she sighed aloud in frustration.

"I'll bring you a present, then. And the vegetable ribbons aren't until tomorrow anyway. I've read the schedule." His tone was cajoling.

She pouted.

"And if you're feeling better, you can go tomorrow. But if you're not, I'm having Dr. Knepp come round."

"For a cold?"

"*Ya* . . . you could have strep throat or something."

"My throat's fine." She scrunched down beneath the quilts and sneezed again.

He laughed and bent forward to kiss the tip of her nose. "All right, little mouse. But today you rest. And wish me a blue ribbon with that bull I've been fostering for your father. I've never seen such a huge animal."

She sighed. "A big hunk of meat on four legs."

"That's right." He grinned. "And some nice prize money in the bank."

His soft beard rubbed her chin as he kissed her good-bye, and she listened with a forlorn ear to his and her father's voices as they talked, then left the house.

She buried her head in the covers and fell back to sleep. She was awakened several hours later by heavy footsteps downstairs and hopped out of bed to yank her clothes on. Everyone should still be at the fair. She did her hair with haste, then tiptoed out of the room to the top of the stairs.

JOSEPH SAT ON THE KITCHEN TABLE AND SHOOK HIS HEAD at Dr. Knepp. "No," he rasped, catching his breath. "No drugs."

"Son, you've got three broken ribs. I've got to set them. A touch of something to help ease things off won't send you back."

Joseph shook his head again, groaning faintly. "Just do it."

"All right, then. Put your hands on my shoulders."

Joseph focused everything he had on raising his arms, but he couldn't stifle the cry that came from his lips as he reached the goal.

"Good. Now I'll set them. It will hurt badly."

"I . . . understand."

The doctor sighed and ran his large hands experimentally down the rib cage. Joseph squeezed his eyes shut and bit his lip until the blood came. Dr. Knepp shifted the bones into relative position, and Joseph felt the room swim before his eyes.

"Scream if you want, son. It won't bother me."

Just then the squeak of the steps interrupted the doctor. Abby walked into the room.

"What's going on here?"

Joseph made a faint sound of distress, and the doctor turned his head.

"Wait outside, Abigail, if you please."

"In my own home? I will not. What are you doing on the kitchen table? Joseph, you're awfully pale and your mouth is bleeding. What happened?"

"Abigail, your husband's got three broken ribs. Setting them is about one of the most painful things I can do to a man. Now, please, step outside."

"Well . . . I'll help you, then," she said uncertainly.

"No," Joseph gasped.

Abigail's face fell and she turned dejectedly, easing out the front door.

"Women!" the doctor exclaimed, tightening a strip of linen with such intensity that Joseph nearly gave in to the pull that had been haunting him for the past minutes. He sagged forward, almost unconscious.

"Thank the good Lord," Dr. Knepp murmured, tying off the rest of the bandages.

"*Danki,*" Joseph whispered as the doctor eased him back, full-length, onto the kitchen table.

Abigail clenched and unclenched her hands in distress and kept a keen ear on the goings-on inside. When she heard Joseph cry out, she felt her stomach drop and tears come to her eyes. He'd been so adamant about her not staying; she couldn't understand why. Then a thought came to her mind, almost as though God had whispered it. The pain. He was in terrible pain, and based on what he'd revealed about the pills, she didn't think the doctor would be able to give him anything. Or perhaps he'd be tempted to ask for something, and it would start him off again down that long, dark road.

She straightened her spine. She could help him through the pain, if only she knew how. The screen door opened and Dr. Knepp walked out, drying his hands on a towel.

"He's unconscious."

"What happened?"

Dr. Knepp gave her a wry look. "He took it into his stubborn head to try and ride a wild horse to win some prize money. He fell off and took a good kick to the ribs."

"*Ach,*" she murmured weakly. "Will he . . . be all right?"

"He's going to need careful nursing for the next week or so. Will you do it?"

"Of course . . . I–I'm his wife."

"So you are, and you can do this, Abigail. Help him through this time."

She swallowed. "He wanted me to leave, but I think I understand."

"Of course he wanted you to leave. What man wants to appear weak in front of the woman he loves?"

"But . . ." She stopped as the doctor's words sank in. *The woman he loves?* But he couldn't—could he?

"I'll fetch your father; we'll put the boy downstairs in the master bedroom before he comes round completely."

The doctor stalked off the porch, and Abigail tiptoed inside.

Joseph lay sprawled and pale as death across the kitchen table. His shirt lay on the floor in ruins, and his rib cage was bandaged tightly. He seemed to rasp when he breathed. She drew closer, fearful of rousing him. His glasses were nowhere in sight, and blood still dripped from the corner of his mouth. She gently lifted a corner of her apron and pressed it against his lips, and he moaned in response. She stepped back, anxious now for the doctor to return.

Joseph turned his head and opened his eyes, peering up at her in an owl-like fashion.

"Ab-by?" Even the syllables were obviously painful for him to get out, and she hastened to shush him.

"Shh . . . yes, Joseph. It's Abby. I'm right here. Do you—want me to go?"

He shook his head. "*Nee* . . . promise . . . stay." He tried to cough, then half sobbed with the effort.

She caught up one of his dirt-stained hands and pressed it close to her cheek. "*Ach*, Joseph. I'll stay," she whispered. "I promise."

"*Gut,* " he mumbled, then he slipped into unconsciousness.

She stared down at him, her husband, and the doctor's voice rang in her head. "*The woman he loves . . .*"

CHAPTER EIGHTEEN

Joseph awoke to the feeling of crushing pain in his chest and the realization that each breath tortured with jagged awareness. The overwhelming desire to beg for something to help ease the pain simmered at the back of his consciousness until he felt the cool press of a cloth on his damp forehead. He opened his eyes to see Abby peering anxiously down at him, her blonde hair hanging loose in a blurred shimmer.

"Glasses?" he whispered, surprised that he had to visualize the word before he could actually get it out.

She shook her head so that he felt the soft curtain of her hair brush the top of his bare chest and trail down to cover his shoulders in a languid fall.

"The pain, Joseph . . . it's really bad, isn't it?"

Yes, he wanted to scream, but doubted he'd get enough air in his lungs to do anything but squeak. He settled for nodding, not wanting her to know how much it hurt.

"I know," she soothed, her voice softer and more womanly than he ever remembered hearing it.

He stared up into the twin pools of her blue eyes, wanting to see her better.

"I know you want the medicine, Joseph . . . the pills. I want you to know that I'm going to help you instead . . . so that you don't want, so that it doesn't hurt as much."

She leaned close to his ear to whisper the last words, being careful not to put any weight on his chest. He closed his eyes when she pressed her gentle mouth to his ear and began to sing a traditional Amish lullaby.

"*Schlof, bubeli, schlof* . . ." Sleep, baby, sleep . . .

He half smiled at the sweet, long-forgotten words and wondered just how lengthy his convalescence could be. He felt the pain melting away as visions of her singing to their own child danced across his mind. *She would be a wonderful mother,* he thought. *Strong. Patient. Loving.* He sighed and gave in to his body's need for rest, falling asleep with her soft voice still bringing peace to his mind and spirit.

ABIGAIL SLIPPED FROM THE BEDROOM AND AVOIDED HER father's gaze. She knew it was night and that she should still probably have her *kapp* on. But at the moment she didn't really care. She knew that her cheeks were flushed fever bright, and she was amazed that *Derr Herr* had brought it to her mind to sing to Joseph. But she was his wife, and she was determined to do anything she could to help her husband.

"How is the boy, then?" her father questioned in a gruff tone.

She was surprised that he was still up and that he'd asked, and she busied herself refilling the water pitcher before answering. "He is—in pain, but he fell asleep."

"Doc should have given him something for it. It's foolishness to me why he should suffer along when he doesn't have to."

Hot words surged forward on Abigail's lips, but she bit them back. How could she explain to this cold, unfeeling man what her husband was going through? He'd probably just judge Joseph and find him lacking. So she said nothing.

Her father cleared his throat. "It won't be the same—working without him, I mean. He's a *gut*, hard worker."

Abigail turned to face him. "*Ya*, he is." She lifted her chin and uttered a silent prayer. It was time for her *daed* to know.

"Father . . . Joseph never did anything that day at the picnic. It was all me. I made it up because I wanted to get even with him for not being as interested in me as I would have liked. I betrayed him, and he still stood up for me. I don't expect your forgiveness or your understanding, but I want you to know. *Derr Herr* has prompted my heart many times to tell you, but I've never had the courage." She swallowed hard. "I know that you've never approved of me even when I was a child. I don't know why, nor does it matter really. Joseph has taught me a lot about the kind of person I had become, and it's not been a pretty thing to look upon. But I've changed, I think. Or at least, I'm trying to. I just wanted you to know so you'd stop blaming him for something he never did."

She turned back to the water pitcher, her heart pounding in her chest. But she was amazed at how good it felt to finally speak the truth. The Bible verse "And the truth shall make you free" drifted across her mind, and she knew that it was true. No matter what her father's reaction might be, she had told the truth before the Lord and she felt more clean inside than she ever had before.

She jumped when she felt a light touch on her arm and turned to see her father standing close. She gazed up at him and was amazed to see his bleary blue eyes awash with tears.

"Abigail . . . I . . . I, too, have much to confess. I knew that Joseph did nothing that day."

"What?"

"I . . . was watching you both. I saw him turn from you. I saw him walk away."

"I don't understand. Then why would you . . ."

Her father took out his hankie and swiped at his eyes with his head bowed. "I worried for you. I—always have. I wanted to keep you safe. I thought if you were married, perhaps you'd stop wanting to go away. I also used the boy—it was just too easy an opportunity to pass by."

Her mind whirled, but one thing struck her especially. "But, Father, how did you know that I wanted to go away?"

He gave a heaving sob, and she instinctively laid a hand on his brawny forearm.

"Because . . . she . . . went away."

"She?"

He caught his breath. "Your *mamm* . . . I've always told you she died in a buggy accident. That much was true. But she was driving that buggy to leave the community, to leave the Amish and me . . . and you."

Abigail dropped her hand and sagged back against the counter. All of the idealized images she'd nursed of her mother over the years swirled in her brain until she thought she might pass out, but then a thought struck her.

"Why should I believe you?" she asked. She had to ask. He'd been so cold, so unfeeling for years. Perhaps, even now, he was telling her this to hold her somehow.

He nodded. "You've a right to ask that. Come with me."

She followed him as he walked to the master bedroom door, then eased it open. He entered the room soft-footed, and she glanced at the bed. Joseph was still asleep.

Her father went to a small cedar chest that sat on his bureau. Abigail knew it held important papers and various letters from relatives, but she was surprised when he turned the chest over. He felt the bottom of the wood, and then she watched as he slid back a hidden panel, revealing a secret compartment carved into the depth of the wood.

In the dim light of the single kerosene lamp she'd left burning, she caught the shimmer of a silver thimble as it fell into her father's large palm. Then he pulled out a piece of paper, crumpled and yellowed with age. He slid the bottom back into place and set the chest back. Then he turned and reached out his hand to Abigail.

"Take these," he whispered.

She obeyed, not wanting Joseph to wake, and left the room with her father following as the press of the small thimble burned in her palm.

CHAPTER NINETEEN

MY DEAREST SOLOMON, MY LITTLE ABBY,

SOMEDAY I HOPE THAT YOU CAN BOTH FORGIVE ME FOR WHAT I AM DOING, BUT I CANNOT GO ON ANY LONGER AS THINGS ARE. I'VE TRIED. THE LORD KNOWS HOW HARD I'VE TRIED. FIRST, I BELIEVED THAT MARRYING WOULD EASE THE RESTLESSNESS IN MY SOUL. THEN I HOPED THAT THE PRECIOUS GOLDEN-HAIRED BABY WOULD MAKE A WAY FOR ME. BUT THERE IS NOTHING THAT HAS BEEN ABLE TO TAKE AWAY THIS DESIRE, NO, THIS KNOWLEDGE THAT I DO NOT BELONG WITH THE AMISH. IT DOESN'T MATTER HOW I WAS RAISED OR HOW LOVING AND KIND THE COMMUNITY IS TO ME. I NEVER BELONGED. I'VE KNOWN THAT SINCE I WAS A CHILD AND WANTED TO THROW APPLE PEELS AT MY MOTHER WHEN SHE INSISTED IT WAS MY DUTY TO HELP WITH THE AUTUMN CANNING. I'VE KNOWN IT SINCE THE DAY I MARRIED. I KNEW IT ON THE DAY YOU WERE BORN, ABBY. I JUST WANT OUT. I WANT ANOTHER WAY OF LIFE THAT DOESN'T INVOLVE THE TERRIBLE CONFINING PRESSURE OF BEING AN AMISH WOMAN.

SOLOMON, THERE IS NO ONE ELSE—I SAY THIS BECAUSE I KNOW THAT YOU WILL THINK IT. THERE IS NO ONE ELSE BUT MYSELF. IF I STAY I WILL POISON OUR DAUGHTER, HER THOUGHTS, HER HEART UNTIL SHE, TOO, SENSES MY DESIRE TO RUN AND THEN WANTS TO RUN AS WELL. I WILL

*NOT LEAVE THAT LEGACY TO HER. I KNOW THAT YOU WILL
DO RIGHT BY HER AND CHERISH HER AS YOU ALWAYS HAVE.*

    *ABBY, SOMEDAY, IF YOU ARE READING THIS, I WANT
YOU TO KNOW THAT I STARTED A QUILT WHEN YOU WERE
TWO YEARS OLD. EVEN NOW, WHEN YOU ARE FIVE AND
DEEPLY ASLEEP, THE QUILT IS NOT FINISHED. I DOUBT
THAT YOU WILL EVER SEE IT, BUT THE PATTERN IS CALLED
"ABBY'S WISH." I COULD NOT FINISH IT BECAUSE I CANNOT
BEAR THE WISH THAT I HAVE FOR YOU, THAT YOU, TOO,
COULD BE FREE. BUT IT IS NOT FAIR TO TAKE YOU FROM
YOUR FATHER, FROM YOUR HOME. PLEASE FORGIVE ME
SOMEDAY, MY DEAREST DAUGHTER. I LOVE YOU.*

    *SOLOMON, I LOVE YOU AS WELL. PLEASE KNOW THIS, FOR
ALWAYS. TELL EVERYONE THE TRUTH, THAT I ABANDONED
YOU AND MY CHILD. IT DOESN'T MATTER. PLEASE GO ON
WITH YOUR LIFE. MARRY A GOOD AMISH WOMAN, SOME-
ONE WHO WILL BE KIND TO ABBY, BUT KEEP LIVING. I AM
NOT WORTH YOUR GIVING UP OR CLOSING UP AS I KNOW
YOU MIGHT DO.*

    *IT IS LATE NOW, AND I MUST GO. I WILL LEAVE THE
HORSE AND BUGGY IN TOWN. I HAVE LEARNED TO DRIVE
AND WILL BE AWAY BEFORE SUNRISE. PLEASE DO NOT TRY
TO FIND ME. I LOVE YOU BOTH.*

    RACHEL

Abigail pressed the silver thimble into the palm of her hand
with such force that she thought for a moment that she could still
feel the warmth of her mother's finger within its hold. But she knew
now that there was nothing but the truth. She lifted her eyes to her
father's as he sat still and quiet across from her at the kitchen table.

Her eyes filled with tears. "I have felt like this, like her—
before Joseph."

"I know."

She impulsively reached to him. "But, Father, since Joseph and I . . . Well, the feeling's gone away. I am content to be his wife. I want to have a life with him. And we want to share that with you."

Her father gave a giant sniff. "I don't deserve that. I've treated you harshly all these years, because I was afraid and I was angry at her. But you were just a little thing who needed a *daed*. I haven't been one to you."

She drew a deep breath, her thoughts teetering between childhood expectation and the reality of life as she'd come to know it.

"*Nee*, you weren't the perfect father, but you did the best you could. And I accept that. I wouldn't change a thing if I could." And she realized that it was true. She wouldn't have become as strong-willed and resourceful if she'd been raised a different way. And it was *Derr Herr* who put people together in families, and it was He who allowed her to have the father that she did.

Then she did something she had not ever been able to do. She rose and came near to where her father sat. Stretching out her slender arms, she bent and embraced his broad shoulders, laying her face against the back of his neck. She felt him shake, then sob, and then he turned and hugged her tightly to his chest.

"My daughter, my child." He wept.

"My *daed*," she returned, her tears falling freely.

A sudden low moan from the adjoining bedroom broke the moment, and they both sniffed. Then her father dried her tears with his handkerchief, and Abigail gave him a brilliant smile.

"Go on, now. Tend to your husband. You're a good wife, Abby."

She nodded and moved toward the bedroom door.

ON THE SECOND DAY, JOSEPH DEVELOPED A FEVER, WHICH made Dr. Knepp frown with concern while Abigail anxiously watched the examination.

"I suppose a bit of a fever is to be expected, but I don't want him getting an infection. I'll leave these antibiotics for him. See that he takes them three times a day—morning, noon, and night. How's his pain?"

The doctor avoided her eyes, and she whispered her reply in a steady voice. "I know about the drugs, Dr. Knepp, and why he can't have the pain medicine. He told me. I—I've been trying to—distract him—as best as I can when he's awake."

The doctor cleared his throat. "I see. Well then, keep up the good medicine." He patted her shoulder.

She would help Joseph get well. But as the doctor left and she was alone with only the quiet sound of her husband's breathing, she realized that getting him well was the least of what she wanted. She wasn't sure how or when, but somehow she had fallen in love with him. Deeply in love. And there was an honesty in admitting it that liberated her thinking and drove out all shame about how their marriage began. If the doctor was right, if Joseph loved her and she loved him, then Joseph might be right that the Lord had a plan in all of this. She was only too happy to follow along.

Joseph awoke by slow degrees, his pain half swallowed by tangled, warm dreams of Abby and her singing. But now something was tickling his nose, and he opened his eyes. He stared up at her, realizing that it was broad daylight and that she was properly *kapped* and dressed. But his nose still itched. He peered sideways and she laughed, a melodic, charming sound that he'd not heard often enough.

"You need to go into town as soon as you're able and get new glasses. The last ones were trampled by the horse. But in the meantime, two tokens from the fair . . ." She stopped twitching his nose and pulled away two prize ribbons, one blue, one red.

"What . . ."

"Your big, nasty bull took the blue ribbon, and my sweet corn took second place with the red. Aren't you happy?"

He gave her a lopsided smile. "Very . . . but my ribs still hurt quite a bit."

"I'm sorry. Is there anything that I can do?" she murmured, bending over him.

"*Ach*, I don't know . . . It seems that while I've been ill, some wondrous nurse has visited my bedside. Might she still be about?"

Even without his glasses, he recognized her flush and enjoyed it. She bit her lip and giggled, then she straightened to adjust his pillows. Her arm brushed against his face and he caught the sweet scent of her and wished he wasn't an invalid and could act like a man with his new bride. But for now he'd settle for her closeness.

"Dr. Knepp says that you're to sit up today, and if you're very, very good, you can sit in a chair tomorrow."

He grimaced. "I hate being down."

She laughed. "But I plan to keep you properly entertained, so you needn't worry about that." She pulled back and lifted a tray from the bedside table to settle on his lap.

"Really?" he asked. "How? Maybe just telling me will make me feel good."

"Well, I thought first of all that I'd help feed you."

He frowned. "I'm not a babe."

"No," she whispered in a husky voice that sent shivers down his spine. "I can see that. But there's something very intimate about letting someone else give you—sustenance." She drew out the word suggestively, and he decided right then and there that he'd eat anything from gruel to noodles from her hand.

She took her time adjusting the cotton napkin around his neck, letting it trail up his chest above the bandages, then leaning close while she fooled overlong with the knot. He felt himself growing increasingly warm and not with fever this time. At least, he thought wryly, not the ill kind of fever anyway.

But as it turned out, Abby's sliding one delicious spoonful of vegetable soup after another into his willing mouth was more than satisfying.

CHAPTER TWENTY

THE FULL MOON OF AN EARLY NOVEMBER NIGHT CAST ITS luminescent beams in shadowy play across the master bedroom. Abigail shifted in the rocking chair where she'd slept for the past weeks of Joseph's recovery and cringed when it squeaked. She nearly jumped, though, when he spoke from the shadows.

"It's foolishness, Abby, you know?"

"Are you dreaming, Joseph? What's foolishness? Do you have a fever again?"

He rose up on one elbow on the bed, and she could see the moonlight stray across his chest. Dr. Knepp had removed the bandages yesterday and had said that Joseph might resume light daily activities.

"What's foolishness?" she asked again, reaching to massage her neck where it rested against the hard wood of the chair.

"It's foolishness that one of us has to sleep either on the floor or in the chair. This bed is big enough for two people, and the weather is getting colder. Your father told me yesterday that he's quite comfortable upstairs in the spare bedroom, so why don't you get out of that miserable chair and come over here and lie down?"

There was a long pause.

He sighed aloud. "No, Abby, I'm not asking for anything except that you stop being uncomfortable. It makes me uncomfortable even to look at that chair. I'll tell you what. I will roll up our lovely double wedding ring quilt and put it like a fat, happy sausage down the middle of the bed. And you can stay on your side, and I'll stay on mine."

She considered further. "I might roll over, though, and reinjure your ribs."

"Oh, Abby, come on. Grow up just a little bit."

"What does that mean?"

"Okay. I have said what I'm going to say on the matter. If you want to freeze and contort yourself in that torture chair, it's entirely up to you. Good night."

Abigail listened to the sheets rustle as he made himself comfortable. It would be lovely to stretch out fully, but her pride was nicked by his words, and she kept her stubborn seat.

I'll wait until he falls asleep, she thought. *Then maybe I'll do as he suggests.*

So she waited, and the idea of being close to Joseph grew more and more appealing. When she thought he was finally asleep, she rose to tiptoe across the room, nearly tripping over George the cat as she moved toward the bed. She settled as gingerly as she could on the edge opposite Joseph and felt for the reassuring bulk of the "sausage," as he called it. She lay down on her back and adjusted her hair, staring up at the ceiling.

"Are you scared of sharing the bed with me?" a soft voice asked.

"No," she lied.

"I used to be scared of storms when I was a kid, especially when I was living on the streets and had no shelter. The whole idea of home or just having a home was so unfamiliar and seemed so out of reach to me then. It's just wonderful to be able to lie here with you and know that we're safe."

"I've never thought about what life must be like for a homeless person."

"The homeless face the brutal elements of the weather, but they also battle physical and emotional and spiritual storms."

She turned slightly, interested now in what he was saying. "Can you tell me about your time on the streets without it bothering you too much?"

"There's not a whole lot to say except that I met a lot of people who were hurt and in need of the Lord's help, but in some cases, they had never even heard of His name."

She played with the pattern of the quilt with a fingertip and shook her head. "I guess I never thought of what it would be like to really leave here. I had this idea that it would be easier somehow or more fulfilling, but I realize that life is just as hard, just as challenging no matter where you are."

"Yes, but having a community of people behind you makes it so much easier. You know the rules. You know what to expect. You know how to fit in. For some people, I guess all of that would be pretty boring, but I've had my taste and my fill of a life with no rules."

She stretched her open palm across the lump of a quilt in between them and felt his hand enclose hers. She fell asleep with a smile on her lips.

JOSEPH AWOKE TO THE DOUBLE SENSATION OF WARM SUN-shine on his face and an even warmer Abby next to his side. Somehow she had leapt the quilt barrier and was nestled against him as comfortably as if she'd always slept there. He kept his breathing shallow and even for fear of waking her and breaking the moment. It was enough just to hold her and smell the fresh mint of her hair and that delicate scent of Abby that was something between a storm and the sea. Soon enough, though, she opened her eyes and jumped like a scalded cat.

"What are you doing?" she asked, outrage in her voice.

"What am *I* doing?"

"You are supposed to stay on your side of the quilt."

"I'm sorry. I may need new glasses, but it's you who appears to have forgotten about the barrier."

He watched her gaze around the bed, and a bright blush stained her cheeks as she realized he was right. She started to pull away, but he caught her back. "Just a minute. Where are you going?"

"To my side of the quilt."

He laughed and then groaned lightly as the pain in his ribs stabbed him.

"Now see what you've done," she admonished. "Let me go."

He reached beneath her arm with unerring fingers and began to tickle her. "When was the last time you played, Abigail Lambert?" he teased.

She squealed and, in her attempt to get away, accidentally knocked him aside the head.

"Oh, I'm so sorry, but—I'm really not." She laughed as she got away. "And maybe it's me who should remind you of what real play is like."

He rubbed his head as he considered her words. "I would be glad to see anything that you have to offer in the line of play."

She danced around the room in her nightdress, her hair a golden cloud, and picked up her clothes and small toiletries here and there. Then she caught up a towel from the back of a chair. "Unfortunately, it's time for my bath, Mr. Lambert, and you will have no play in that." She turned on her heel with her nose in the air and left him smiling on the bed.

He wondered how often she would continue to move in the dance between girlhood and womanhood. He would always find her entertaining, but he longed for a more mature relationship with his wife. She had told him once that she was patient, but he knew deep inside that he was just as patient. And, he thought with a grin, maybe just a bit more plotting than she was.

With a light heart, Abigail dragged the hip bath out near the woodstove. Her father greeted her with a smile and rose from his rocker to leave the room. She thought how wonderful it would have been to have had his smiles all her life, but she knew that it was never too late to have something put right. So she dropped a light kiss on his cheek and put a kettle of water on the stove to heat.

"There's one thing more that I wanted to talk to you about, Abby," her *daed* said. "I've been wrong also all these years about keeping that quilt up in its frame. I want you to have your own quilting and to make a wedding quilt for you and Joseph."

Abigail paused as she watched slow bubbles begin to form in the bottom of the kettle. Her father's words were a balm to her spirit, but she was struck with inspiration at the same time.

"You know, Father, I've been thinking, too, about the quilt and *Mamm's* letter. I wondered if you'd mind my finishing the Abby's Wish quilt?"

He gazed at her across the kitchen. "Why would you want that?"

She thought hard and examined her heart. "Because part of accepting who I am in the Lord is accepting who my mother was. I want to finish that quilt with some joyful women who will remind me that this life is more than worth living, even if the people we love don't always turn out the way we hope they will. I wanted a mother for years, but I've come to realize that I can be mothered in other ways, by other women and friends. The quilt would be a celebration of all of that."

For a moment she thought he might cry again, but he simply nodded.

"That's good enough for me, and very wise for such a young woman as yourself to realize."

"Thank you, Father."

He cleared his throat. "Well, I'll just take the sheet and cedar off of the quilt, then, and tighten the rolls of the frame up a bit so that it can be ready for you. When do you want to have your quilting party?"

Abigail considered. If she were through with her housework and Joseph remained well in the afternoon, she might be able to take Carl around and deliver individual invitations to a quilting for Saturday. That gave her three days to prepare. She glanced around the rather dim kitchen with some doubt but decided that true friends would accept her home in any condition.

"Saturday," she told her *daed*.

"Fair enough. I'll take Joseph somewhere that day to get away from all the female fussing."

"I'm sure he'll enjoy that."

Her father nodded again, then he left the room, going out the back door. Abigail pulled the screen around the tub and emptied the kettle full of hot water into the bath. She filled yet another and dropped a bar of homemade mint soap into the tub. She played dreamily with her hair as she thought about waking up in her husband's arms. He was so strong and so handsome, but he was also smart and funny. She realized that she liked the edges of his humor and that it was a fair complement to her own.

When the rest of the water was heated, she slipped into the tub and began a leisurely wash. A thumping noise, followed by the opening creak of the master bedroom door, drew her upright in the tub, and she squeaked in surprise. "Who's there?"

"No one," Joseph answered, and she could hear the smile in his voice.

"You get back in that bed and stay outside of this screen."

"I just wanted to get some milk. I had no intentions of playing in your bath. Is that all right?"

"Just get the milk and go." She hugged her chest to her bended knees and longed for the towel or her dress, which hung out of reach atop the screen. She would not give him the satisfaction of seeing even so much as a silhouette of her form, which he could probably do by the light of the stove and the thinness of the screen.

She heard Joseph moving about the kitchen.

"Father will be back soon."

"Well then, you'd better get out of that tub, hadn't you?"

She fumed at his good humor and decided to concentrate on finishing her bath. She caught up the soft mint soap and squished it between her fingers, enjoying the feel and the smell. She made haste to scrub her arms and shoulders and decided she'd wash her hair at a more convenient and private time. Suddenly the towel, which had hung out of reach, was flipped down atop her head, and she blinked in surprise.

"Thought I'd help you out a little bit," he said, very near the screen.

She clutched the towel. "I don't need any help, and I really think that you're overdoing things and should just lie down."

"Well . . ." And then her skirt fell on the floor beside the tub. "You didn't mind my help last night when that chair was so uncomfortable. I thought we were making some progress toward understanding each other better."

He flicked her blouse off its perch to land next to the skirt, and she stared with fury at the outline of his body on the other side of the screen.

"Oh, I understand you perfectly," she replied. "And I am going to catch pneumonia if I don't get out of this tub soon."

Her apron landed atop the other clothes.

"We can't have that, can we? All right, I'll leave the lady to her bath and me to my milk."

With great relief she heard the master bedroom door creak, but then he called out in a loud voice, "Do you know, it's an interesting fact that ladies used to actually take baths in milk. It softened their skin."

She couldn't reply, and hoped for a wild second that he would trip on the way back to his bed.

CHAPTER TWENTY-ONE

JOSEPH WAS WELL ENOUGH THAT AFTERNOON FOR THEM TO make a trip to town to get him fitted for new glasses. Abigail bundled up in a warm cloak, as the weather had changed and winter was truly upon the area. It had even begun to snow a little.

She had to drive Carl, as Joseph couldn't see two feet in front of him, and she thought it funny that her husband was nervous about her handling the horse. She decided to pull on Carl's reins and make him break trot just to tease Joseph.

"Do you need me to drive?" he asked in a gruff tone.

"No," she replied sweetly. "I'm quite capable."

"Then you're either as blind as I am or you are deliberately baiting me. Which is it?"

"I'd go for the baiting."

He was silent for a moment. "So you're actually playing with me, your husband, right?"

She turned to smile at him. "*Ya.* You need more play in your life."

He rolled his eyes.

They passed the rest of the ride in companionable silence and arrived at the office of the *Englisch* optometrist, Dr. Stokes.

Abigail came around to Joseph's side of the buggy. "Do you need help down?" she asked.

He jumped beside her with ease and caught her close in a hugging embrace. "Yes, you can hold me and help me up the steps so that I don't break my neck."

She pushed him away and they both laughed. He then caught her arm, and they walked together up the steps to the office door.

Abigail was struck by how modern the room was with its glossy magazines and the well-dressed receptionist who greeted them with a smile. A few months ago, her first impulse would have been to dive for the magazines and catch a glimpse of the outside world. She now knew that the man giving his name at the reception window was her world, and the thought thrilled her to her core. She took a seat on one of the comfortable leather couches, and Joseph soon joined her.

"Look," he said, "do you want to go and get some shopping done while I'm here? It might take a bit to get an exam and pick out some glasses. Although"—he laughed—"I know there's not much potential for style in Amish glasses, so I'll just have to do the best I can."

"You'd look good in anything," she said in a matter-of-fact voice, and he leaned forward to brush his lips against hers.

"Thank you, Abby. That's quite a compliment coming from the most beautiful girl I know."

He left her to go with the nurse, and Abigail decided to begin offering invitations to her quilting while she had the chance. She crossed the busy street and made her way to Yoder's. She was glad to see Tillie, who gave her a bright smile.

"And where's that handsome husband of yours?"

"He's getting new eyeglasses. I came over to invite you and the other ladies from the kitchen to come to my house this Saturday for a quilting. It'll be my wedding quilt since I never really had the chance to do one before we married."

She felt no shame in bringing up the hurriedness of her marriage. It all seemed like part of what was supposed to happen, now that she thought of it.

Tillie agreed at once. "I know I can be there, and I'm sure Judith and the other ladies would love it. What time should we come?"

Abigail settled on ten o'clock, knowing that there was actually only a small part of the quilt to finish. Normally a quilting would begin very early and last the whole of the day.

"I have an idea," Tillie said. "Why don't we make it a quilting and kitchen frolic too. We can help stock your pantry, eat some good food, and do our quilting."

"That sounds wonderful," Abigail said with a smile. "But I don't want to impose on anyone. I'll just be glad to have you all there."

Tillie waved away her words. "It's no imposition. I'll tell the other women, and I know that they'll be so glad to help. Food is easy for us around here, and so is friendship."

Abigail blinked back tears at Tillie's spontaneous generosity and kindness. It was almost as if the Lord was revealing to her that, by being patient, by waiting for Him to work, she would see Him bring forth an abundance in her life. An overflowing cup . . . or an overflowing pantry. Both were wonderful, but the friendship was especially something to be treasured.

Abigail left the restaurant feeling a deep contentment in her spirit, which increased when she saw Joseph coming down the street toward her.

"Well, how did it go?" she asked, staring up at his handsome face.

"Great. My new glasses will be ready in about an hour, so we have some time to ourselves," he said. "Abby, your father has paid me well these last months, and I'd like to buy my bride a gift. What would be your heart's desire, madam?"

Abigail thought hard. She couldn't remember the last time someone had bought her something just for pleasure.

"You got me George as a wedding gift," she pointed out.

Joseph frowned. "I like the cat, but that is not a true wedding gift. You deserve something beautiful."

She was aware of people passing them in the street as they stood together, but it didn't matter. She felt like the very world could go by and she'd be content just to stand with Joseph forever.

"George is beautiful to me. And . . . so are you." She whispered the last words shyly, and he reached down and caught her hand.

"You continue to amaze me, Abby." His voice was hoarse. "You've got me coming and going, and I never know which end is up with you. It feels so good that I want . . . I want . . ."

The sudden appearance of an *Englisch* woman with bright red curls broke the moment. For a moment Abigail's heart dropped to her stomach, then she realized that it was not Molly. But she recognized in that moment that she still felt vulnerable and a little insecure, especially toward these tender new feelings for her husband.

"Did you see that redhead?" she asked in a small voice.

"Yep."

"So . . . do you . . . think of Molly?"

"No. I think about how much time I wasted in foolishness and pursuit of the things and people who I thought would make me happy. The truth is that I've never felt more content than to be here with you, in the middle of a little country town, while the rest of the world goes by in a blur of colors and all I can truly see is your beautiful face."

She blushed. "You need those glasses."

He laughed aloud. "All right, Abby Lambert. Now tell me what you want for a wedding gift, or I'll buy you chocolate in a cardboard box and write you a bad card."

She couldn't bring to mind anything that she actually needed. It seemed that the Lord had supplied her with all that a heart could want, but then an idea came to her. "All right," she said, smiling. "Let's go to Stolfus's Dry Goods."

"Dry goods? That doesn't sound very romantic."

"Oh, you'd be surprised."

They walked along the sidewalk together, and Abigail noticed how many Amish people mixed with the *Englisch*, and how many women, both *Englisch* and Amish, threw interested glances in Joseph's direction.

She put her hand in his and squeezed, and they walked up the broad wooden steps to Stolfus's together. They entered to the familiar scent of spices, soaps, and a myriad of good things, but it was the fabric that drew Abigail's eye.

She had taken Joseph's measurements for a new shirt when he was ill and figured she might make him a new one in a color besides white. But knowing his stubbornness, she knew he wouldn't want to buy the fabric if he realized it was for him. So she pretended a great interest in a sky blue material that she said would be just right for something personal that she had in mind.

As she turned away from the counter after giving her order for the dry goods, she accidentally bumped into a small display of soaps and sachets. Catching a rose sachet in her outstretched hand, she lifted the pouch to her nose and breathed in deeply.

"Mmm, this is lovely." She held it up for him to try.

He shook his head. "No. I have a particular preference for mint, especially soap."

She blushed and put the sachet down, and then he was serious.

"Abby, do you like that perfumy thing? If you want it, I'll be glad to get it for you."

She shook her head as Mrs. Stolfus handed her the fabric across the counter. She couldn't help but notice the more than curious glances the woman cast in their direction, but she ignored them and turned back to Joseph, who was studying the sachets with an indifferent eye.

"Joseph, I've got everything I need except some thread and needles. I better get some extra needles for the quilting too. And I was thinking about making teaberry cookies for Saturday. I need some dried teaberries."

She led him back to the dried spices and found the small red berries. Soon they had checked out and were headed back to the optometrist's. She clutched her brown-paper-wrapped fabric and thread with secret pleasure, trying to decide when she'd get a chance to sew for him.

At Dr. Stokes's office, Abigail thought Joseph looked even more handsome in his new circular frames and lenses than he had in his old pair.

"Now you're Amish," she declared, and Dr. Stokes laughed.

Joseph smiled, and she thought how endearing he was to her heart, even though he could drive her to temper sometimes. She decided that they made for a good stew together, like one of Judith's best recipes. A little spice mixed with the taste of love could make for a sumptuous life.

They were soon back behind Carl and headed out of town when it occurred to Abigail to invite both Katie Stahley and Mrs. Knepp to the quilting.

"Do you mind making a few more stops?" she asked him.

"Not at all. Where are we going?"

Soon they turned down the Stahleys' narrow lane, and Abigail hopped out to give a quick invitation for Katie through her husband. She was back in the buggy within moments.

"Is she coming?" Joseph asked.

"I don't know. Her husband is kind of shy. He wouldn't even look me in the eye when I was giving him the invitation."

"Blinded by beauty," Joseph declared.

"Ha."

"And where else do we have to go?"

"Just to Dr. and Mrs. Knepp's, and that's all."

"Maybe we can stay and visit with them for a while, if you wouldn't mind," Joseph suggested.

"That would be nice. I'd like to thank Mrs. Knepp once more for the quilt."

"Ahhh. You mean the sausage roll."

"Yes," she agreed. "The sausage roll."

JOSEPH FELT GOOD ABOUT GOING TO VISIT THE KNEPPS. HE would always be very grateful for the role that they had played in his past. They were good, kindhearted people, but more than that, he knew that they lived out the love that was preached about in Amish meetings. He also wanted Abby to have the chance to get to know Mrs. Knepp better, perhaps as a mother figure or someone to turn to.

The Knepps' farmhouse came into sight, and Joseph was glad to see the doctor's truck out front.

"Joseph," Abby murmured under her breath, "I don't think Mrs. Knepp likes me very much."

"What?"

"No, I'm serious. Even though she gave us the quilt and wished us well, I bet she still remembers the time I was a little girl and pulled all of her tulips up by their roots when they were just blooming."

He laughed and turned his head with interest. "Why would you do that?"

"I thought I was saving them from being cut, so I took them home and put them in water—dirt, roots, and all. My father was so mad at me. And Mrs. Knepp's face was as red as a beet when she found out it was me."

"What did the doctor say?" he asked.

"He laughed, as usual," Abby answered.

Joseph smiled. "I'm sure she's forgiven you." He took Abby's hand and helped her down, and they both went to the door.

Joseph knocked on the door, and Mrs. Knepp opened it. Abby ducked her head as if she were still carrying tulip stains on her cloak, but the older woman greeted them both with a broad smile.

"Come in, come in. I'm so glad to see you both. It's chilly out today, and I've got a fresh baking of gingerbread that I just took out of the oven. The doctor is here too. He just returned from delivering twins and is a bit testy from being up half the night."

"Oh," Abby said. "Maybe we should come back another time."

Mrs. Knepp shook her head. "There is no 'better time' in a doctor's life, my dear. Just come right in and make yourselves at home."

With Abby at his heels, Joseph followed the smell of gingerbread, and they soon were sitting around the kitchen table sharing coffee and gingerbread with fresh whipped cream.

The doctor talked with Joseph about crops and the weather, then Mrs. Knepp invited Abby to come into the sitting room for their own conversation.

Joseph noticed that Abby was hesitant to leave him, but Mrs. Knepp pressed a kind hand on his shoulder.

"No, no," she said. "You menfolk stay here while Abigail and I have a woman-to-woman talk."

The doctor laughed. "You go on. Joseph and I will have seconds on the gingerbread."

ABIGAIL FOLLOWED MRS. KNEPP INTO THE COMFORTABLE sitting room. A fire burned with cheerful vigor at the hearth, while comfortable chairs covered with bright afghans and quilts dotted the room. It was not the room of a rich man, as Abigail knew the doctor most certainly could be, but rather the room of a true home.

"I'd like my house to look like this," Abigail said.

Mrs. Knepp smiled. "Yes, I've always found that comfortable

and neat does just as well as fancy and frilly. But, please, let's sit down and talk. I'd like you to tell me the truth, and I give you my word that it won't be repeated to anyone else. How is it going with you two? The doctor told me that Joseph had shared his past with you. That's a big thing for a new wife to swallow. Are you all right?"

Abigail nodded. "*Ya*. We really have spent time talking about it and how both of us need to lean on the Lord for support to get through life. I don't mean just looking ahead long-term, but day-to-day living. Or maybe hour-to-hour living."

Mrs. Knepp gave Abigail a warm smile. She reached out and patted Abigail's hand. "I still remember the tulips, you know."

Abigail blushed. "I just told Joseph about that on the way here. I wish I could take that back. They were so beautiful."

"You were so impulsive, but I wish that I could take back my anger at a little girl who just thought she was doing the right thing. I want you to know that I sense a change in you . . . a calmness of spirit and peace that was not there before. I also want to tell you that I've prayed for you often."

Abigail bit her lip. "Thank you so much. You don't know what it means to me to have the praise of another woman, especially one that I admire." She smiled. "I actually came today to invite you to attend my wedding quilting. I've only asked a few women. The truth is that I haven't spent much time trying to make friends with the women of our community."

Mrs. Knepp smiled. "But you have all the time in the world to do that now."

"I know. I just wish I'd known it sooner."

As they said their good-byes, Mrs. Knepp pressed a small package into her hands. "Just a little something, my dear, to help with Saturday."

Abigail climbed into the buggy and started to unwrap the gift. "What is it?" Joseph asked.

Abigail sat and stared at the contents of the package. It was a beautiful case of quilting needles, some with golden eyes, and a bright silver needle threader. "Oh, they're so beautiful."

Joseph cast an eye over the small gift. "If you say so. They look sharp to me, and I can just see one of the ladies pricking her finger and getting blood all over the quilt."

"Do you have to be so positive?" Abigail asked.

Joseph laughed. "Well, I try."

She sighed. "On a more serious note, there is one more woman I would like to invite to the quilting, but I don't have time to deliver a personal invitation."

"Who is it? We still have half the afternoon."

"Your sister," she said in a quiet voice. "But I know she's too far away."

"Oh . . . that's really nice. She'd love it. I told you that she is an artist, and she'd think quilting with a bunch of Amish women would be just the height of modern art." He pressed her hand. "Thank you for thinking of her."

Abigail nodded and held her new needles in a tight grasp.

CHAPTER TWENTY-THREE

JOSEPH TOOK ABBY'S HOPE OF INVITING HIS SISTER TO heart and stole away in the dark of night to put a call in to New York. Angel said she'd be on a plane Friday night.

"But I don't have any way to pick you up at the airport. The horse just will not do."

She'd laughed, his own laugh, many gentle tones lighter. "You forget that I'm a New Yorker and pretty resourceful, Joe. I'll be there, but don't tell her. Okay?"

He'd agreed and was glad he'd made it back to the master bedroom in time for a cuddle with Abby. It was gradually becoming a regular thing, this touching of her skin to his. One hand against him here, one knee drawn up in sleeper's balance, her cheek resting against his shoulder. It was enough to both lull his sensibilities and make him want to scream at the same time.

THE MORNING OF THE QUILTING DAWNED BRIGHT AND CLEAR but ice cold. A fine frost covered the fields, making enchanted things of the barren trees and the stray bent plants. Abigail was excited as she looked out the window. She'd never been the hostess of a social gathering before and wasn't entirely sure of what was expected of her, but she would make a good try at it. Joseph and her father had already left, the buggy tracks on the driveway proof of their eagerness to get away before any of the invited females showed up.

Joseph had kissed her, though, and wished her well. "I'll pray for you," he'd whispered. "That you will have a fulfilling and peaceful time with your friends."

She clung to that prayer as the first buggy arrived and she saw the ladies from Yoder's all pile out in a ridiculous number from behind one horse. She wondered how they had managed to fit, especially when they came bearing baskets and boxes and bags bulging with supplies. She opened the door, and George the cat skittered outside.

Judith was the first to enter and gave Abigail a big hug. "Thank you, Abby, for having us. It's a good, cold day to stay warm and happy inside."

Abigail tried to help the older woman with her packages, but Judith waved her away. "No, honey. You just go on ahead and greet your guests. I'll take care of all our stuff."

Abigail hugged each woman from Yoder's in turn, ending with Tillie, who had a broad smile on her face.

"We brought just about everything you could think of for your pantry, Abby. And we'll have your quilt finished in no time."

Abigail wanted to cry, but laughed instead. She felt so overwhelmed by the generosity and love that filled the room. She watched as Judith and Ruth made short work of filling the shelves of her pantry and was amazed at the canning jars full of bright colors. Yellow peaches and corn and squash, red tomatoes and jellies and preserves, green beans and peas and bread-and-butter pickles . . . The baskets kept producing. Soon she had a more than an adequately stuffed provision of stores for the coming winter.

"There," Judith said with a smile. "Next year we'll come again at canning time and help you do all of this work, so you can know what you're about."

Ruth interjected, "I say we come in the spring when it's time to order seeds, so she'll know what to plant in the kitchen garden."

A knock interrupted the conversation, and Abigail went to

greet Katie and Mrs. Knepp. They both bore baskets, which turned out to be full of spices of every kind.

"You'll have the best-stocked medicine closet in the district, next to the doctor's," Mrs. Knepp declared once she'd finished putting up her gifts. "And you'll need it, if Joseph keeps insisting on trying to ride wild horses!"

They all laughed together, and Abigail felt the warm camaraderie and power of what a group of women could accomplish together if they set their minds to it. A year ago, stocking a pantry would have been something she would have disdained. Now she saw it as the result of tremendous work and an accomplishment to protect and provide for those you love.

The ladies had just settled around the quilting frame when the sound of a motor vehicle barreling down the lane reached them inside.

"What in the world?" Abigail asked as she rose from her place and hurried to look out the window. Her first thought was that Joseph had been hurt again somehow, but then she saw a slender *Englisch* girl hop out from the passenger side and wave the driver away. The girl began walking toward the porch, a bright patchwork bag swinging jauntily over her shoulder and her long black hair blowing in the wind. Abigail's heart caught, and her eyes filled with tears. There was no mistaking her identity; she was so much a delicate version of her husband.

Abigail ran to the door and flung it wide just as the girl had the screen door open to knock.

"Abby?"

"*Ya*, I mean, yes . . . and you're . . ."

"Angel, Joe's sister. I hope it's all right . . . He called me the other night and said that you wanted—"

Abigail half sobbed and threw her arms about the girl. All of the usual reserve and uncertainty were gone as she hugged her new sister-in-law, who returned the embrace with enthusiasm.

"Come in," Abigail sniffed. "Please come in. I'm sorry I'm so emotional . . . It's just that you look so much like Joseph."

Angel rolled her dark eyes. "I know. It's always been that way. And I have to say that Joe was right—you are one beautiful girl!"

Abigail smiled and caught her hand. "Come and meet my friends. Everyone, this is Joseph's sister, Angel, from New York. She came just for the quilting. She's an art student."

Judith moved over a space and patted the empty chair beside her. "Sit down here, honey, and tell us about yourself. Your brother's become a hero around these parts lately."

Angel smiled. "He's never been one to look before he leaps . . . except, I bet, when he married Abby . . . I bet he did a whole lot of looking then."

They all laughed, and Abigail thanked God that here was someone new and wonderful who was willing to love her and her family. It was almost more than she could bear.

And later, when the remaining three stars had been quilted, the women stopped to admire each other's handiwork. The stitches were marvelous in their uniformity and precision, and Abigail felt a warm glow inside as she surveyed them. She'd used her mother's thimble throughout the quilting and knew a rippling sense of peace that the woman lost to her long ago had still been a part of the day.

Then she served the teaberry cookies and hot tea. They all talked and laughed, and Angel fit right in, sharing stories from New York and listening with obvious, deep interest to the life tales of the women around her. And Abigail felt encircled by love and laughter that melted away all the vestiges of uncertainty in her heart about herself as a person and becoming a wife in truth.

JOSEPH TILTED HIS ROOT BEER BOTTLE BACK AND LET THE rich sweetness slide down his throat. He was playing checkers with his father-in-law in a little country store, and they'd attracted quite an interest from the Amish men looking on. Joseph was an expert at checkers but decided early on in the game that it wouldn't be quite right to beat this particular opponent, so he let himself slip on a last move.

"Aha!" Solomon cheered, taking his king. And the other men murmured in approval. Soon Joseph and Solomon were back in the buggy, shivering a bit against the cold.

"You think we can go back now?" Joseph asked and was surprised when the usually taciturn man laughed out loud.

He still found it hard to match the renewed good humor of his father-in-law with the stoic man he'd worked with all fall.

"*Ya*, we can go back, in time for a cookie or two. I bet they're about finished now except for the talking, and that will never be finished."

Joseph chuckled. "I think I like your sense of humor."

"And I like yours, son. I like yours."

CHAPTER TWENTY-FOUR

IT WAS LATE ON THE NIGHT OF THE QUILTING. ANGEL WAS
ensconced upstairs in Abigail's old room, and the house was quiet
except for the gentle brush of Abigail's nightdress as she put-
tered about the master bedroom putting things away and taking
overlong to brush her hair. A single kerosene lamp burned on the
bedside table, and Joseph sat up against the pillows watching her.
She knew that she was dallying, but she wasn't quite sure how to
broach the subject that had been on her mind since that afternoon.

"So, the quilt is beautiful," he remarked, and she turned to
watch him run his hand over the pattern of multicolored stars.
"Abby's Wish, hmm?"

She nodded. "When your sister found out the pattern name,
she actually went around the table and had everyone make a wish
for me."

He smiled. "That's nice. When are you coming to bed?"

She bit her lip. "Don't you want to know the wishes?"

"I know what I wish." His voice was husky, and she turned on
her bare feet to face him, leaning against the bureau for support.

"What?" she whispered.

He laid aside his glasses and closed his eyes, and his thick
lashes fanned against the flush of his cheeks. He began to speak
in a dreamy tone that made her curl her toes into the wooden
floorboards.

"I wish that you'd put down the hairbrush and that you'd walk
toward me and that you'd smile your beautiful smile and that your

329

eyes would shine. Then I wish you'd look at me the way you did when I was sick and whisper that you'd do anything to help me, because I need help, Abby. I need you, and I . . ." He broke off and opened his eyes, and she stared into their warm, dark depths, almost as if she could see herself reflected there.

And she could see herself as he'd described, coming to him . . . *just as she was meant to do as his wife*. The thought simmered across her consciousness, and she took one small step forward. She saw him swallow and watched as a pulse beat strongly in the bare line of his throat.

"Abby . . ."

She smiled and let the love she felt for him show in her eyes. She could hear him breathing, short, deep intakes of breath as if he'd run a long way and now was finding rest.

She came until she was within hand's reach of him, but he still didn't move. She wet her lips and gazed down at him, all of the love she felt for him heating her heart and her mind. She bent forward from the waist, letting her hair enclose them like a curtain, and then she kissed him.

"Joseph," she murmured.

He opened his eyes. "Is this real?" he asked in wonder. "Do you . . . Are you . . . ?"

Her lips found his once more, and then he reached strong arms up to pull her to him. He pressed hot kisses along the line of her throat and through the cotton fabric of the shoulder of her gown.

"And what do you wish for, Abby Lambert?" he whispered in a breathless sigh, drawing the quilt over their heads.

She stared up at him, then pulled his eager mouth down to meet her own once more. "That's easy," she said between kisses. "As the Lord wills, I wish for a lifetime of joy, and children, and peace, with the husband of my heart."

He smiled. "Well then, Mrs. Lambert, I'll give it my earnest attention to make sure that your every wish comes very . . . very true."

READING GROUP GUIDE

1. Joseph battles an extremely tough addiction but relies on Christ to see him through, moment by moment. What problem does God help you with on a moment-to-moment basis?
2. At first Abby wants to escape her way of life, rather than yielding to God's work in her. What do you wish you could escape that might be yielded to the Lord for transformation?
3. How does the idea of "play" develop intimacy between Abby and Joseph?
4. Abby learns to feel safe with Joseph. Who do you feel most safe with in your own life—safe to be yourself, express your ideas, and so forth?

ACKNOWLEDGMENTS

I'D LIKE TO ACKNOWLEDGE MY EDITOR, NATALIE HANEMANN, that encourager of words! Thank you for listening . . . Beth Wiseman and Kathy Fuller, two delicious word users . . . LB Norton, my line editor . . . Dan Miller, my Amish consultant and good ear . . . Brenda Lott, my critique partner and encourager . . . my family, both near and far . . . and, most importantly, the living God who has given me the opportunity to write for Him.

Amish Recipes

DONNA'S RAISIN-FILLED COOKIES

    1 egg
    3 teaspoon cream of tartar
    1 cup mill
    2 teaspoon soda
    2 cup sugar
    ½ teaspoon salt
    1 cup shortening
    flour (start with about 4 cups)

Mix ingredients together, adding enough flour to make a soft dough. Roll out dough, cutting to desired size. Place on cookie sheet and put a spoonful of raisin filling on top. Top with another cookie and seal around edges.

Bake in 350° oven until slightly brown.

Filling

    1 box raisins
    2 eggs
    1 cup sugar
    1 tablespoons butter
    2 cup water
    2 tablespoons flour

Cook the raisins until tender. Add the sugar and butter. Mix eggs and flour together and stir slowly into raisins. (May be slightly lumpy but it won't matter.) Cook slowly, stirring constantly. Cool.

Hints: *Make the top cookie thinner than the bottom one. I take the top cookie and sort of flatten it a little in my hand and then form it around the bottom cookie, sealing the edges. I use about a box and a half of raisins. That way you can put plenty of raisins in each cookie. I use a medium-size glass to cut out my cookies. You can make any size you want.*

TEABERRY COOKIES

A teaberry is a low-growing, creeping evergreen plant with white flowers, aromatic leaves, and spicy edible scarlet berries. You can order teaberry extract at www.country-pantry.com/candy_making.html and teaberry candies at www.nutsonline.com.

> 1½ cups vegetable oil
> 1½ cups white sugar
> 2 eggs
> 4 cups all-purpose flour
> 1 teaspoon baking soda
> 1 teaspoon baking powder
> 1 cup buttermilk
> ¾ teaspoon salt
> ¾ teaspoon vanilla extract
> 1 teaspoon teaberry extract
> optional: teaberry candies

1. Preheat oven to 350°F.
2. Mix together vegetable oil (yes, 1½ cups!), sugar, and eggs.
3. Mix in flour, baking soda, baking powder, buttermilk, salt, vanilla, and teaberry extract.
4. Pour teaspoon-sized amounts of batter onto cookie sheets,

leaving plenty of room in between. Cookies will puff up and get large.
5. Bake for 8 to 10 minutes.

—Courtesy of Gilbert Stout

Amish Icebox Cookies

 1 large egg
 1 egg yolk
 1 teaspoon vanilla extract
 ½ teaspoon salt
 1 cup (2 sticks) unsalted butter, softened
 1 cup sugar
 2½ cups all-purpose flour
 1 teaspoon of any extract you like—vanilla, root beer, etc.

Mixing the Dough
1. In small mixing bowl, whisk egg, egg yolk, vanilla, and salt until well blended.
2. In large mixing bowl, beat butter and sugar with an electric mixer on medium-high speed until light and fluffy, about 3 to 4 minutes. Stop mixer and scrape down sides of bowl with rubber spatula.
3. Add egg mixture and beat until blended and creamy.
4. Add flour and blend with the mixer on low speed or with a wooden spoon just until soft dough forms.
5. Divide dough into two equal portions and stir flavoring of your choice into each half of dough.

Preparing/Storing the Dough
1. Line your counter with plastic wrap and scrape one portion of dough onto it.

2. With lightly floured hands, roll dough into log about 9 inches long and 1½ inches in diameter. Repeat with second portion of dough.
3. Wrap each log separately in plastic and refrigerate for at least 1 hour or up to 24 hours. (Wrapped logs of dough can also be placed in a freezer bag in the freezer for up to a month. Slice and bake cookies directly from the freezer.)

Baking the Cookies
1. Position oven rack in middle of oven and preheat to 375°F.
2. Using a sharp knife, slice log into ¼-inch thick slices, rotating the log as you cut so it maintains its round shape.
3. Transfer slices of dough to ungreased cookie sheets (line sheets with parchment paper if desired), spacing them at least 1 inch apart.
4. Bake, one cookie sheet at a time, for 12 to 14 minutes (a minute or two longer for frozen dough), until cookies are pale golden around the edges but still soft on top.
5. Remove from oven and let cool on cookie sheet for 1 to 2 minutes before transferring to a wire rack to cool completely.

Yields about 6 dozen cookies—store in an airtight container or freeze.

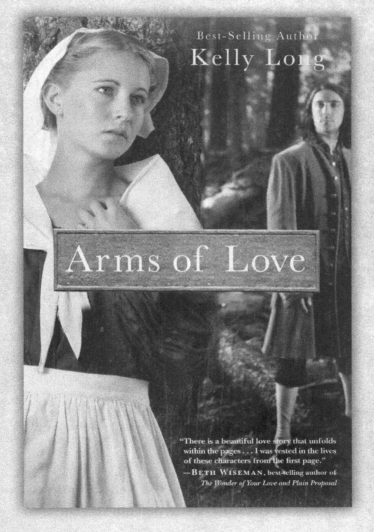

ENJOY THESE AMISH NOVELLAS
FOR EVERY SEASON

Visit AmishLiving.com

LOVE ALL THINGS AMISH?

Join the conversation at AmishLiving.com

About the Author

KELLY LONG is the author of the Patch of Heaven series. She was born and raised in the mountains of Northern Pennsylvania. She's been married for twenty-six years and enjoys life with her husband, children, and Bichon.